THE FLYING BEAVER BROTHERS
BIRDS VS. BUNNIES

MAXWELL EATON III

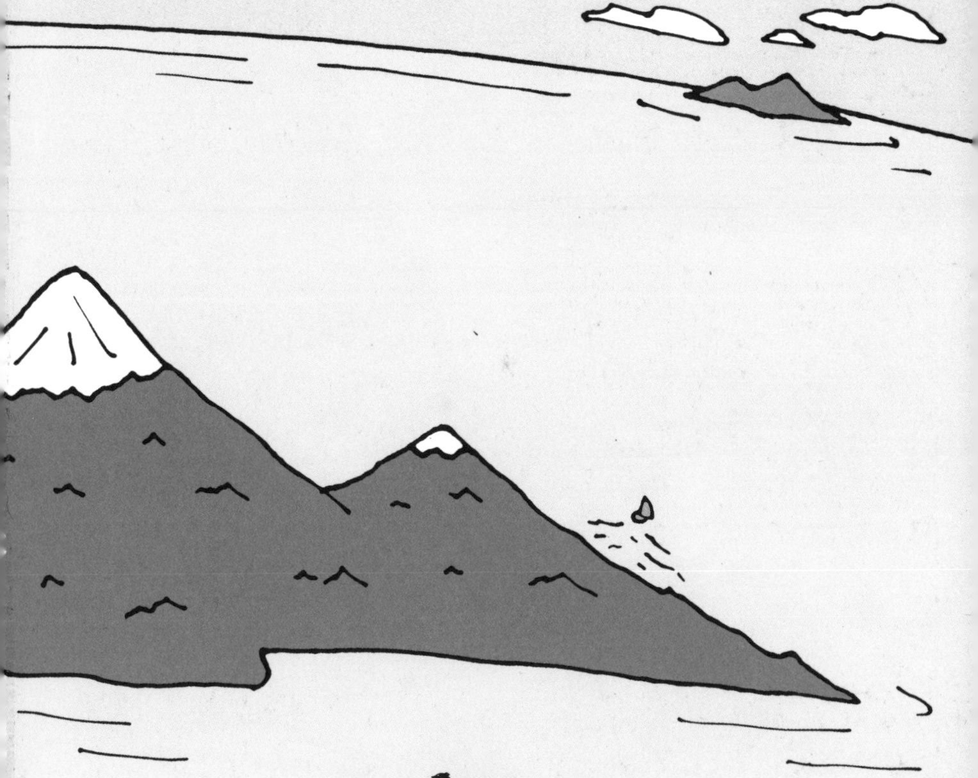

ALFRED A. KNOPF
NEW YORK

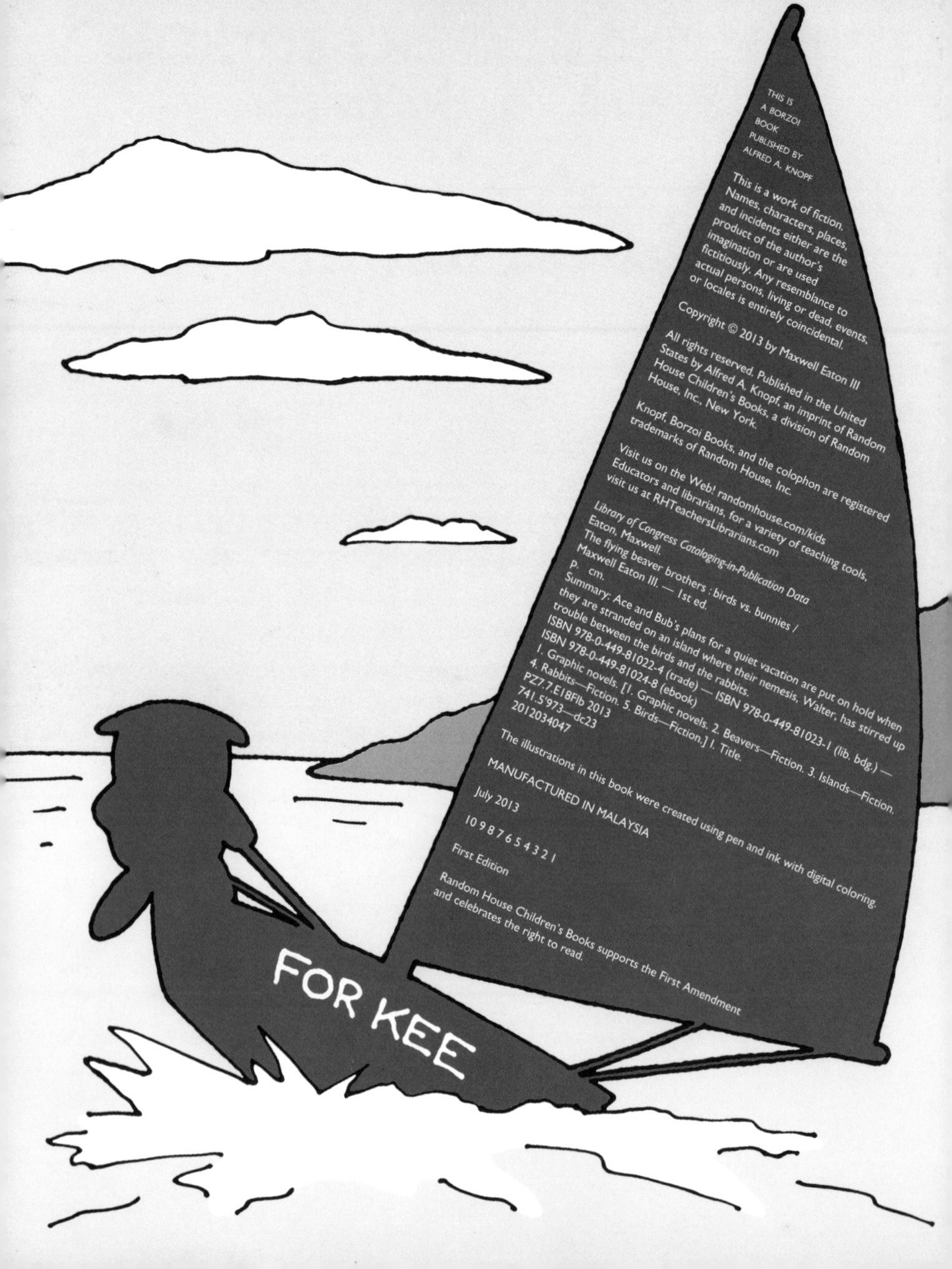
FOR KEE

THIS IS
A BORZOI
BOOK
PUBLISHED BY
ALFRED A. KNOPF

Visit us on the Web! randomhouse.com/kids
Educators and librarians, for a variety of teaching tools, visit us at RHTeachersLibrarians.com

Library of Congress Cataloging-in-Publication Data
Eaton, Maxwell.
The flying beaver brothers : birds vs. bunnies / Maxwell Eaton III. — 1st ed.
p. cm.
Summary: Ace and Bub's plans for a quiet vacation are put on hold when they are stranded on an island where their nemesis, Walter, has stirred up trouble between the birds and the rabbits.
ISBN 978-0-449-81022-4 (trade) — ISBN 978-0-449-81023-1 (lib. bdg.) —
ISBN 978-0-449-81024-8 (ebook)
1. Graphic novels. [1. Graphic novels. 2. Beavers—Fiction. 3. Islands—Fiction. 4. Rabbits—Fiction. 5. Birds—Fiction.] I. Title.
PZ7.7.E18Flb 2013
741.5'973—dc23
2012034047

The illustrations in this book were created using pen and ink with digital coloring.

MANUFACTURED IN MALAYSIA

July 2013

10 9 8 7 6 5 4 3 2 1

First Edition

Random House Children's Books supports the First Amendment and celebrates the right to read.

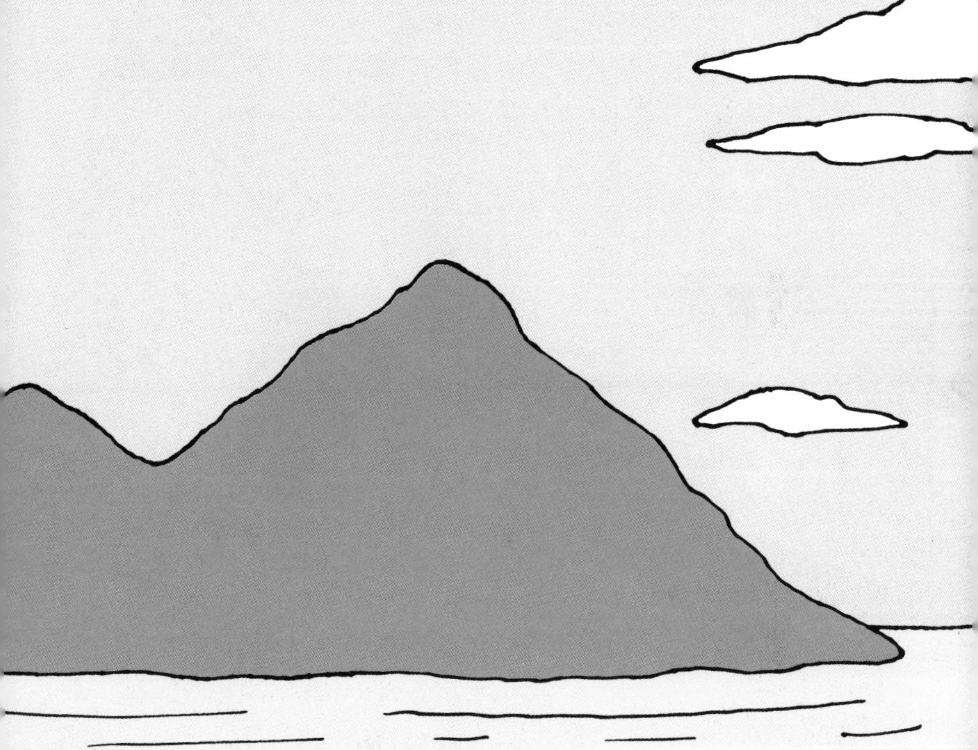

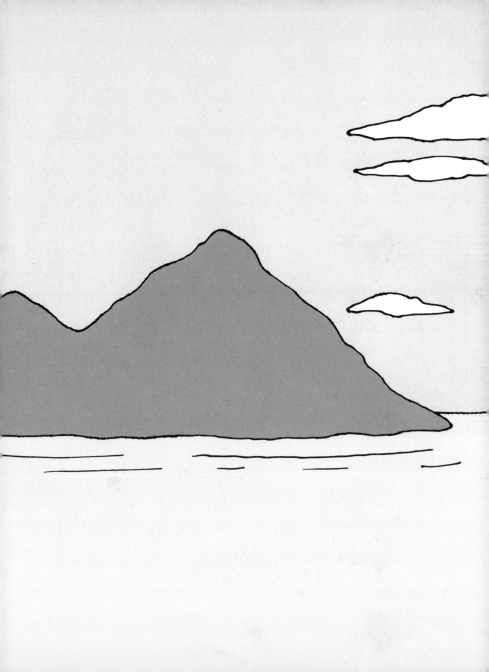

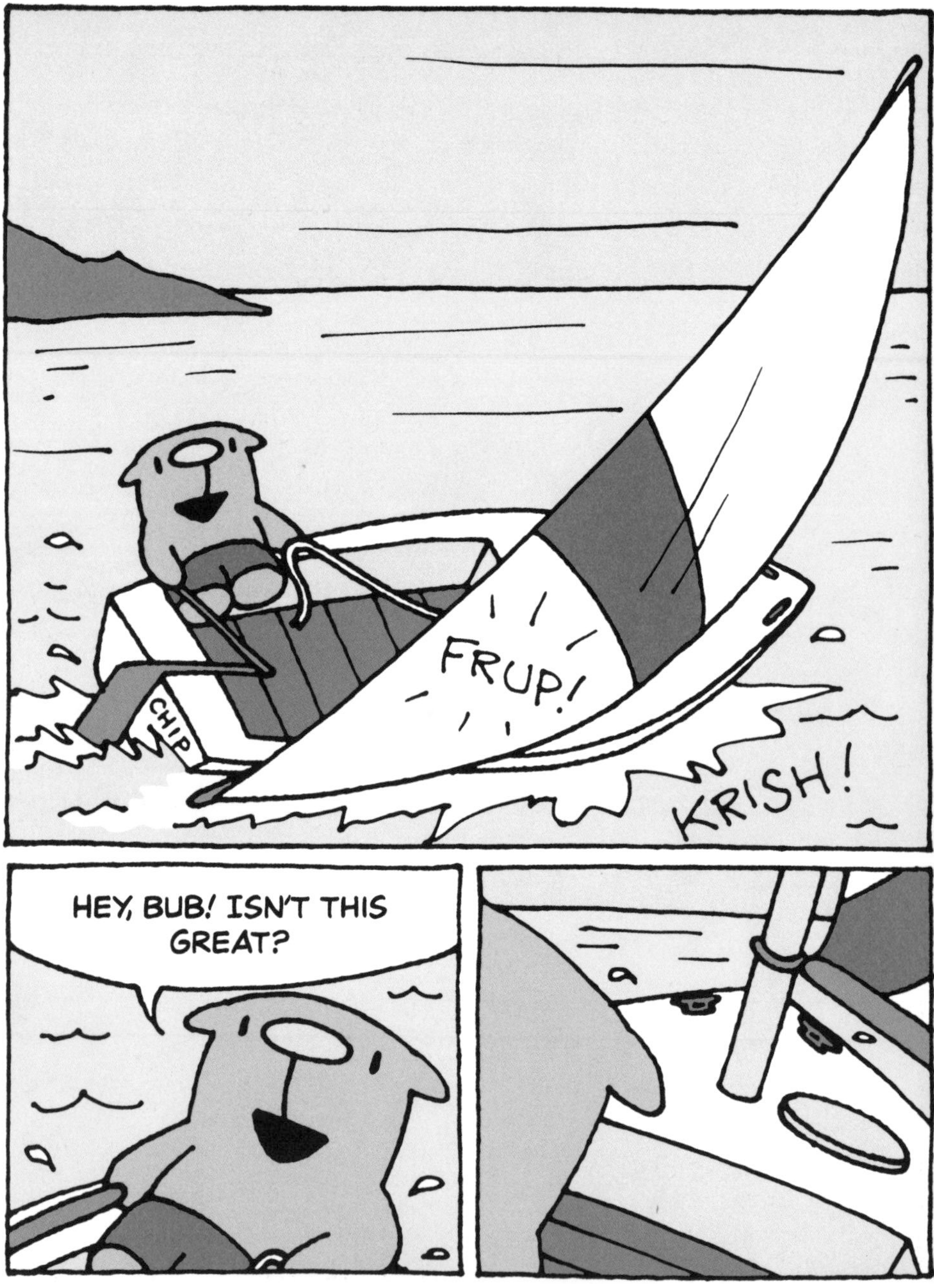
CHIP
FRUP!
KRISH!
HEY, BUB! ISN'T THIS GREAT?

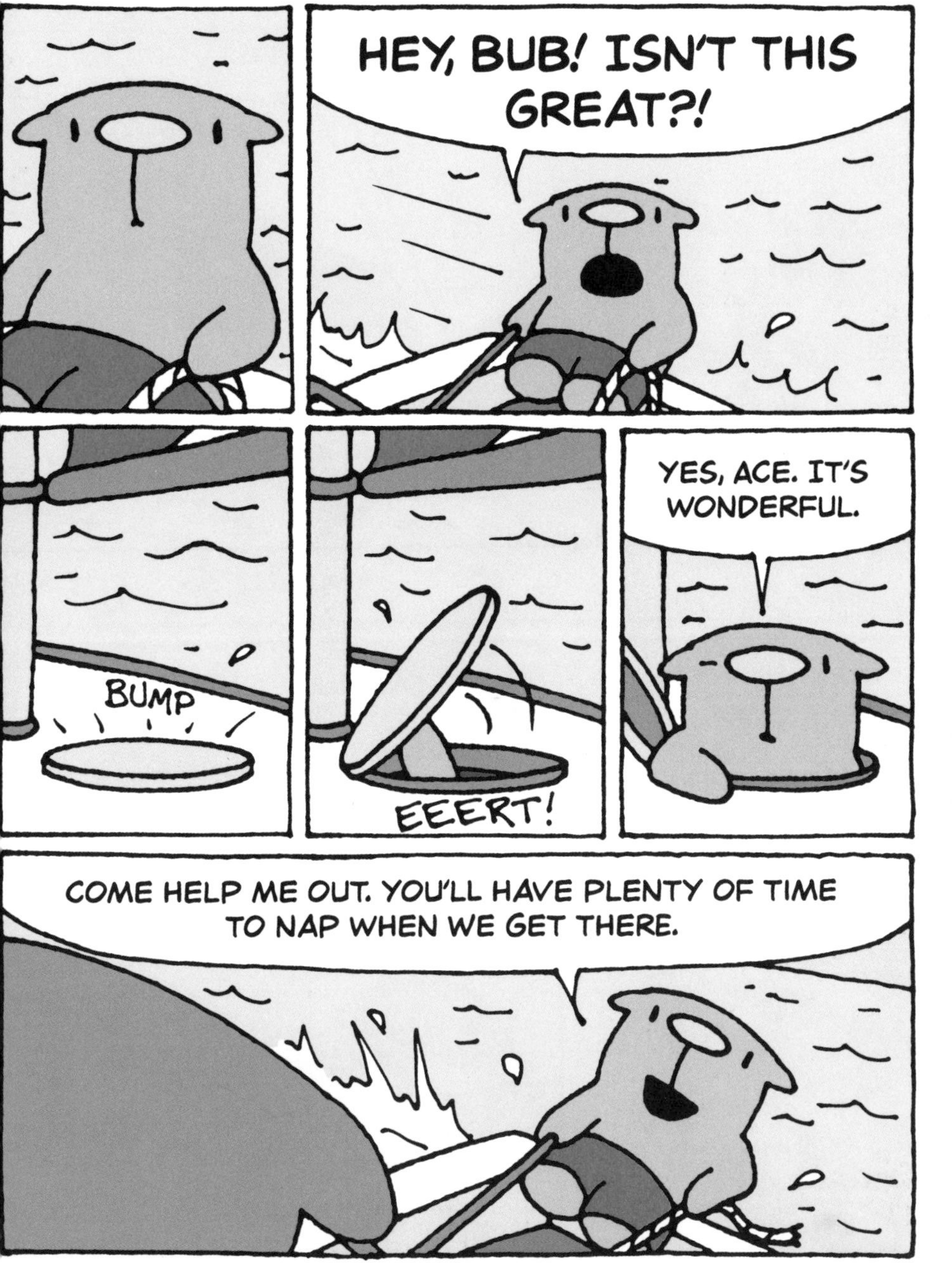
HEY, BUB! ISN'T THIS GREAT?!
BUMP
EEERT!
YES, ACE. IT'S WONDERFUL.
COME HELP ME OUT. YOU'LL HAVE PLENTY OF TIME TO NAP WHEN WE GET THERE.

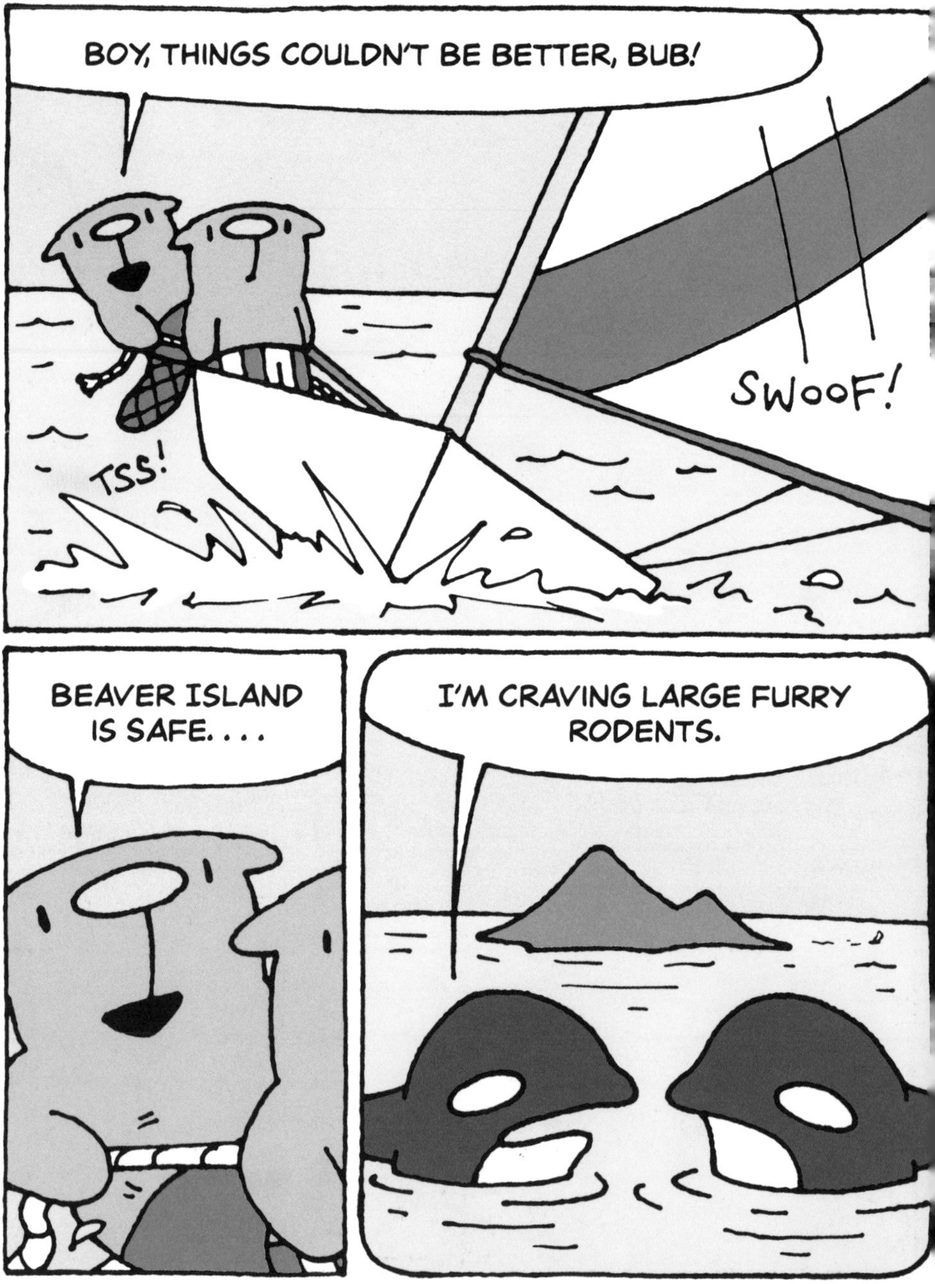
BOY, THINGS COULDN'T BE BETTER, BUB!
SWOOF!
TSS!
BEAVER ISLAND IS SAFE. . . .
I'M CRAVING LARGE FURRY RODENTS.

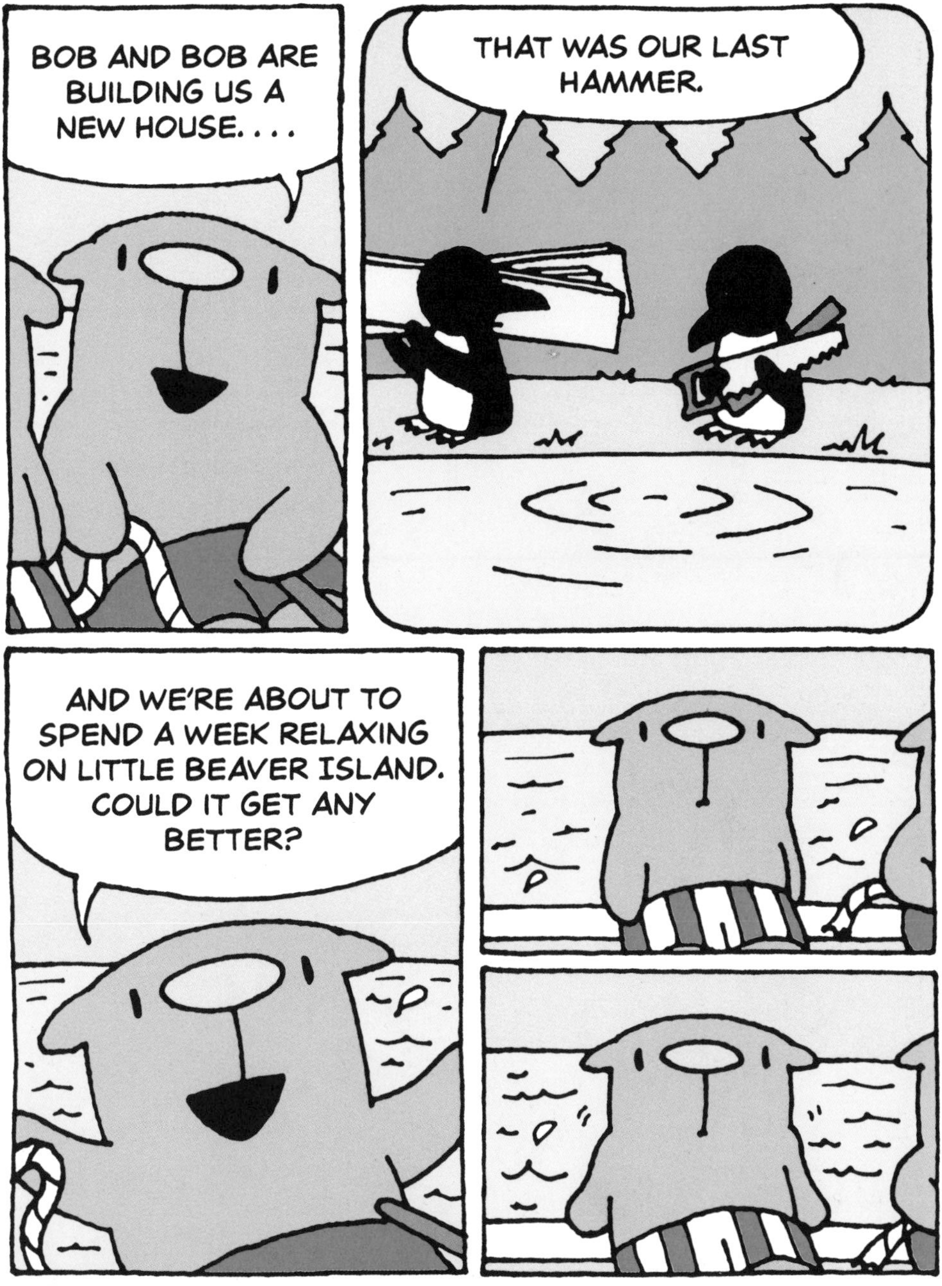
BOB AND BOB ARE BUILDING US A NEW HOUSE. . . .
THAT WAS OUR LAST HAMMER.
AND WE'RE ABOUT TO SPEND A WEEK RELAXING ON LITTLE BEAVER ISLAND. COULD IT GET ANY BETTER?

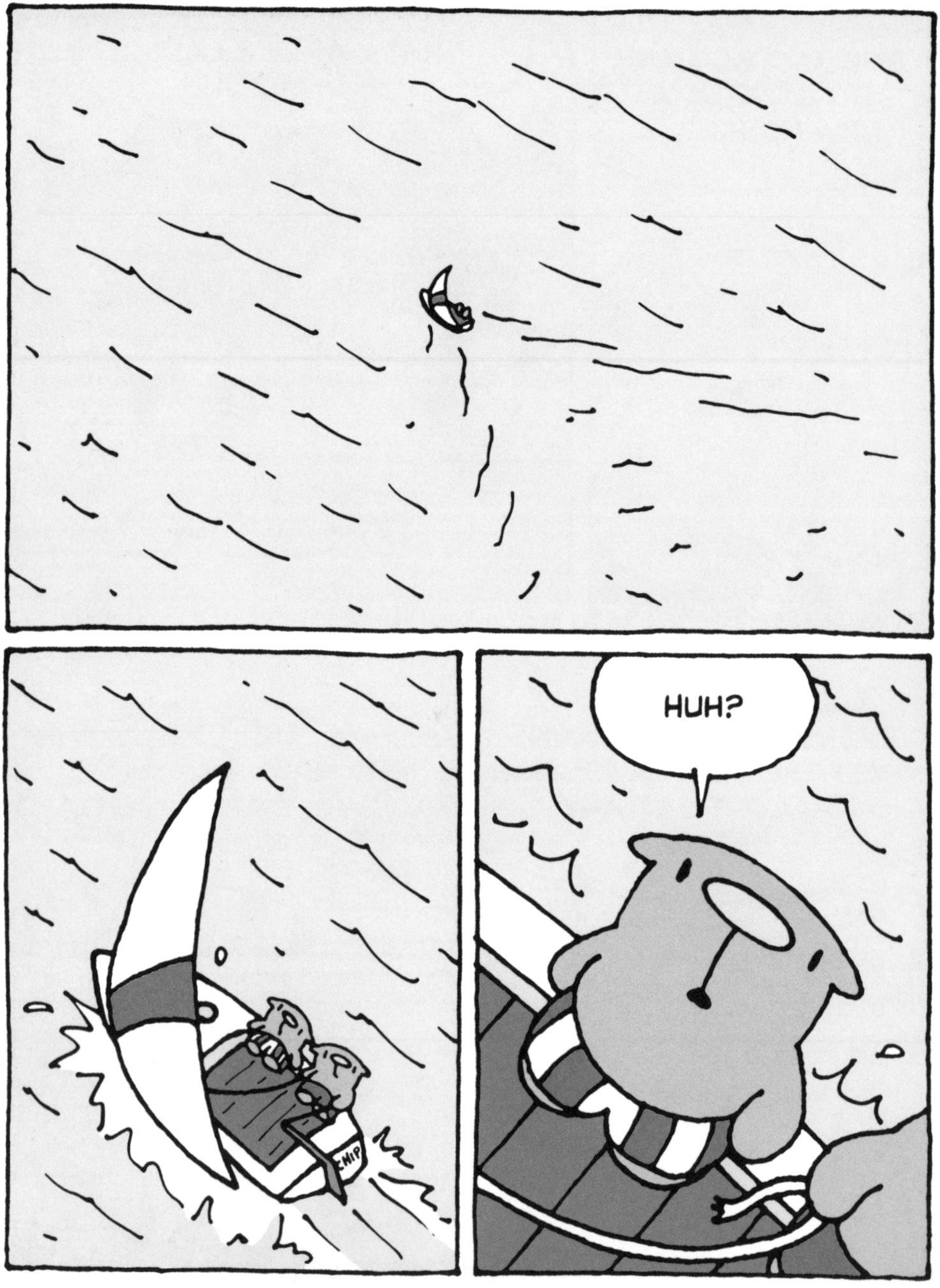
CHIP
HUH?

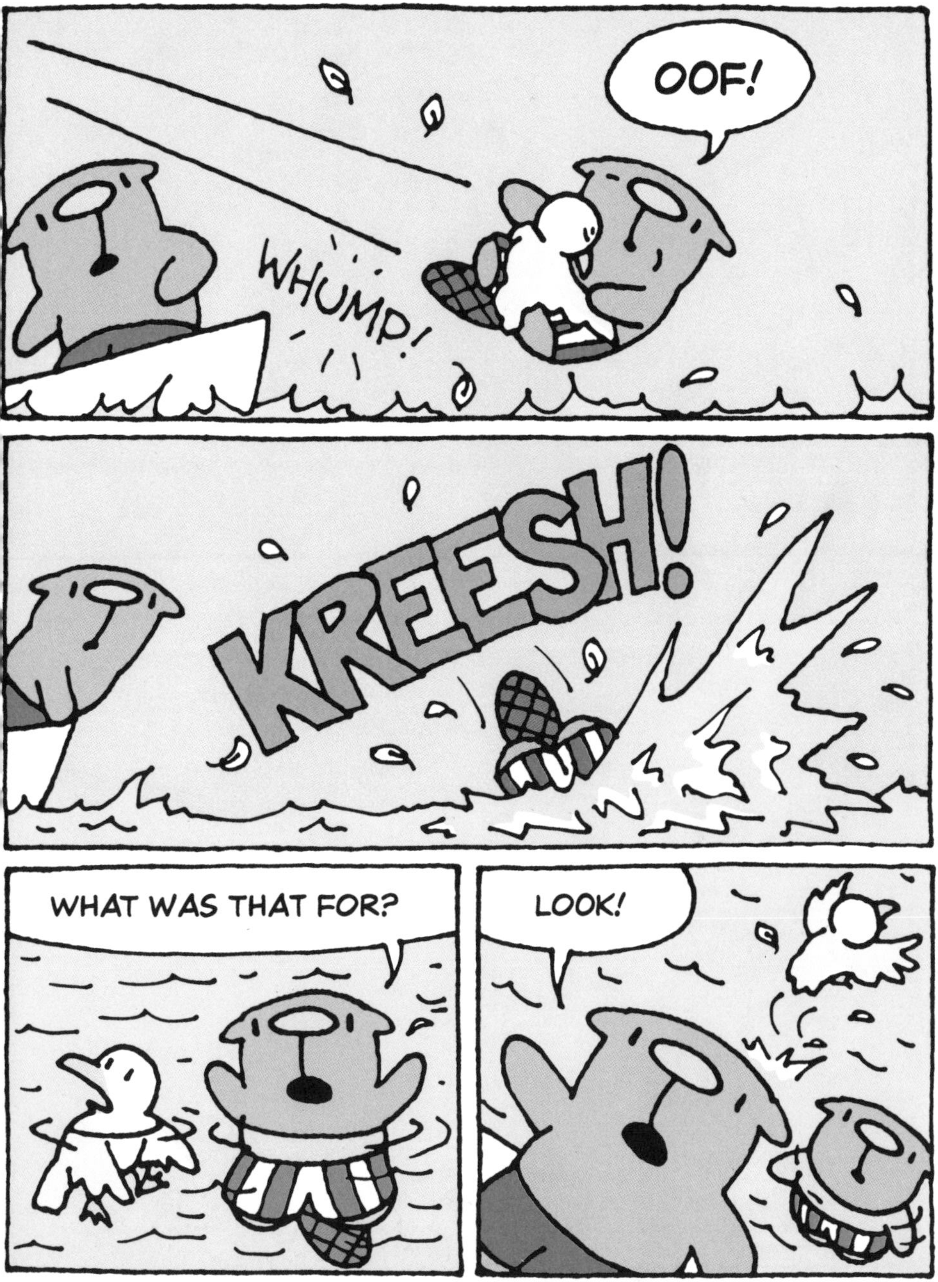
OOF!
WHUMP!
KREESH!
WHAT WAS THAT FOR?
LOOK!

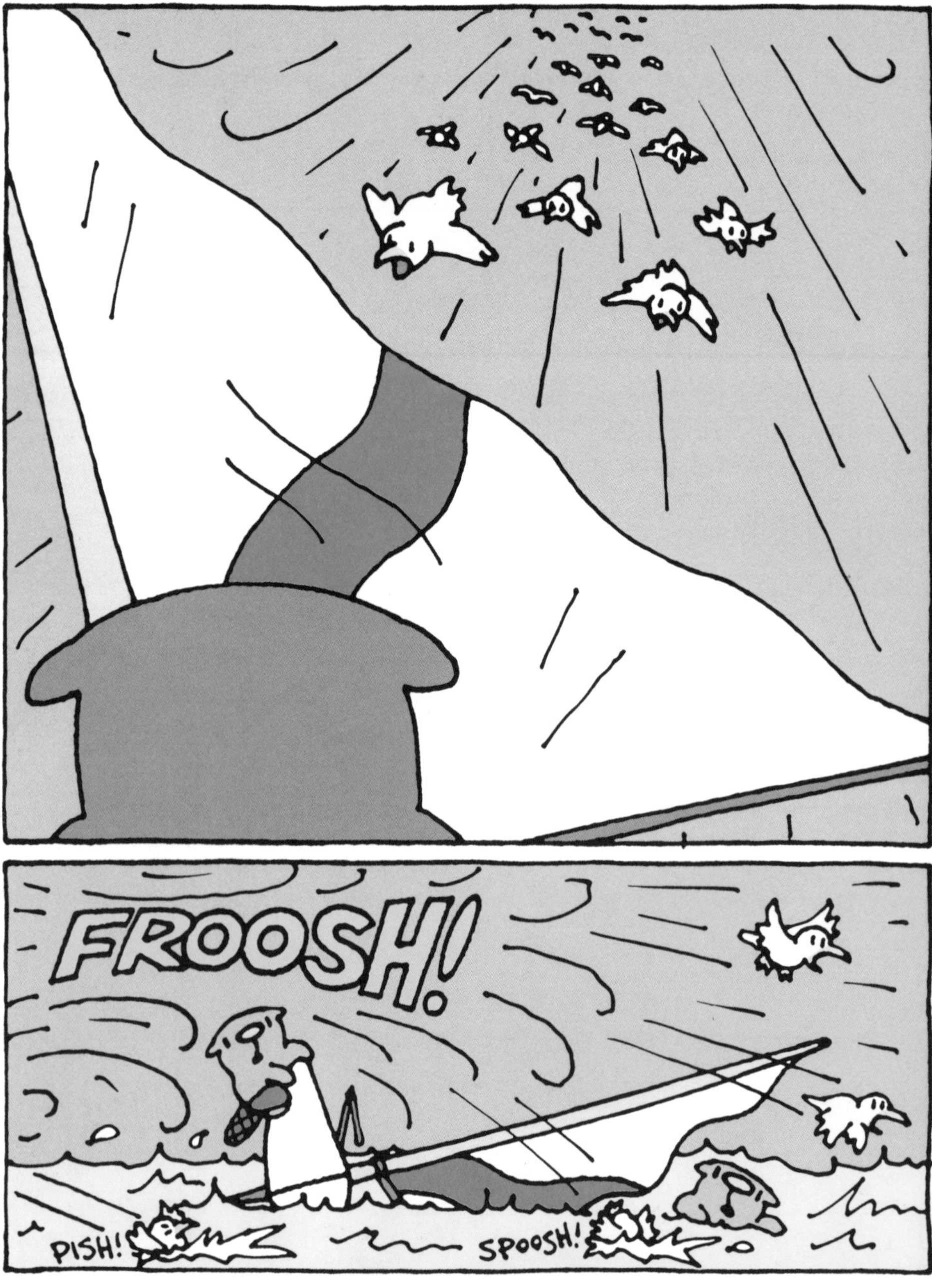
FROOSH!
PISH!
SPOOSH!

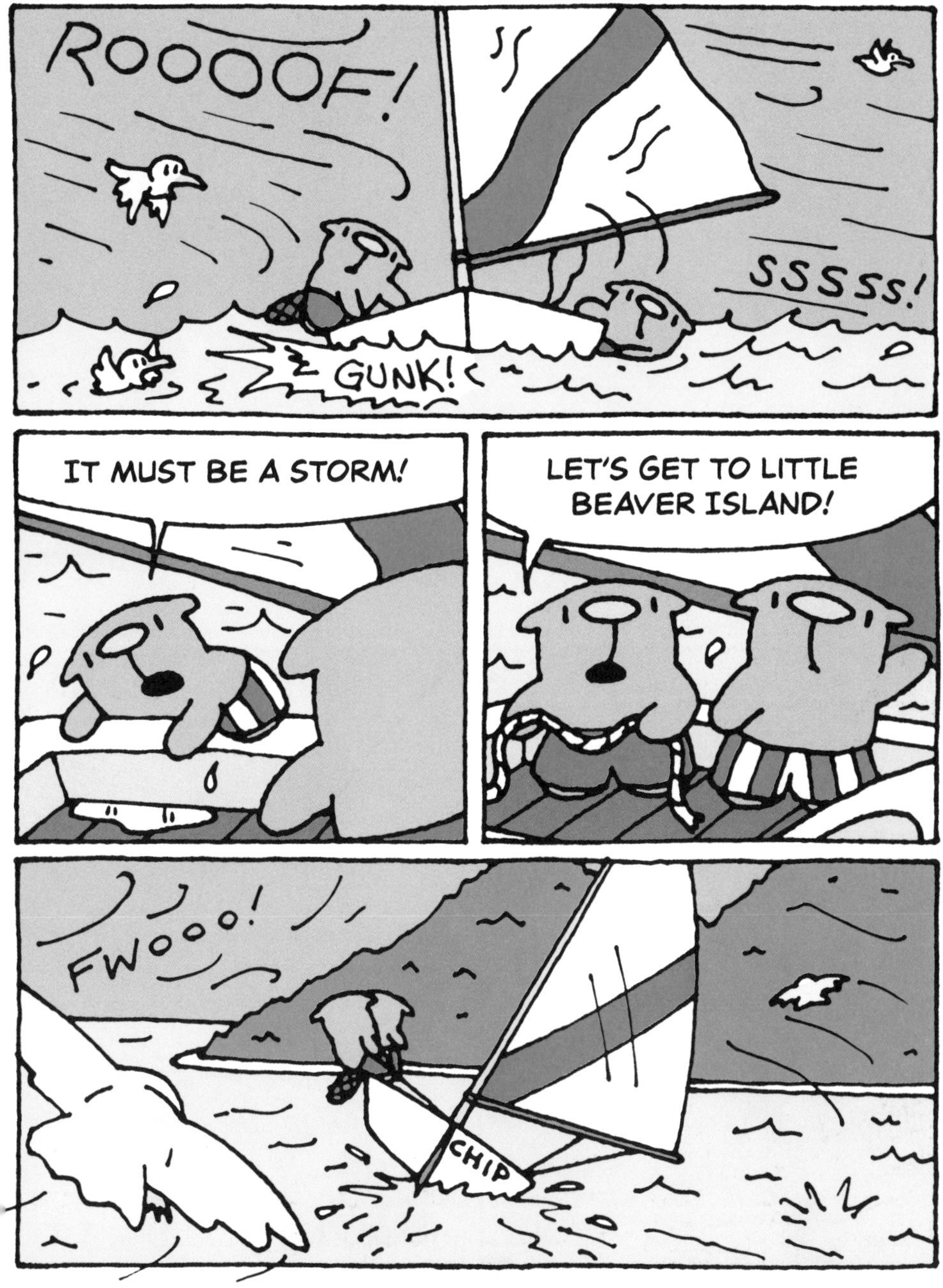
ROOOOF!
SSSSS!
GUNK!
IT MUST BE A STORM!
LET'S GET TO LITTLE BEAVER ISLAND!
FWOOOO!
CHIP

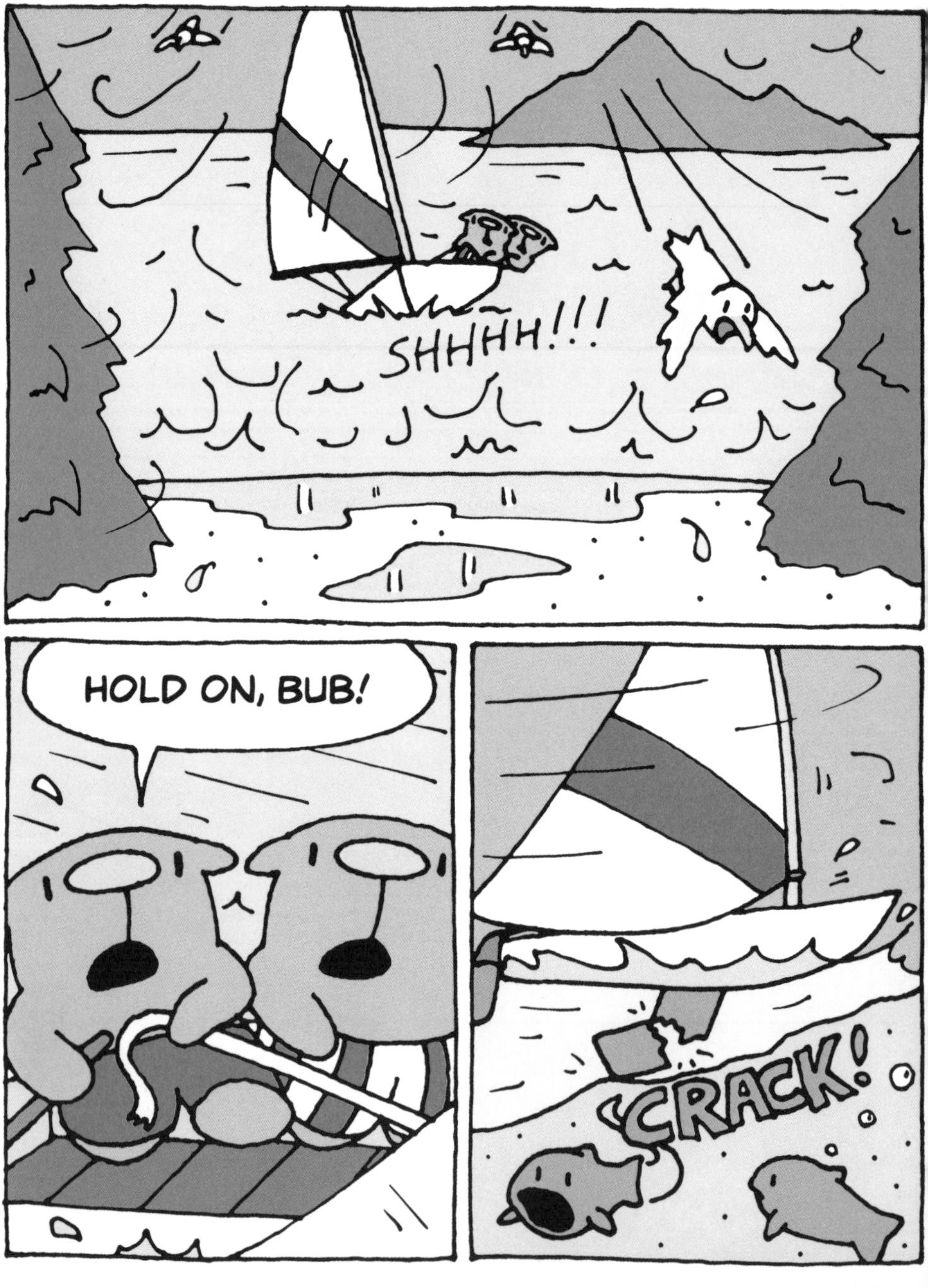
SHHHH!!!
HOLD ON, BUB!
CRACK!

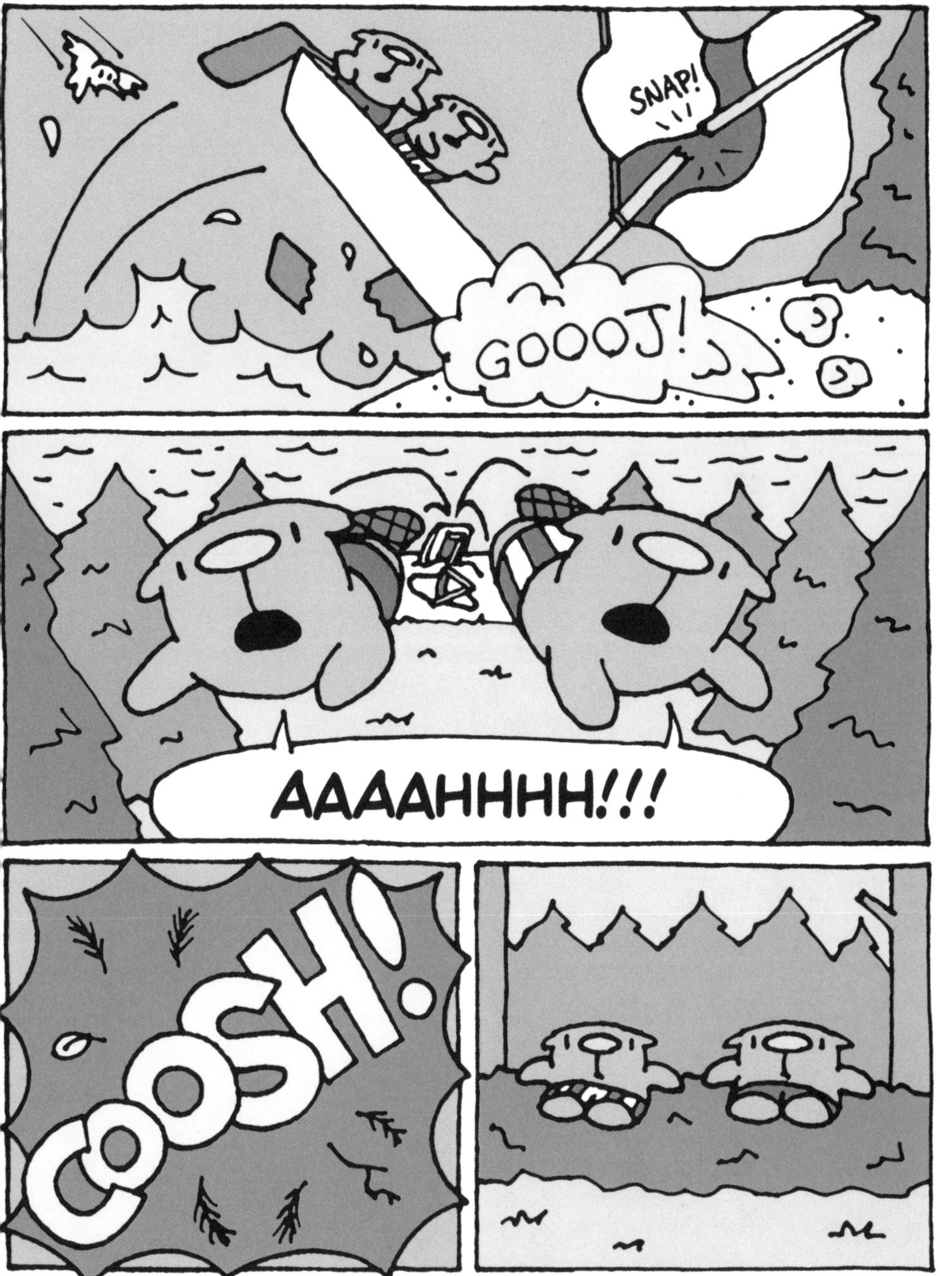

SNAP!
GOOOJ!
AAAAHHHH!!!
COOSH!

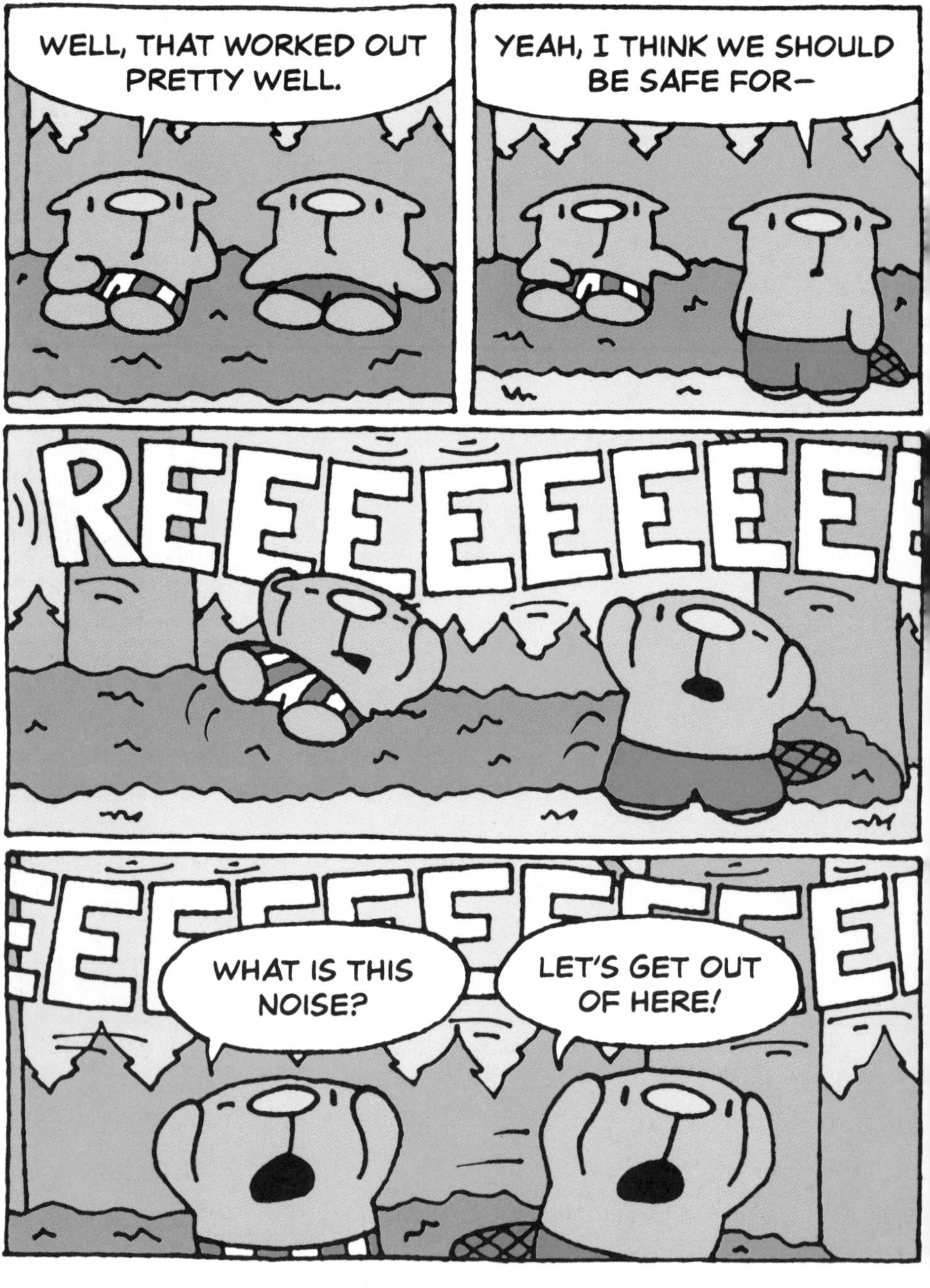
WELL, THAT WORKED OUT PRETTY WELL.
YEAH, I THINK WE SHOULD BE SAFE FOR—
REEEEEEEEEE
EEEEEEEEEE
WHAT IS THIS NOISE?
LET'S GET OUT OF HERE!

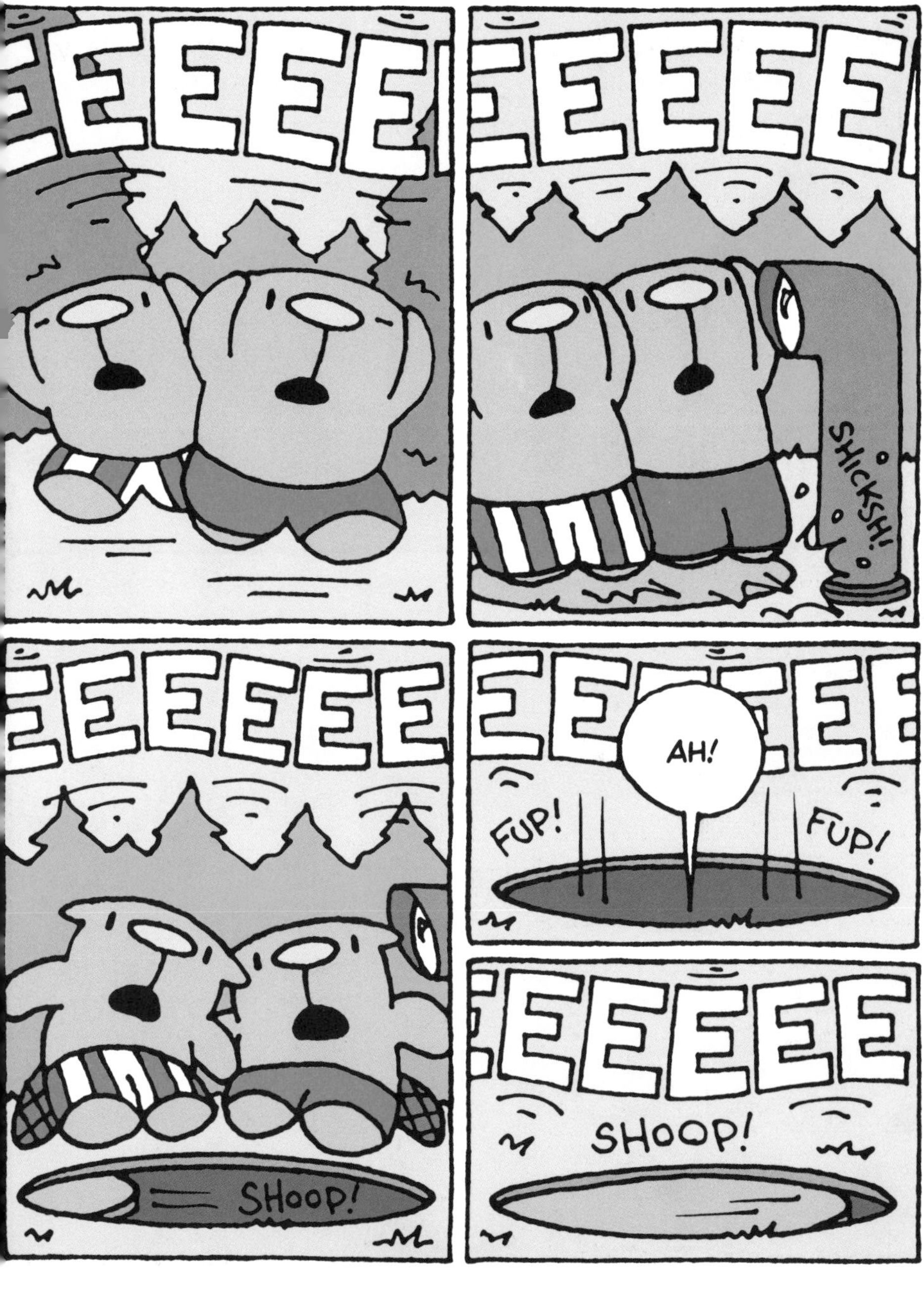
EEEEEE
EEEEEE
SHICKSH!
EEEEEE
SHOOP!
EEEEEE
AH!
FUP!
FUP!
EEEEEE
SHOOP!

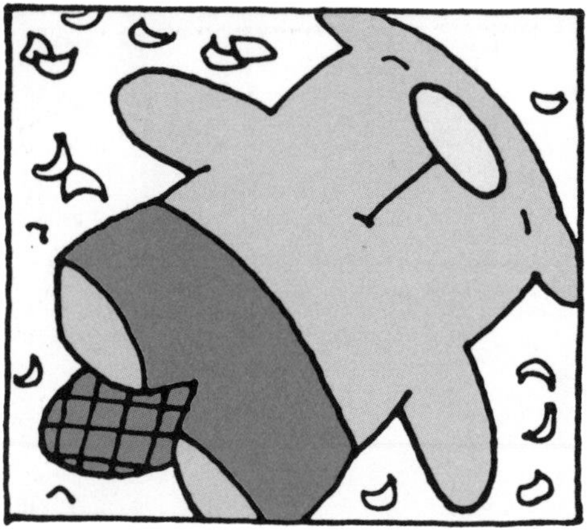
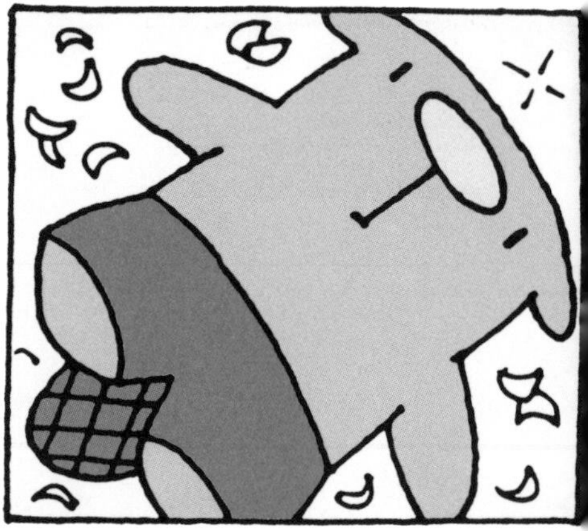
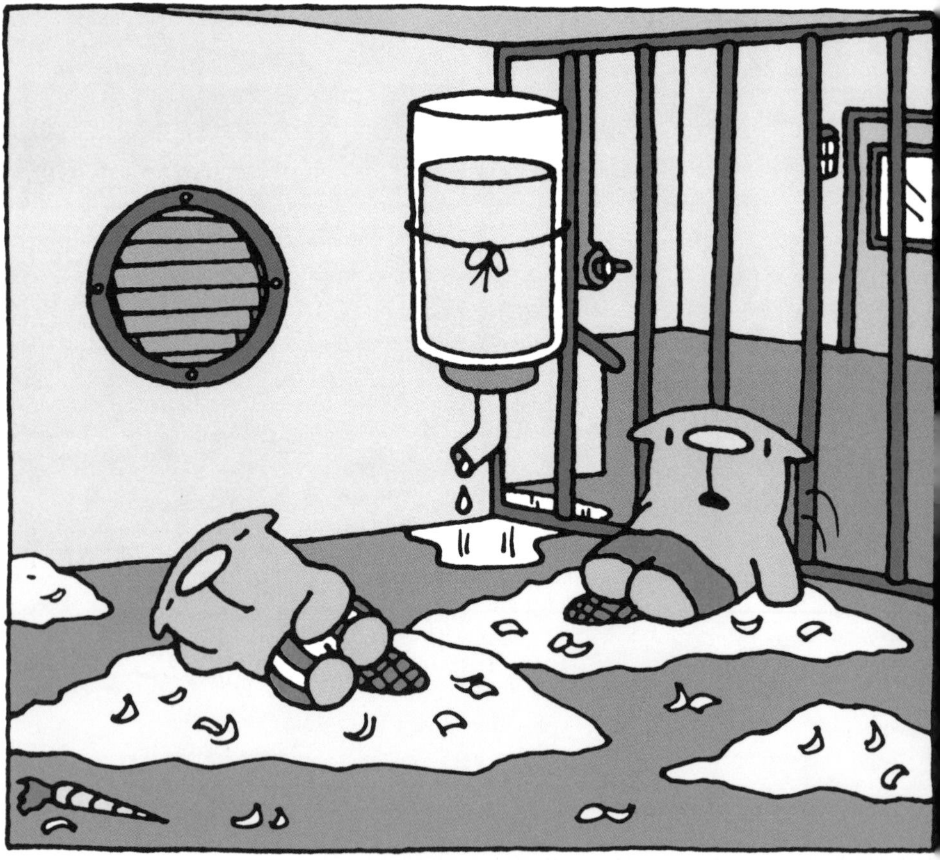

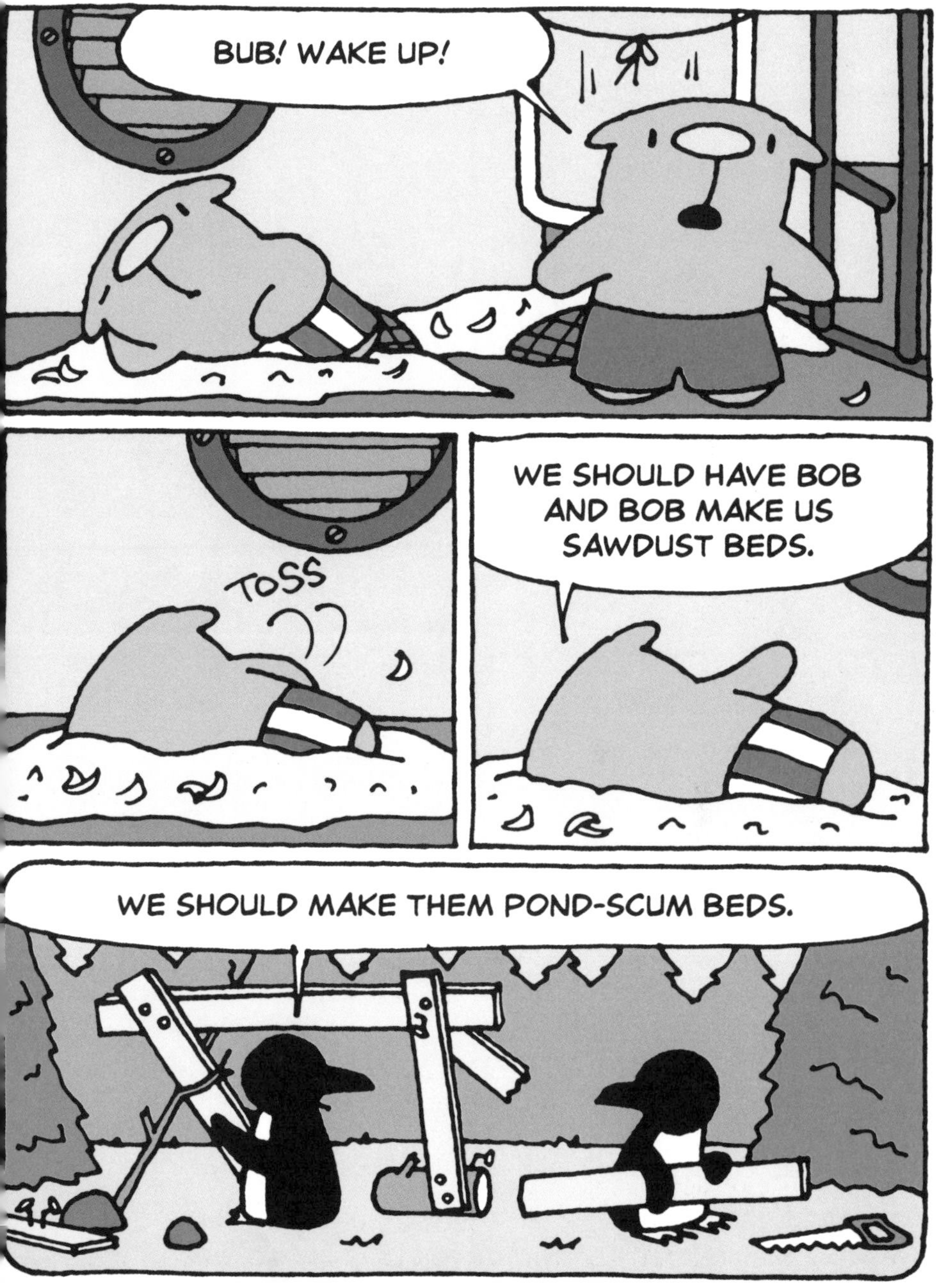
BUB! WAKE UP!
TOSS
WE SHOULD HAVE BOB AND BOB MAKE US SAWDUST BEDS.
WE SHOULD MAKE THEM POND-SCUM BEDS.

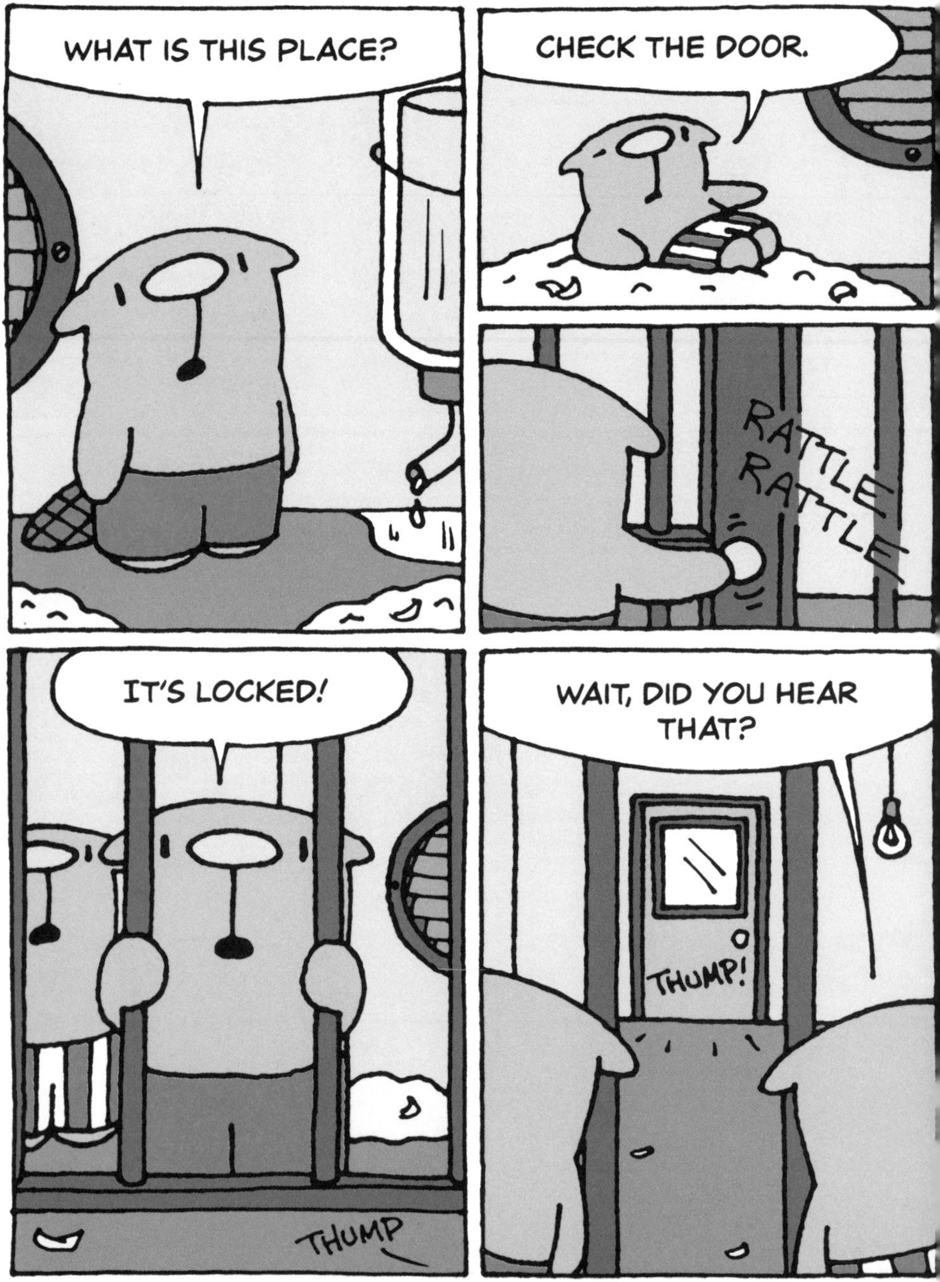
WHAT IS THIS PLACE?
CHECK THE DOOR.
RATTLE RATTLE
IT'S LOCKED!
THUMP
WAIT, DID YOU HEAR THAT?
THUMP!

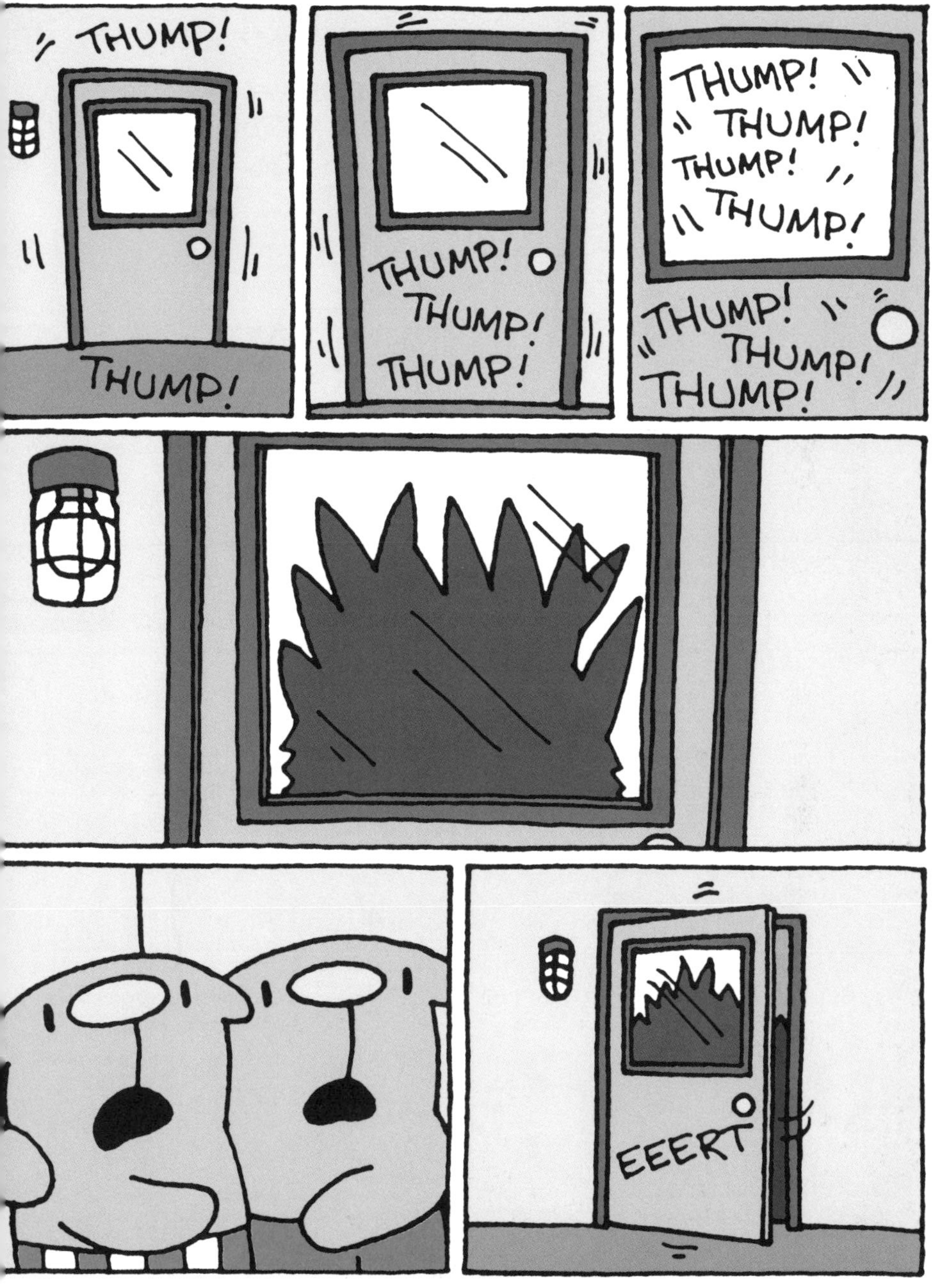
THUMP!
THUMP!
THUMP!
THUMP!
THUMP!
THUMP!
THUMP!
THUMP!
THUMP!
THUMP!
THUMP!
THUMP!
EEERT

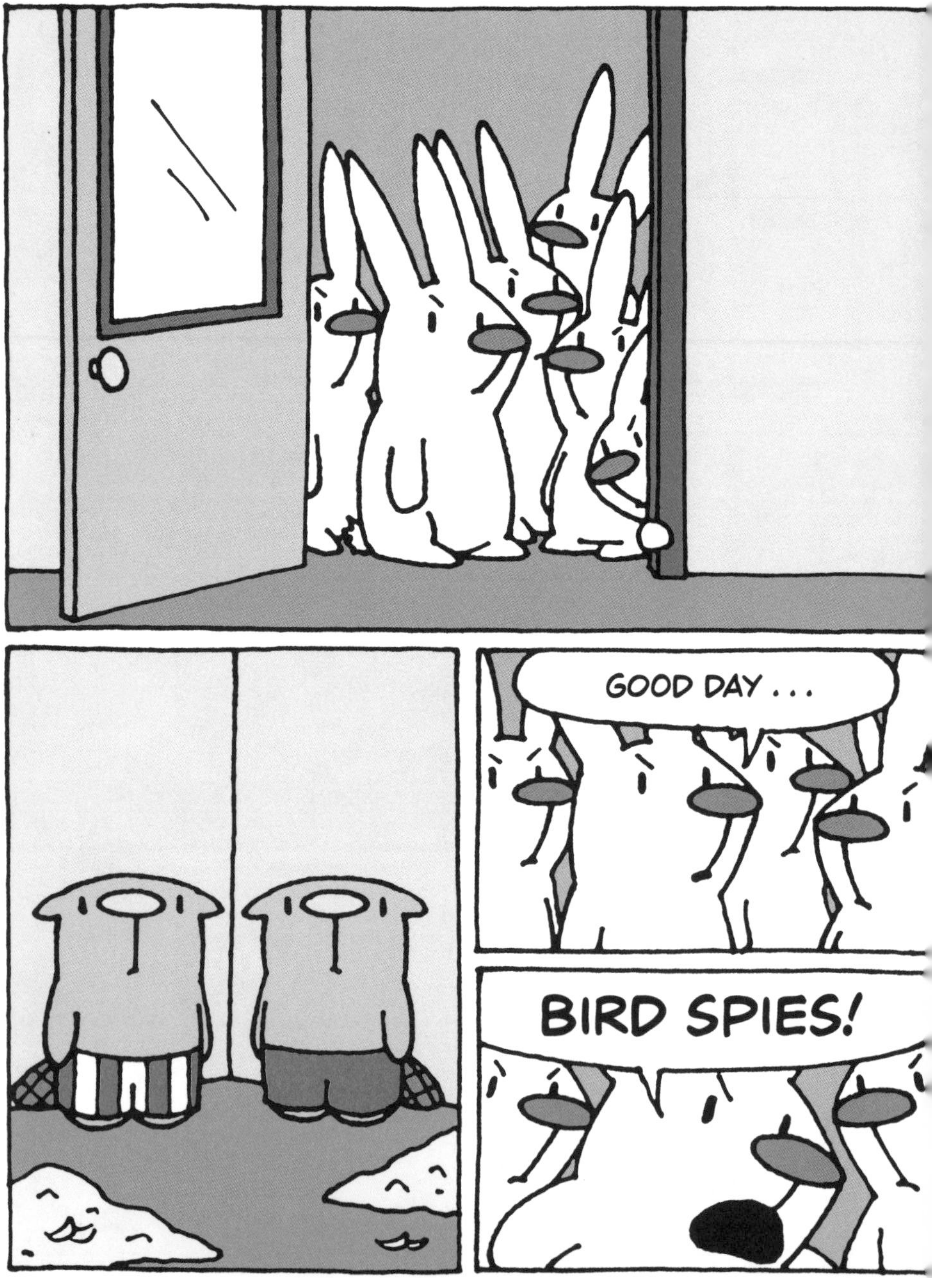
GOOD DAY . . .
BIRD SPIES!

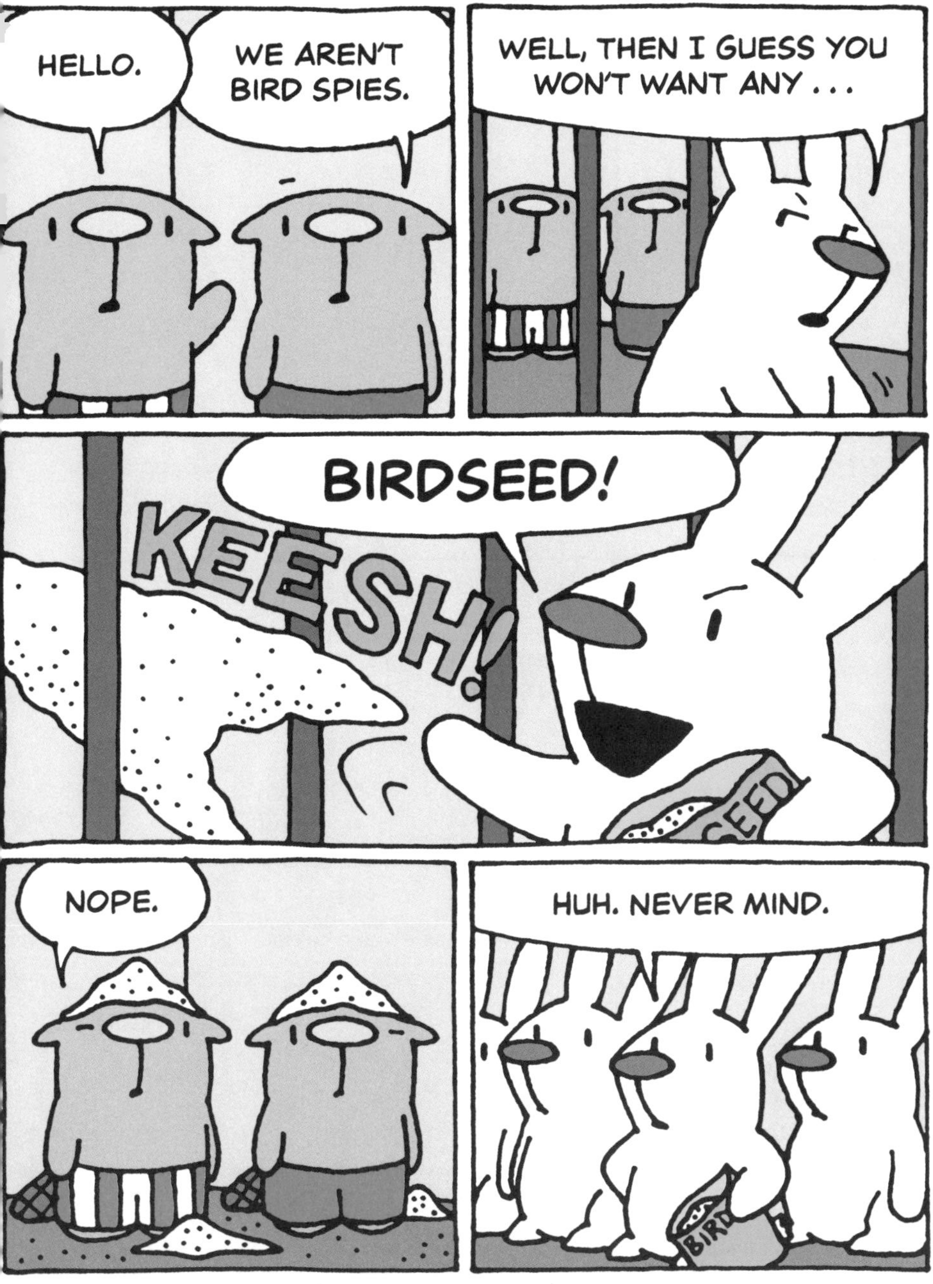
HELLO.
WE AREN'T BIRD SPIES.
WELL, THEN I GUESS YOU WON'T WANT ANY . . .
BIRDSEED!
KEESH!
SEED
NOPE.
HUH. NEVER MIND.
BIRD

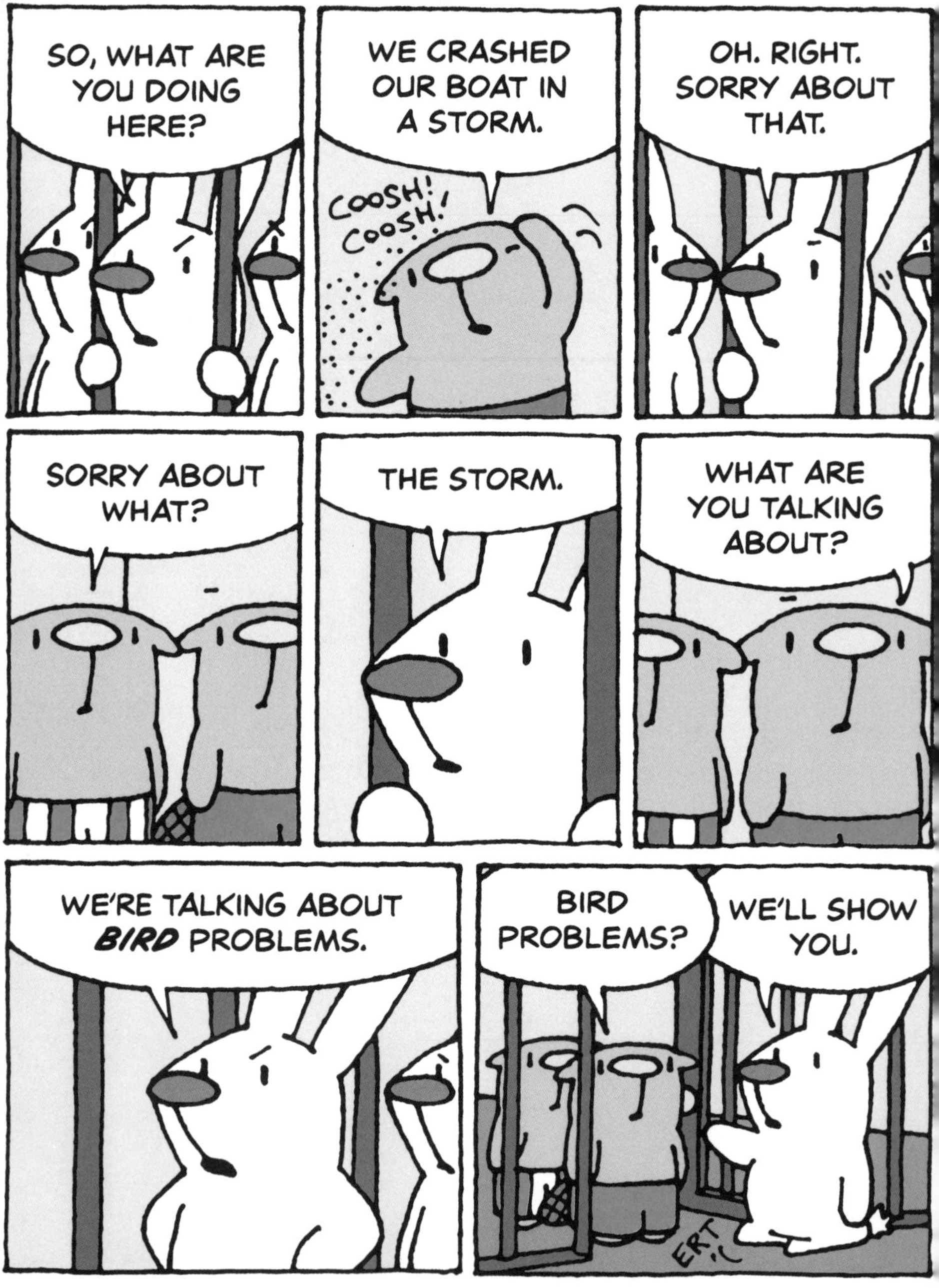
SO, WHAT ARE YOU DOING HERE?
WE CRASHED OUR BOAT IN A STORM.
COOSH! COOSH!
OH. RIGHT. SORRY ABOUT THAT.
SORRY ABOUT WHAT?
THE STORM.
WHAT ARE YOU TALKING ABOUT?
WE'RE TALKING ABOUT *BIRD* PROBLEMS.
BIRD PROBLEMS?
WE'LL SHOW YOU.
ERT

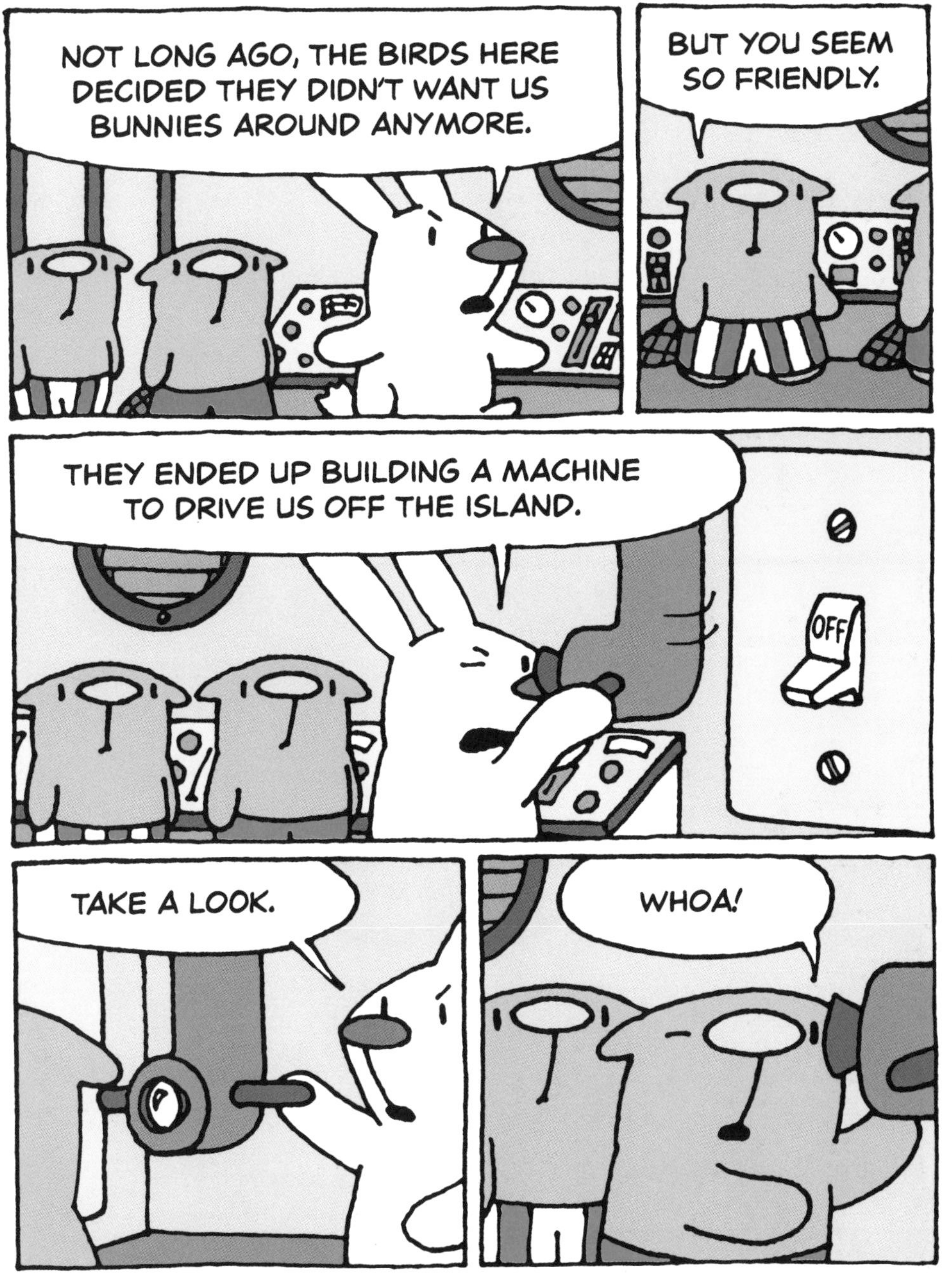
NOT LONG AGO, THE BIRDS HERE DECIDED THEY DIDN'T WANT US BUNNIES AROUND ANYMORE.
BUT YOU SEEM SO FRIENDLY.
THEY ENDED UP BUILDING A MACHINE TO DRIVE US OFF THE ISLAND.
OFF
TAKE A LOOK.
WHOA!

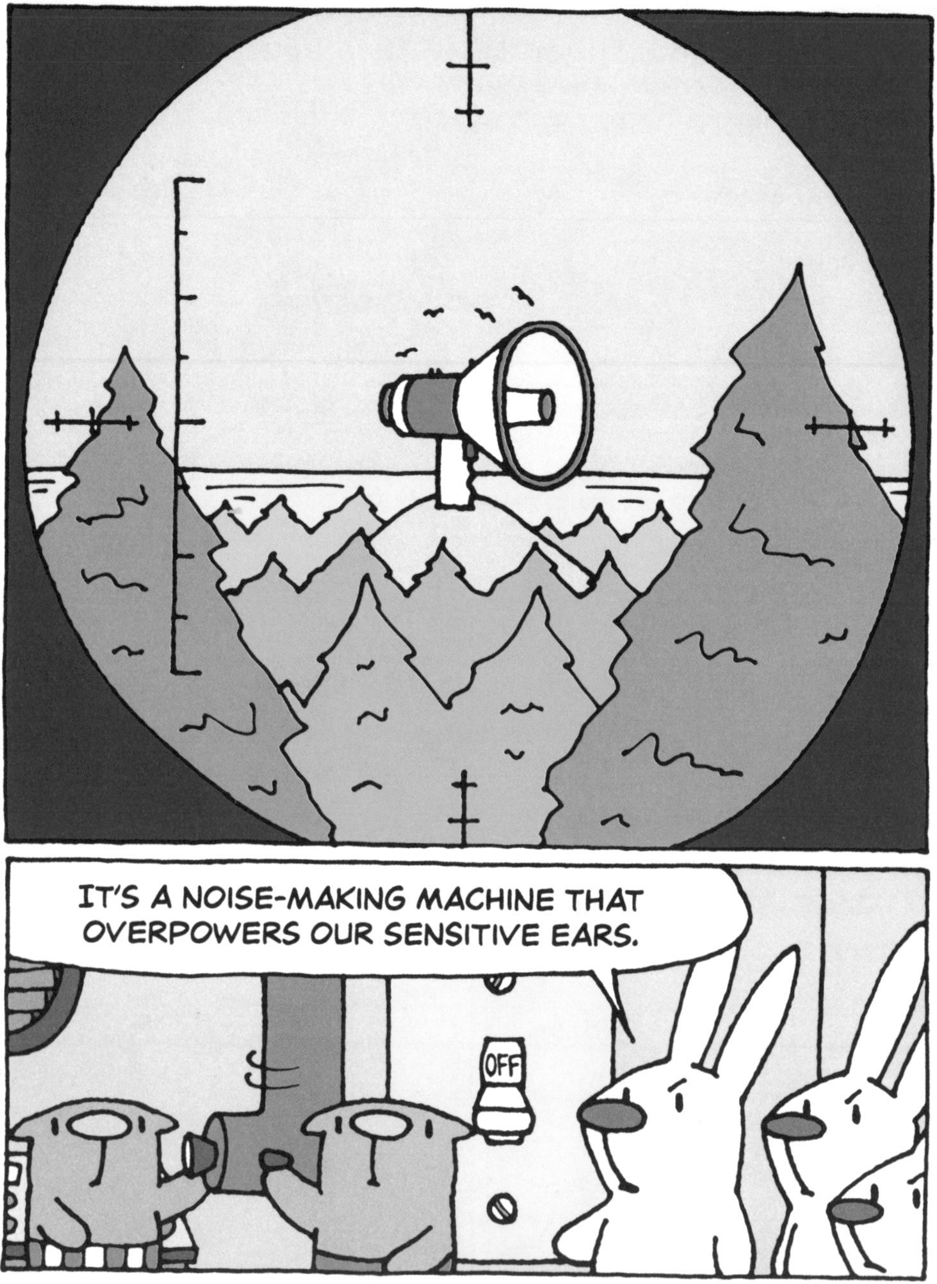
IT'S A NOISE-MAKING MACHINE THAT OVERPOWERS OUR SENSITIVE EARS.
OFF

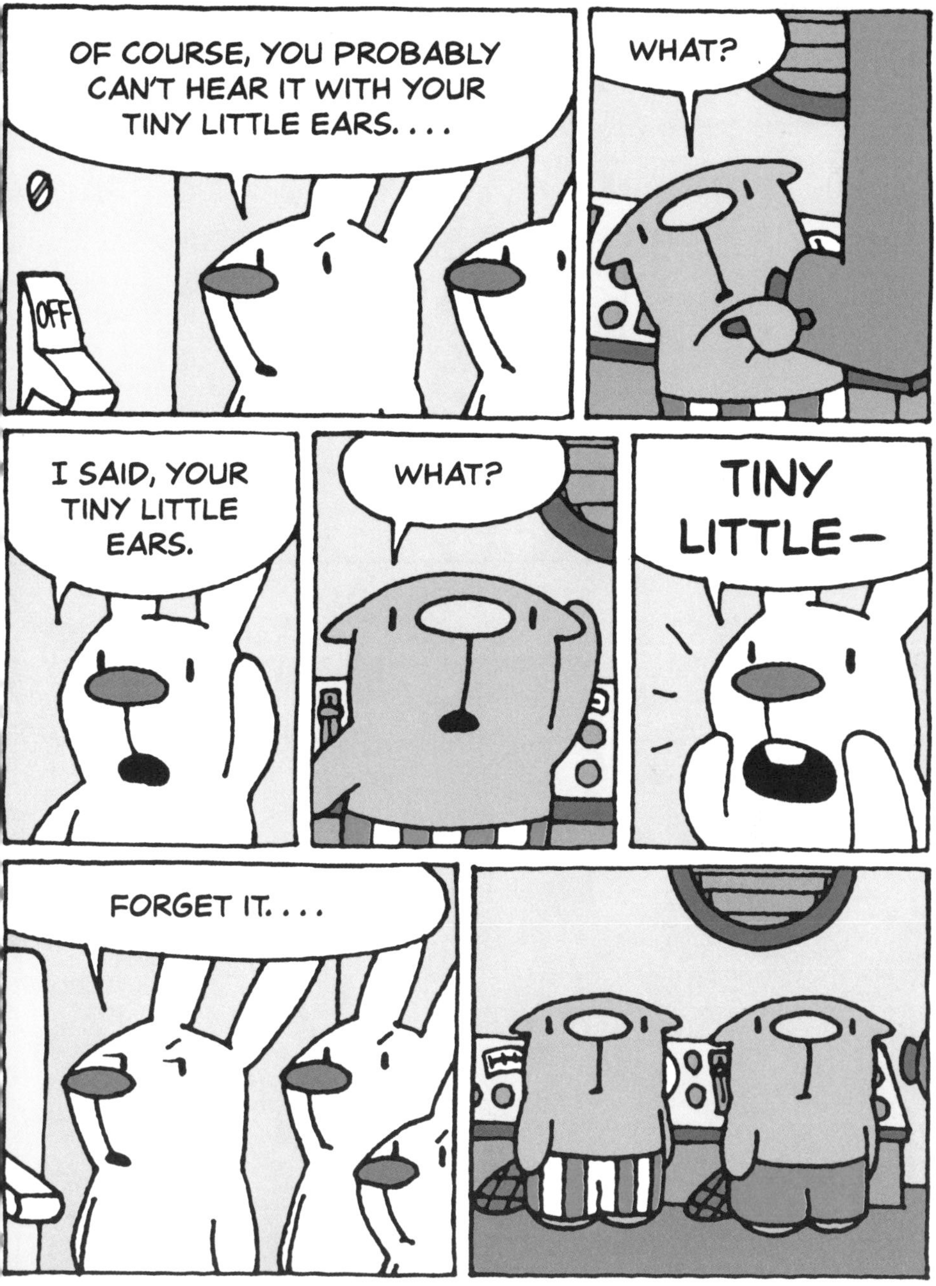
OF COURSE, YOU PROBABLY CAN'T HEAR IT WITH YOUR TINY LITTLE EARS. . . .
OFF
WHAT?
I SAID, YOUR TINY LITTLE EARS.
WHAT?
TINY LITTLE—
FORGET IT. . . .

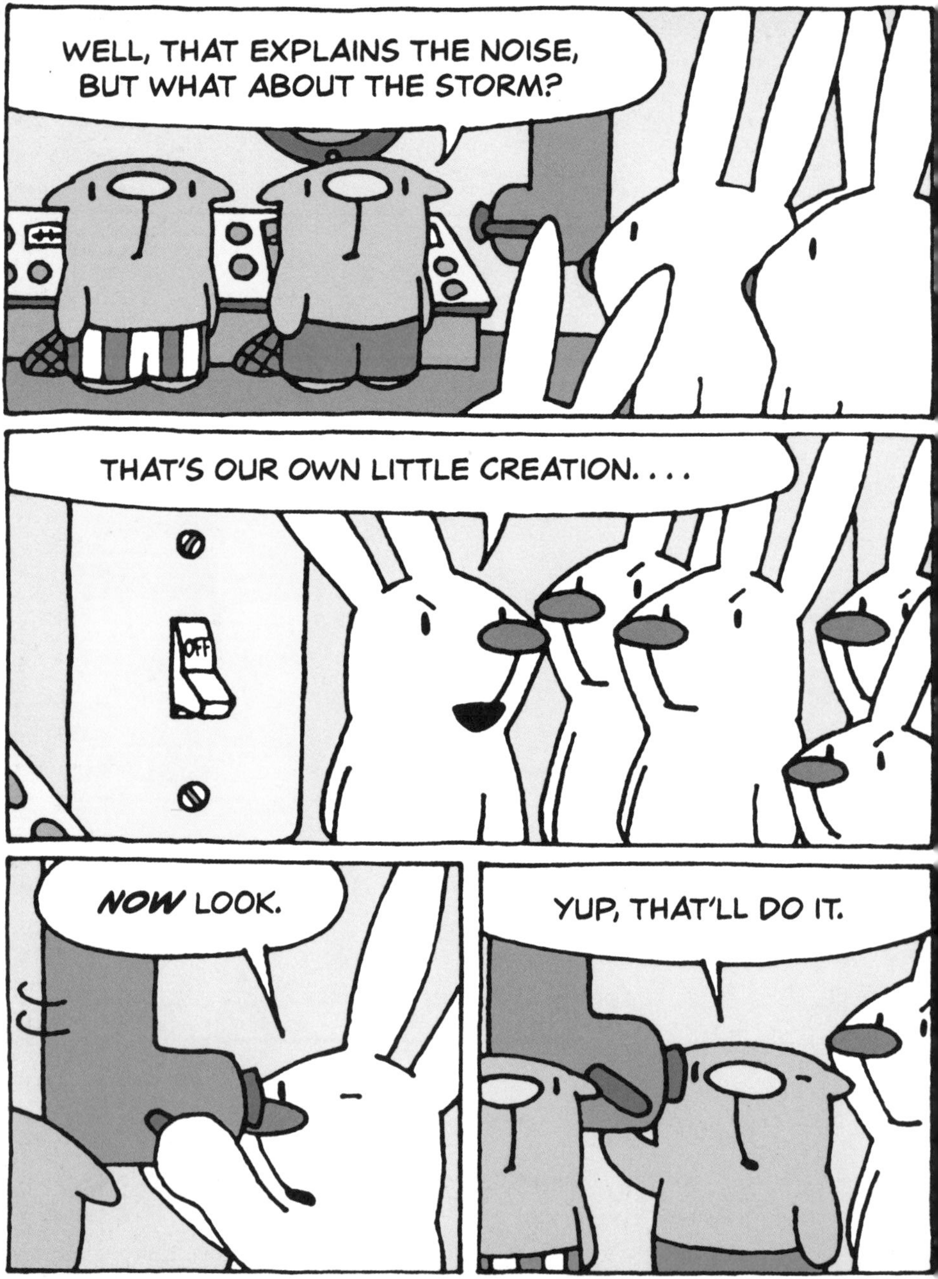
WELL, THAT EXPLAINS THE NOISE, BUT WHAT ABOUT THE STORM?
THAT'S OUR OWN LITTLE CREATION. . . .
OFF
NOW LOOK.
YUP, THAT'LL DO IT.

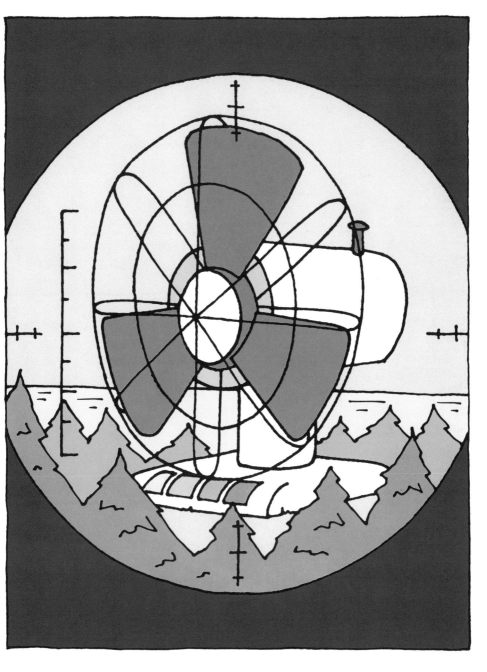

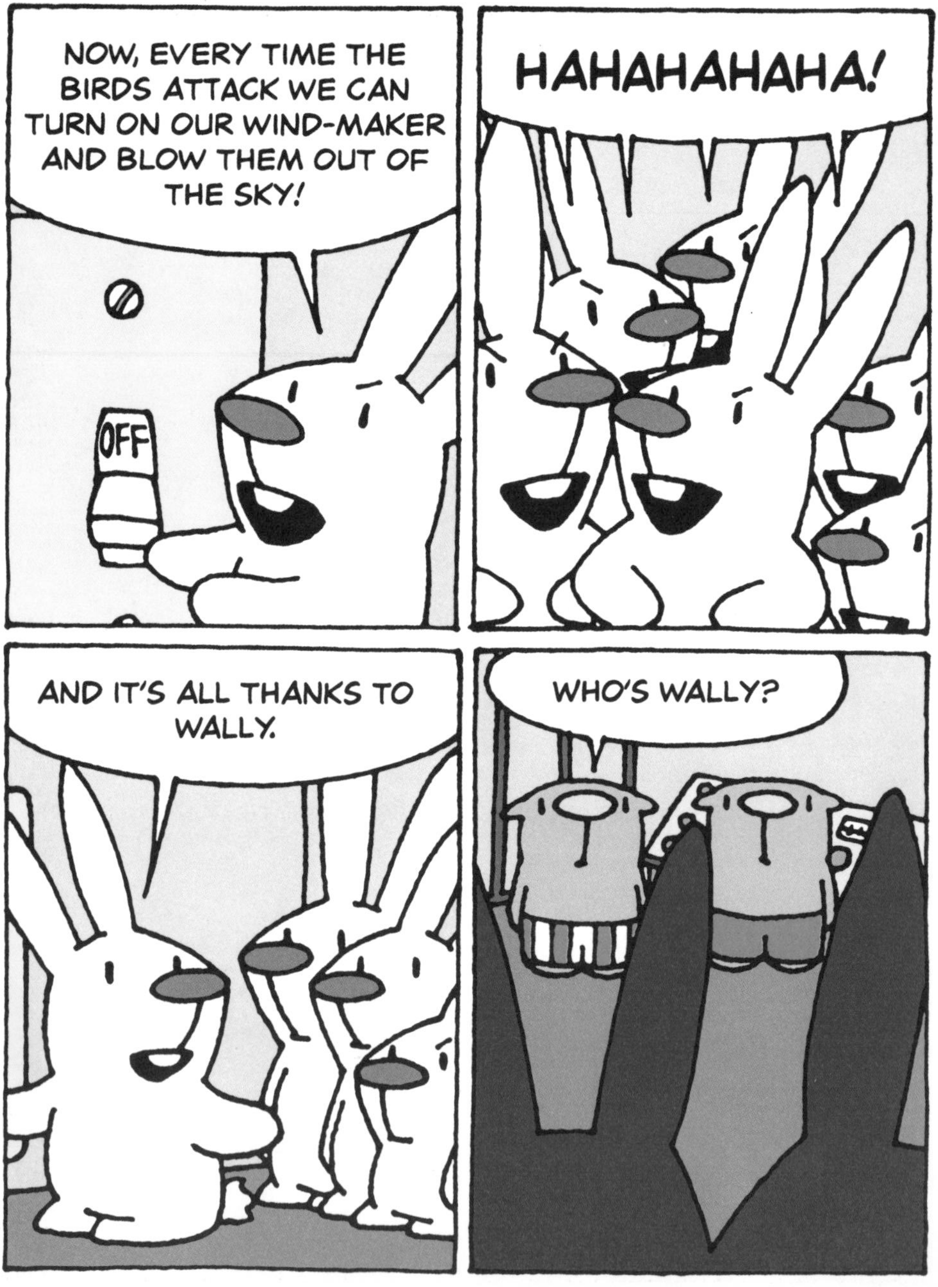
NOW, EVERY TIME THE BIRDS ATTACK WE CAN TURN ON OUR WIND-MAKER AND BLOW THEM OUT OF THE SKY!
OFF
HAHAHAHAHA!
AND IT'S ALL THANKS TO WALLY.
WHO'S WALLY?

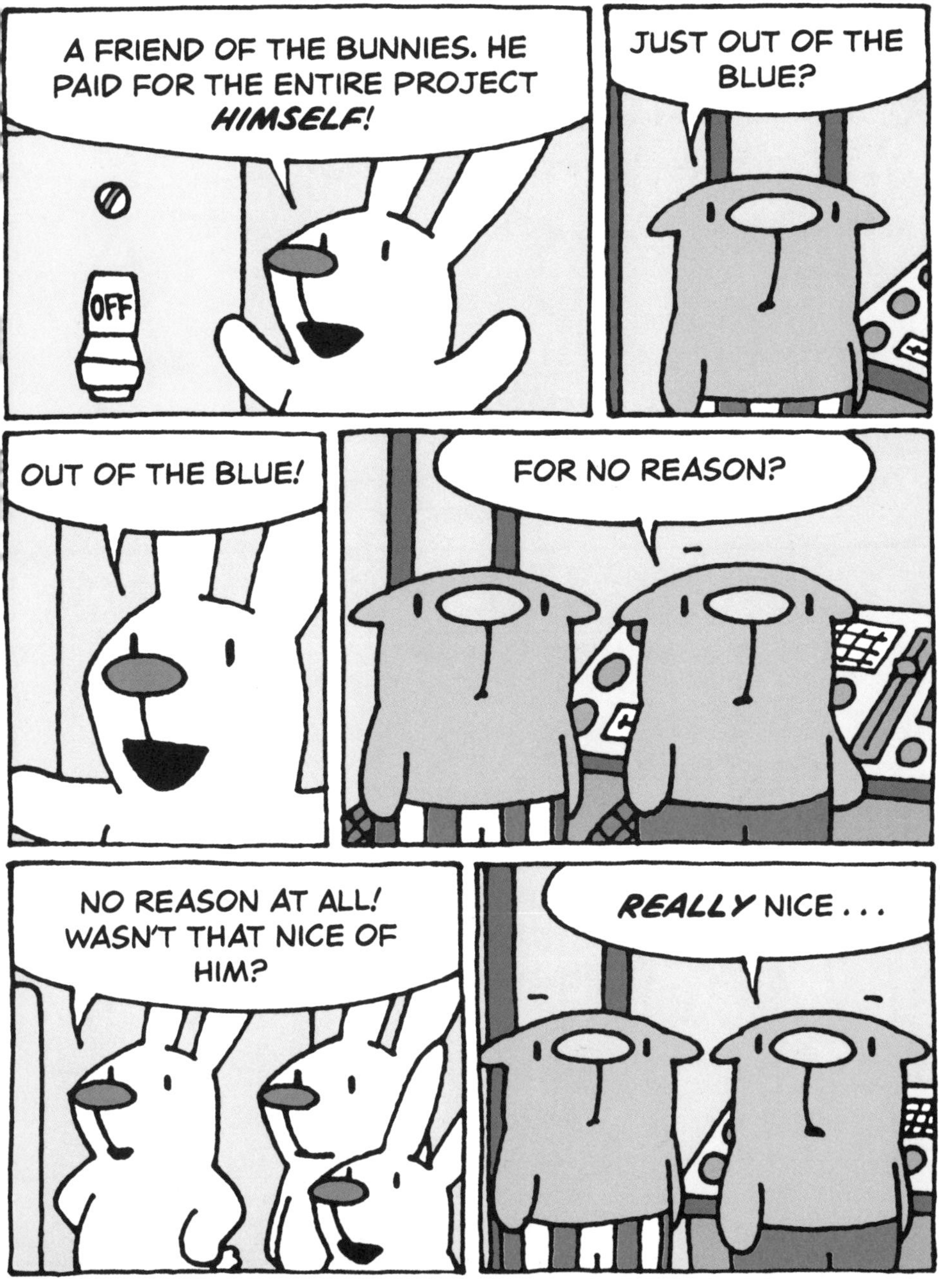
A FRIEND OF THE BUNNIES. HE PAID FOR THE ENTIRE PROJECT *HIMSELF*!
OFF
JUST OUT OF THE BLUE?
OUT OF THE BLUE!
FOR NO REASON?
NO REASON AT ALL! WASN'T THAT NICE OF HIM?
REALLY NICE . . .

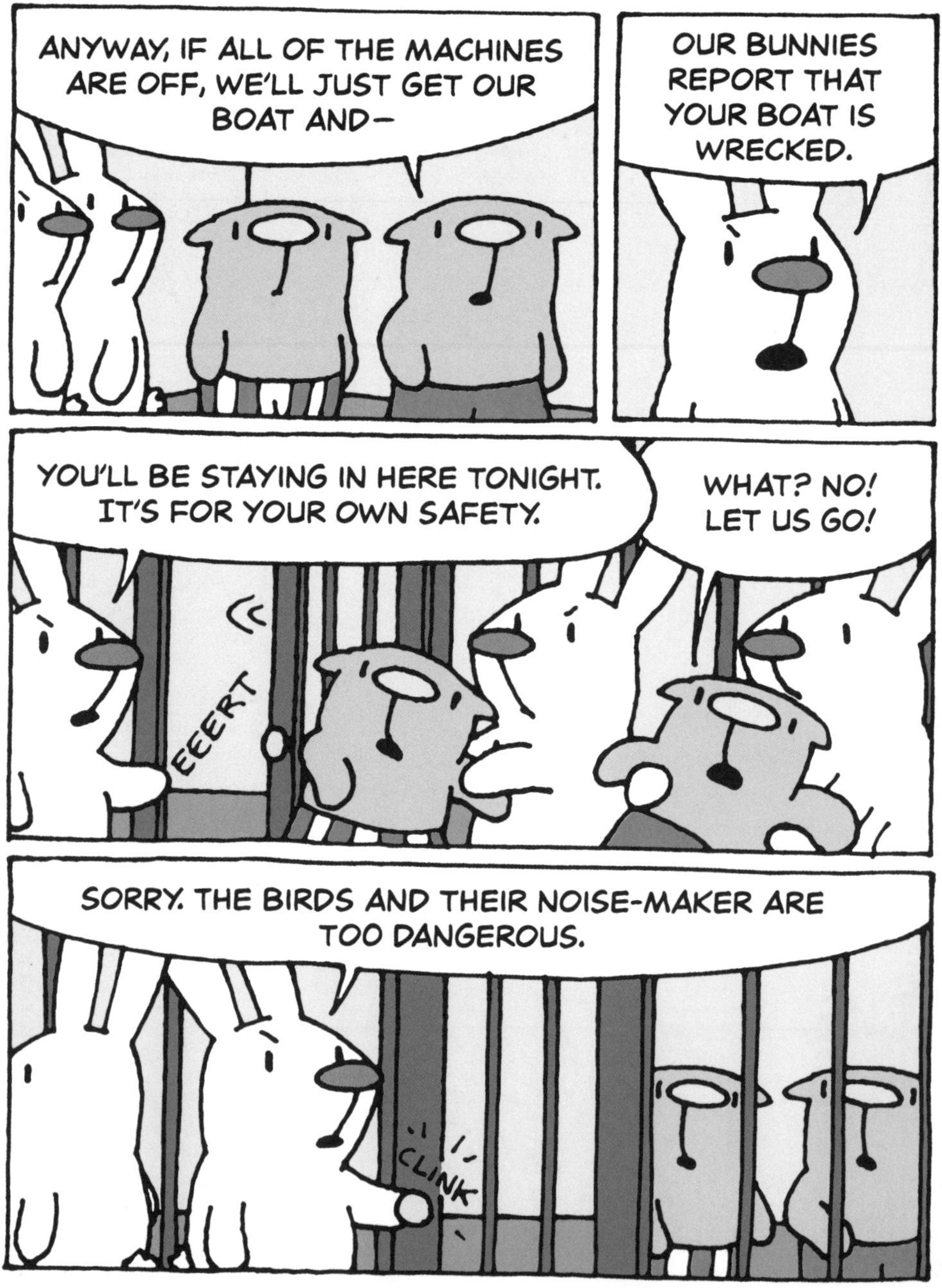
ANYWAY, IF ALL OF THE MACHINES ARE OFF, WE'LL JUST GET OUR BOAT AND—
OUR BUNNIES REPORT THAT YOUR BOAT IS WRECKED.
YOU'LL BE STAYING IN HERE TONIGHT. IT'S FOR YOUR OWN SAFETY.
WHAT? NO! LET US GO!
EEEERT
SORRY. THE BIRDS AND THEIR NOISE-MAKER ARE TOO DANGEROUS.
CLINK

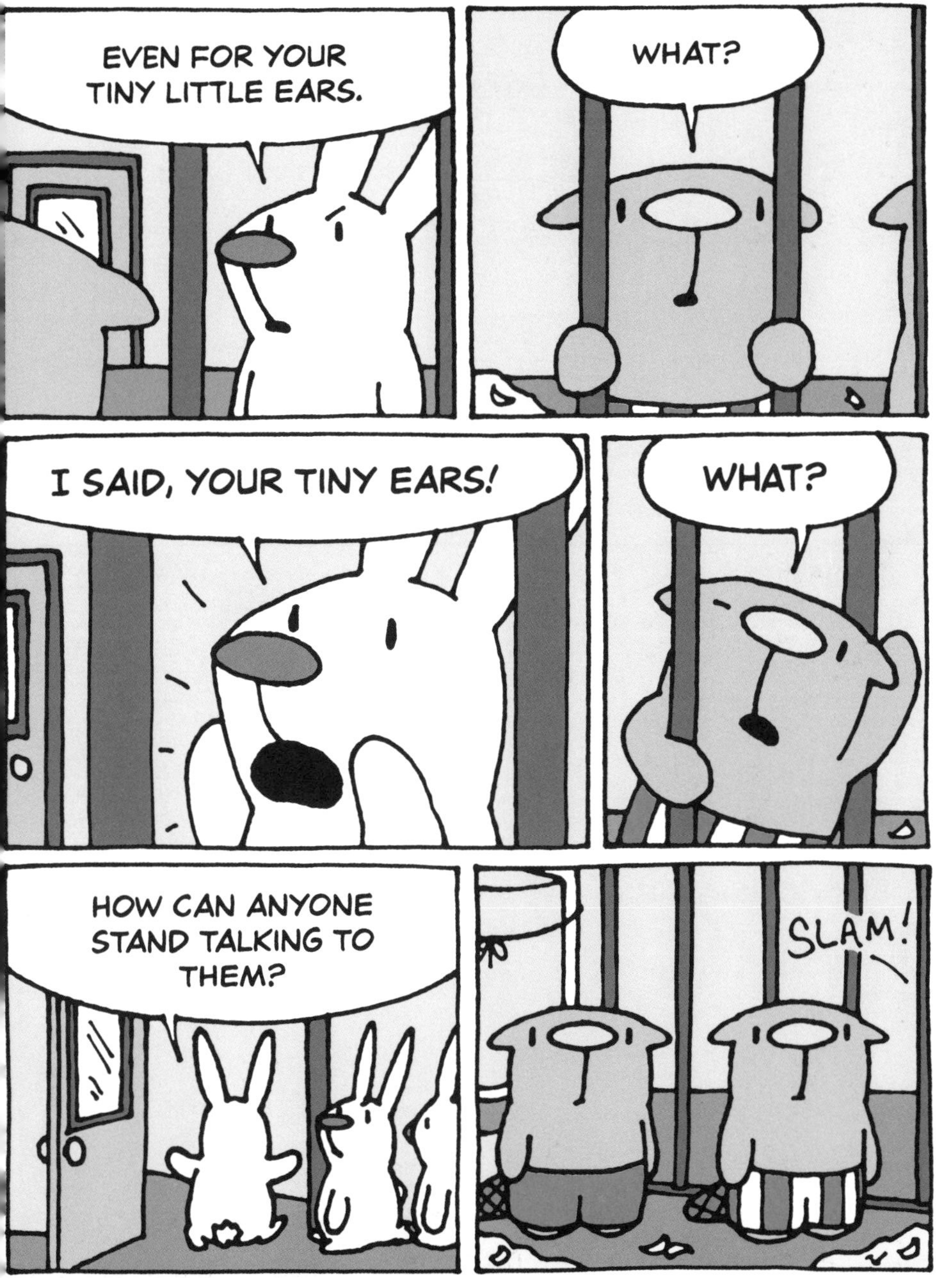
EVEN FOR YOUR TINY LITTLE EARS.
WHAT?
I SAID, YOUR TINY EARS!
WHAT?
HOW CAN ANYONE STAND TALKING TO THEM?
SLAM!

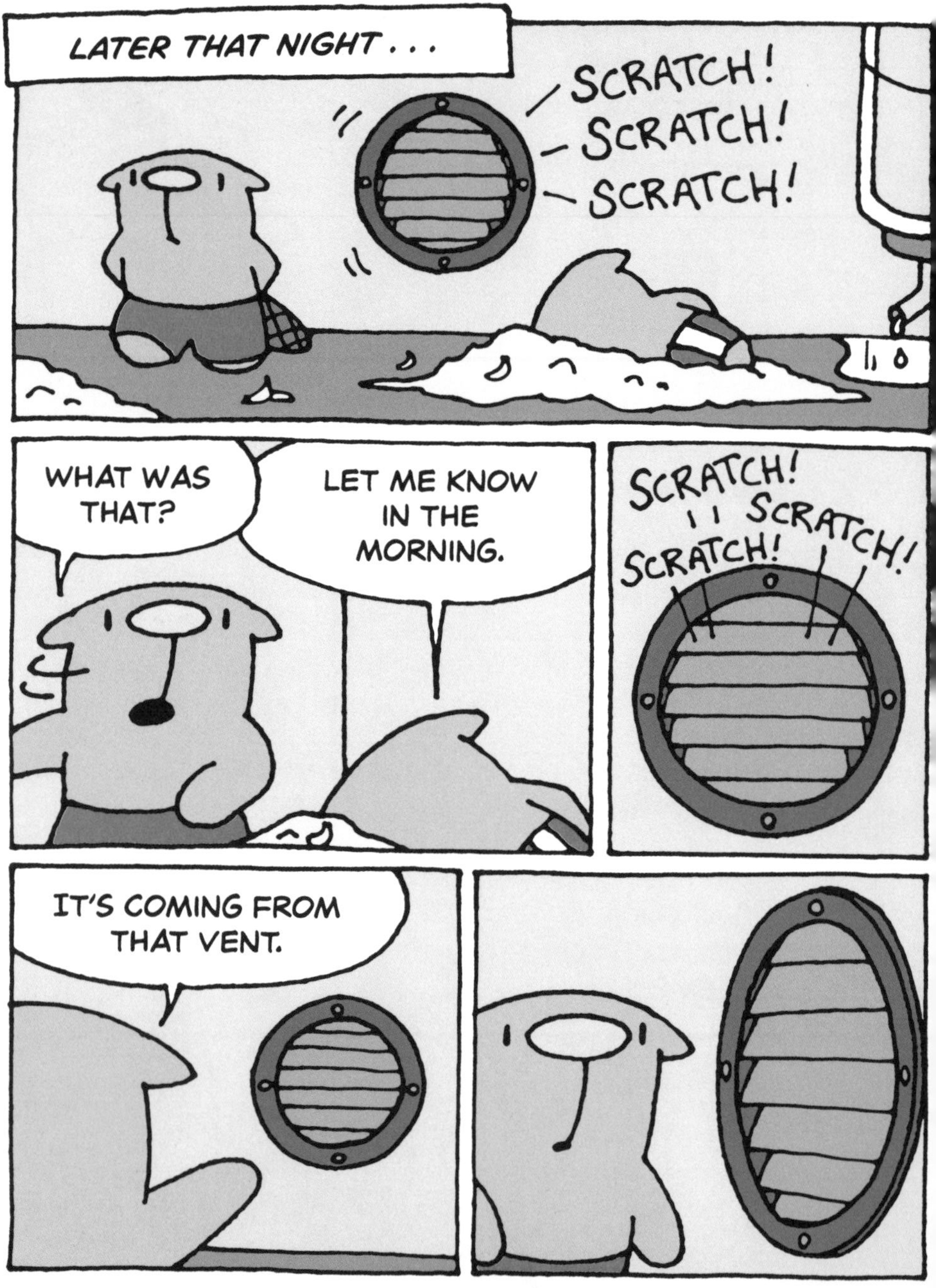

LATER THAT NIGHT . . .
SCRATCH!
SCRATCH!
SCRATCH!
WHAT WAS THAT?
LET ME KNOW IN THE MORNING.
SCRATCH!
SCRATCH!
SCRATCH!
IT'S COMING FROM THAT VENT.

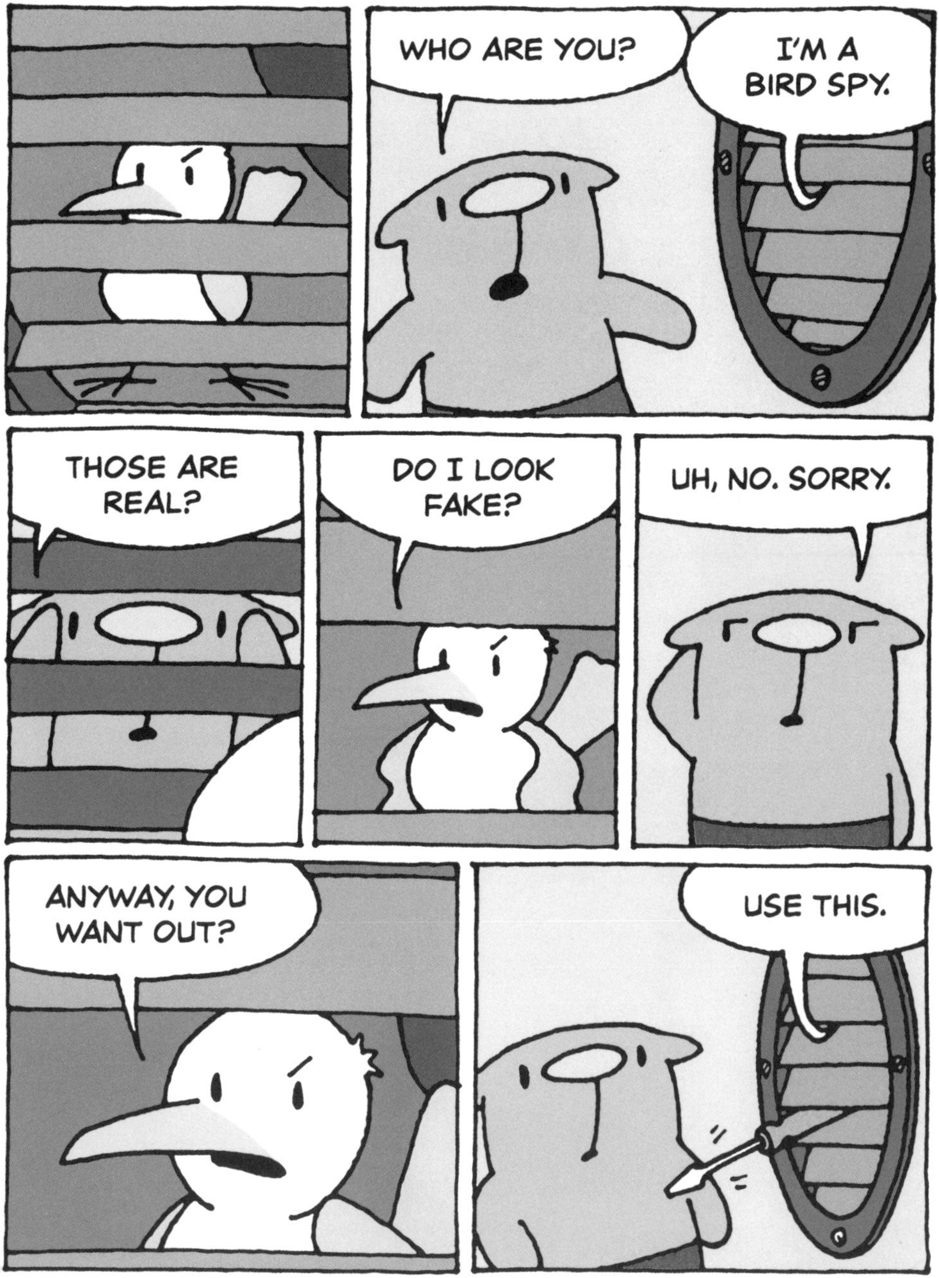

WHO ARE YOU?
I'M A BIRD SPY.
THOSE ARE REAL?
DO I LOOK FAKE?
UH, NO. SORRY.
ANYWAY, YOU WANT OUT?
USE THIS.

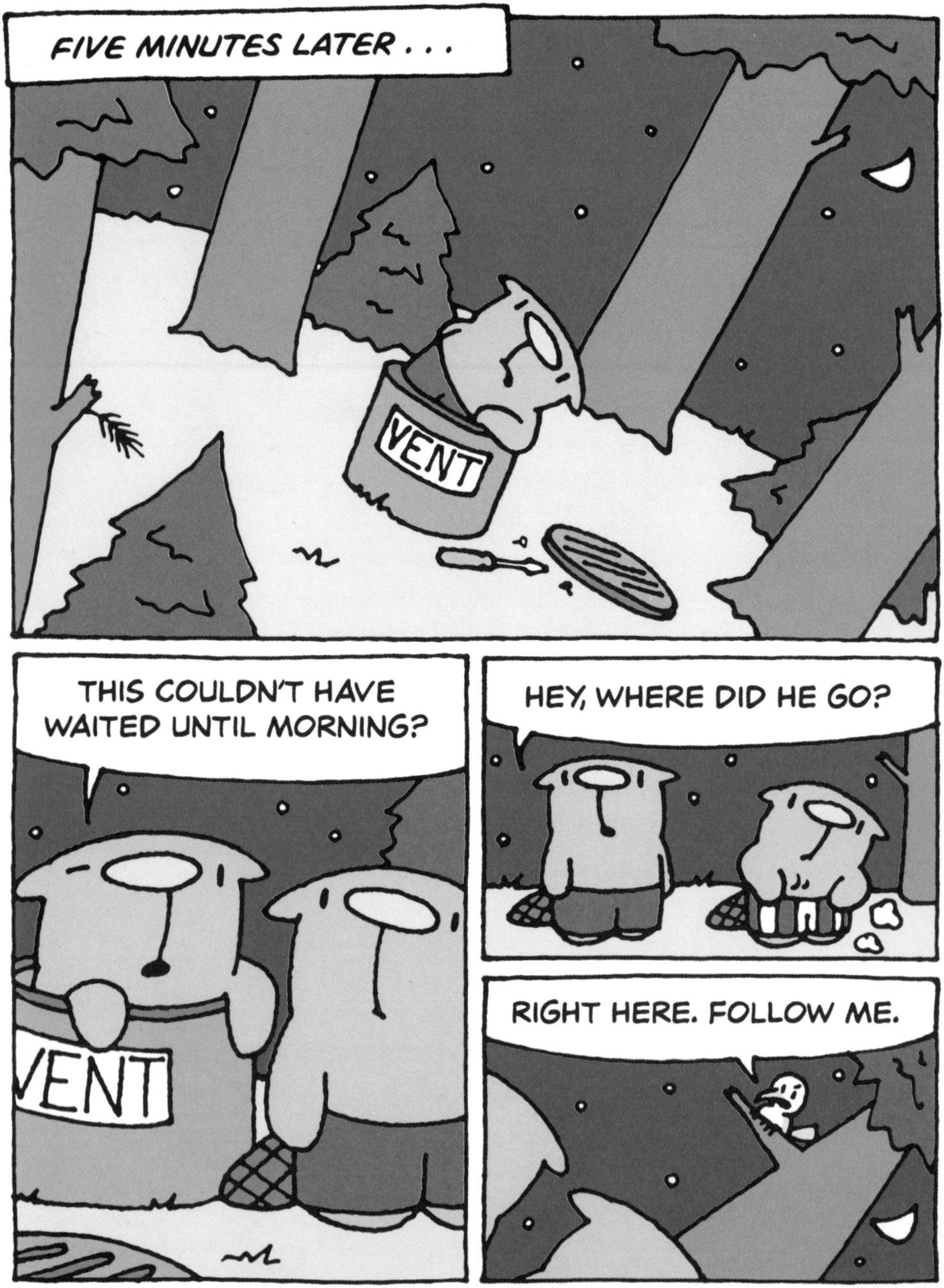
FIVE MINUTES LATER . . .
VENT
THIS COULDN'T HAVE WAITED UNTIL MORNING?
VENT
HEY, WHERE DID HE GO?
RIGHT HERE. FOLLOW ME.

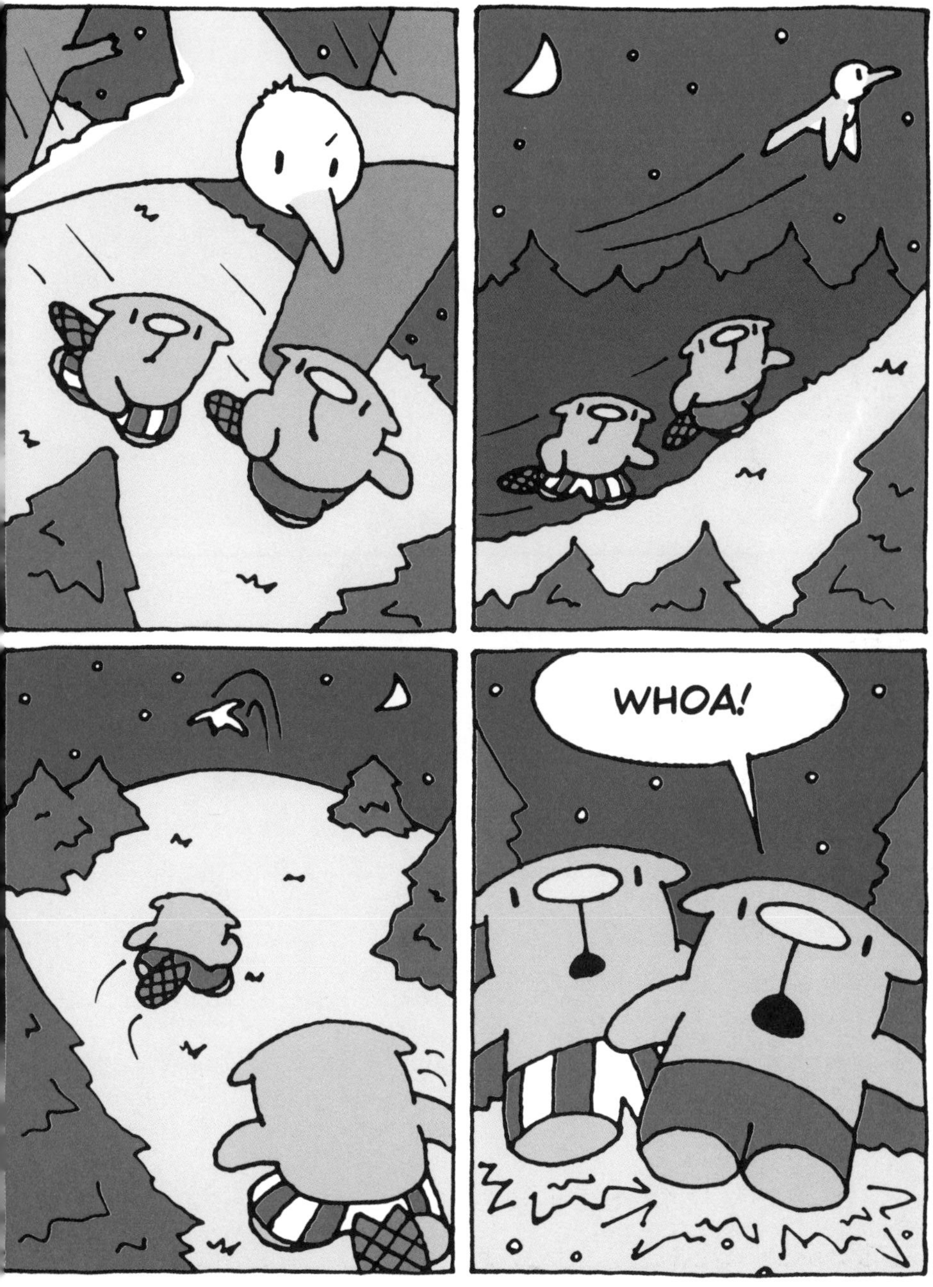
WHOA!

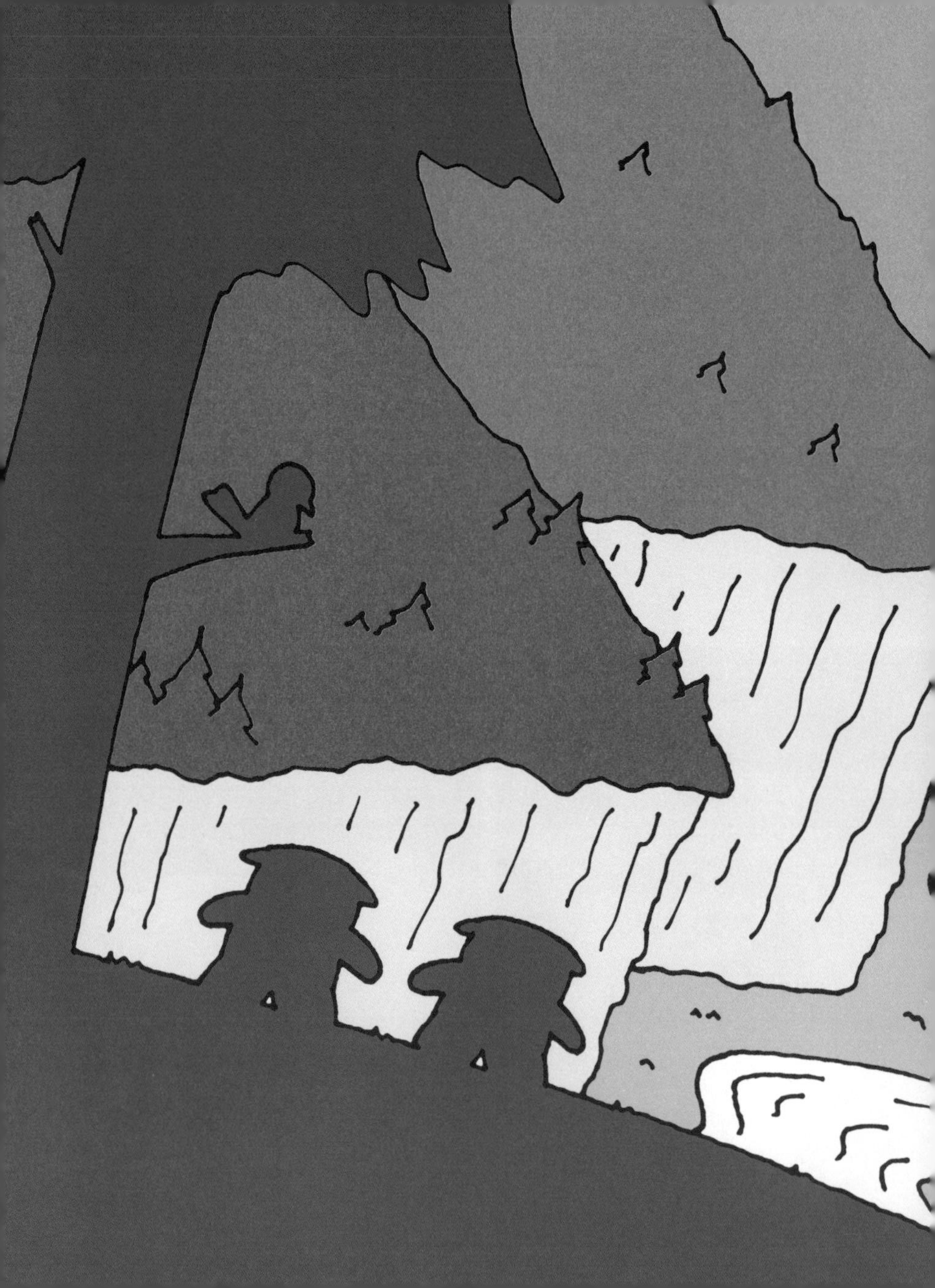

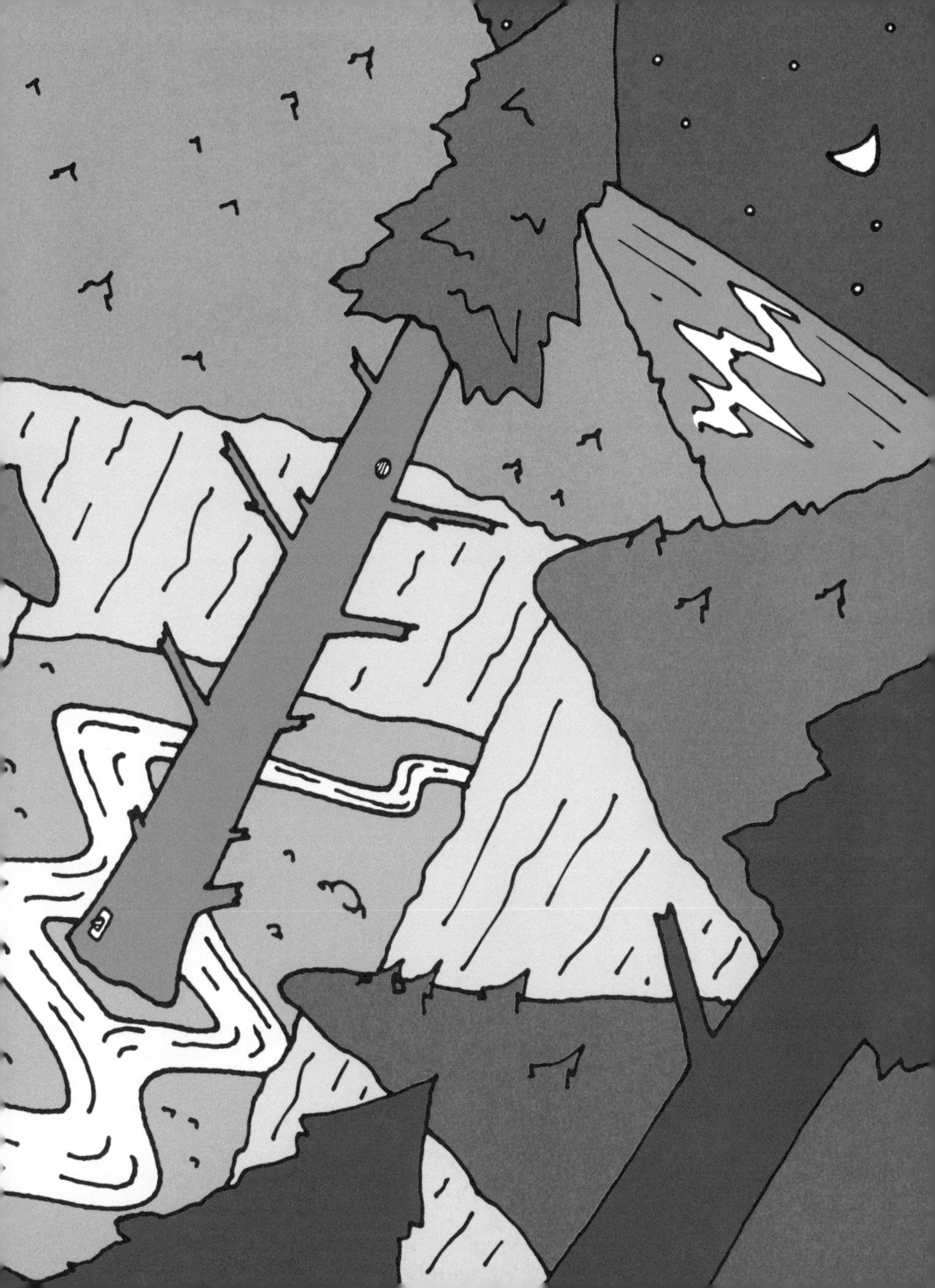

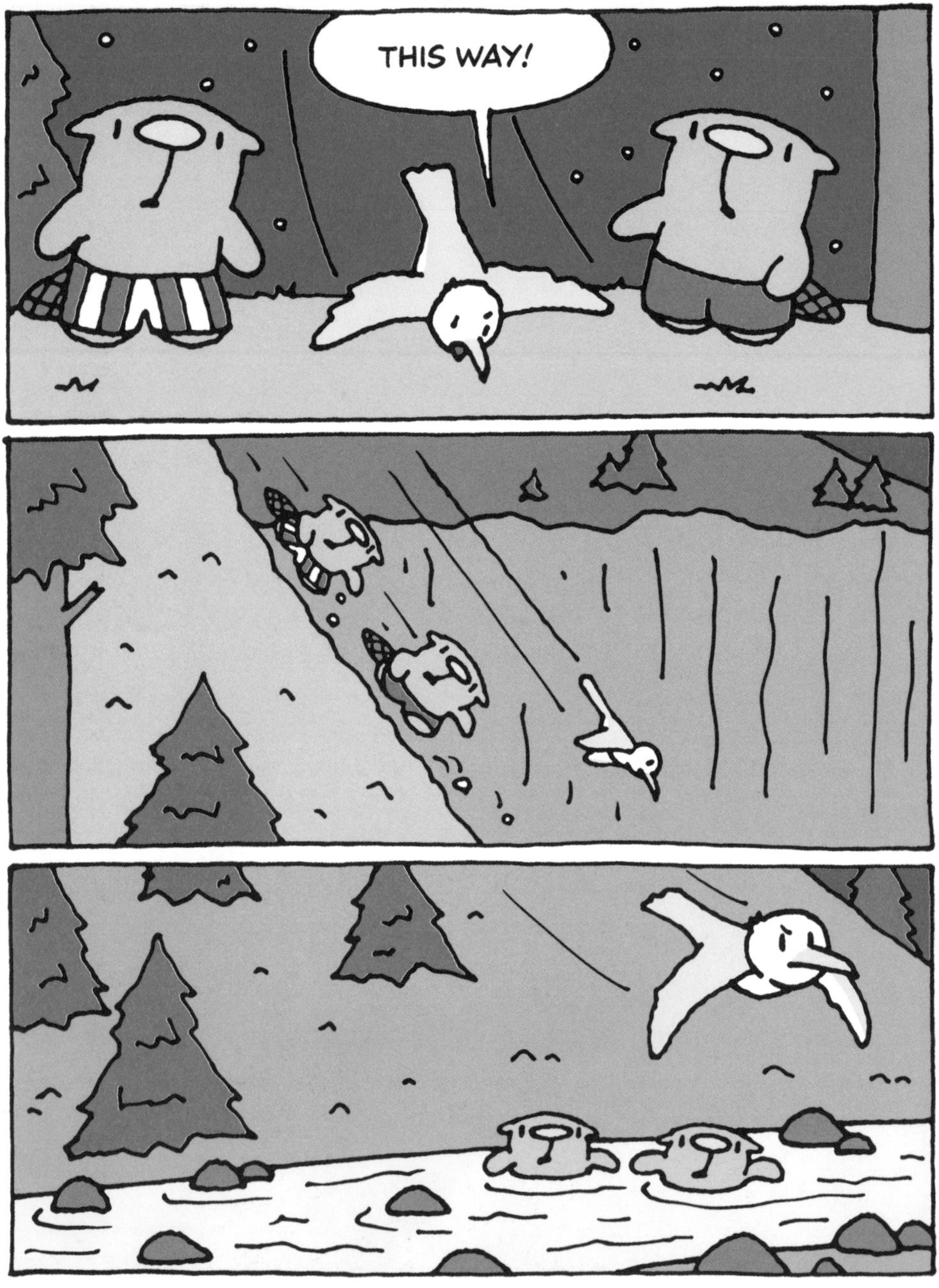
THIS WAY!

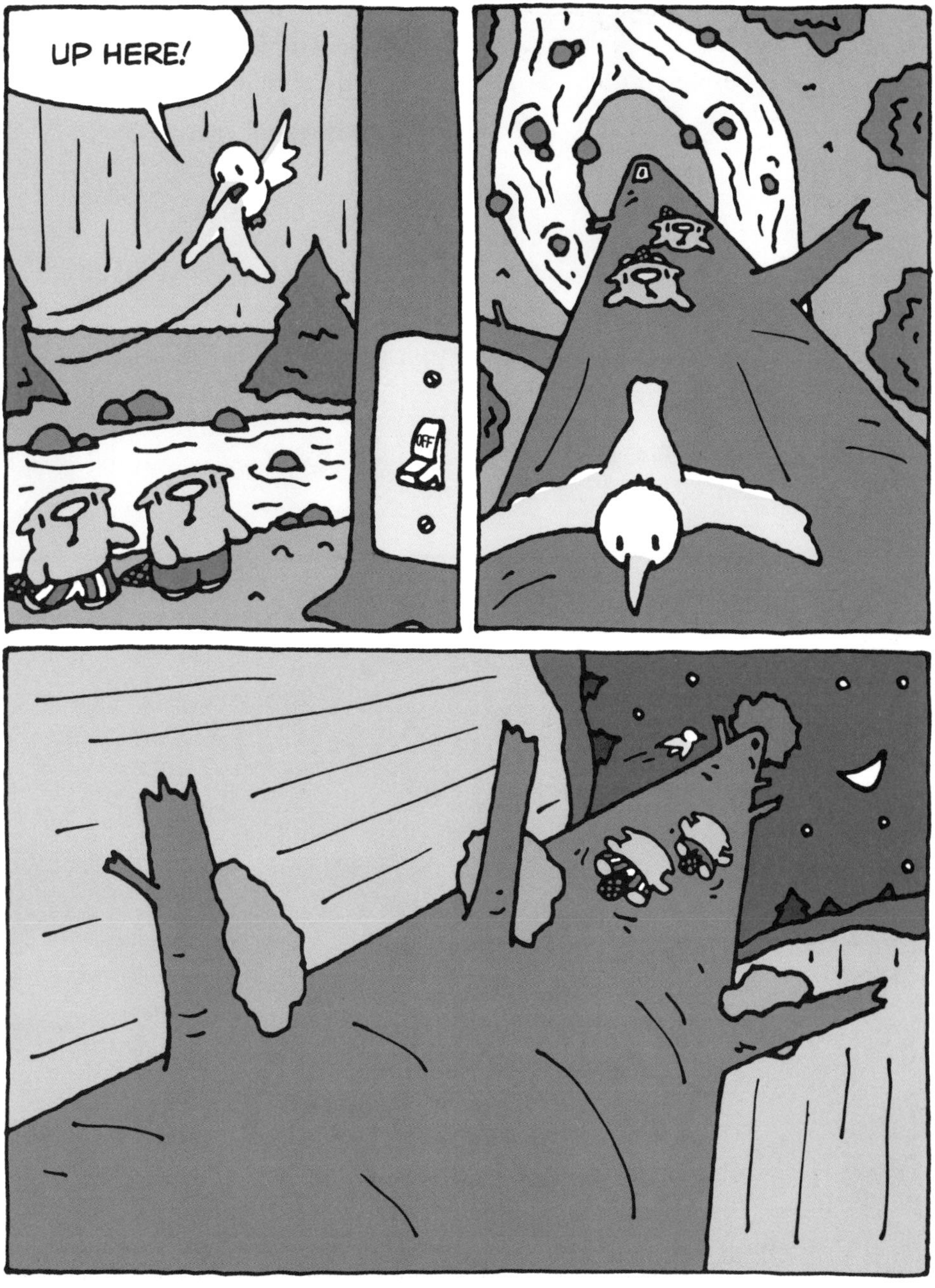
UP HERE!
OFF

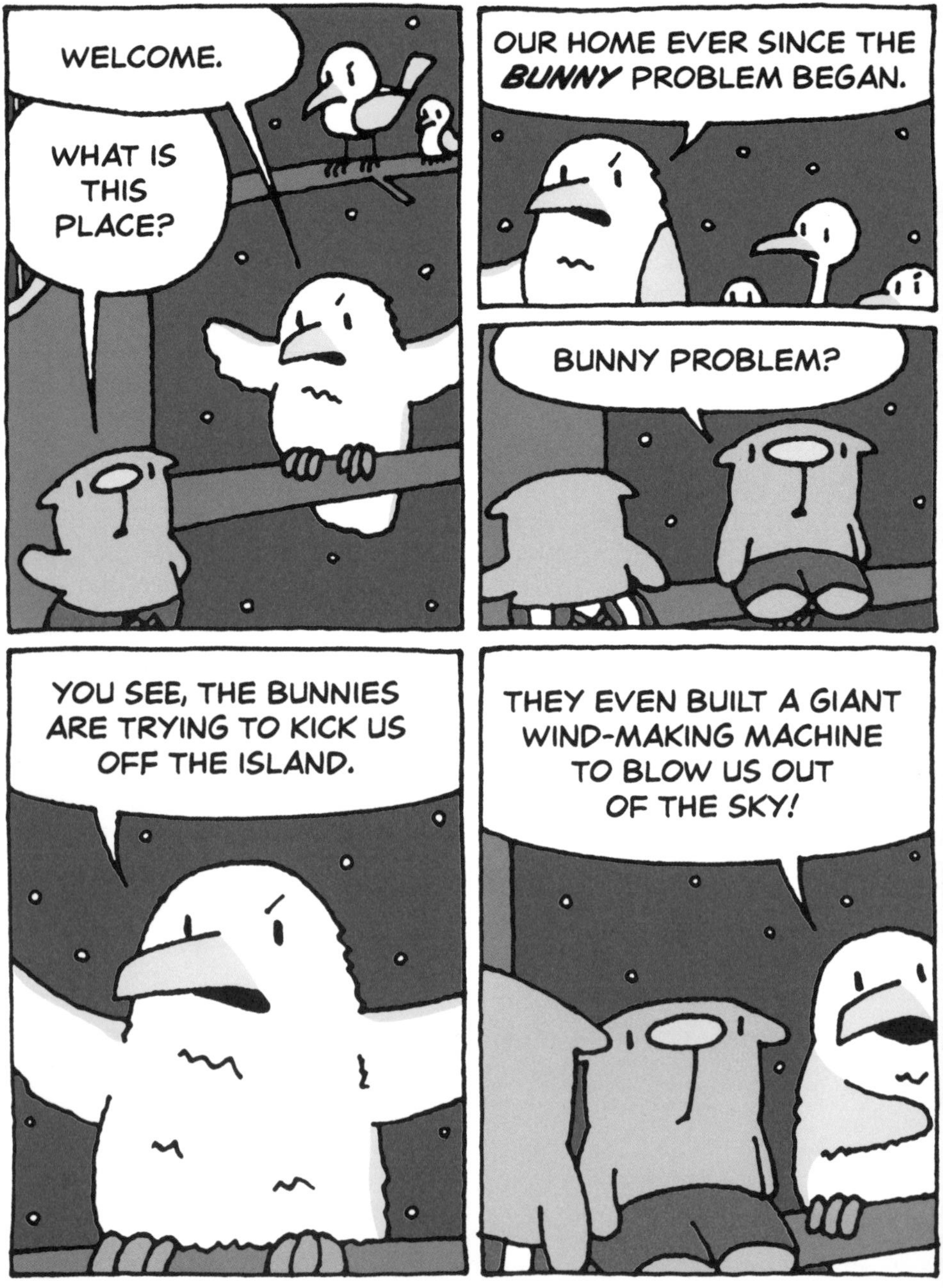
WELCOME.
WHAT IS THIS PLACE?
OUR HOME EVER SINCE THE *BUNNY* PROBLEM BEGAN.
BUNNY PROBLEM?
YOU SEE, THE BUNNIES ARE TRYING TO KICK US OFF THE ISLAND.
THEY EVEN BUILT A GIANT WIND-MAKING MACHINE TO BLOW US OUT OF THE SKY!

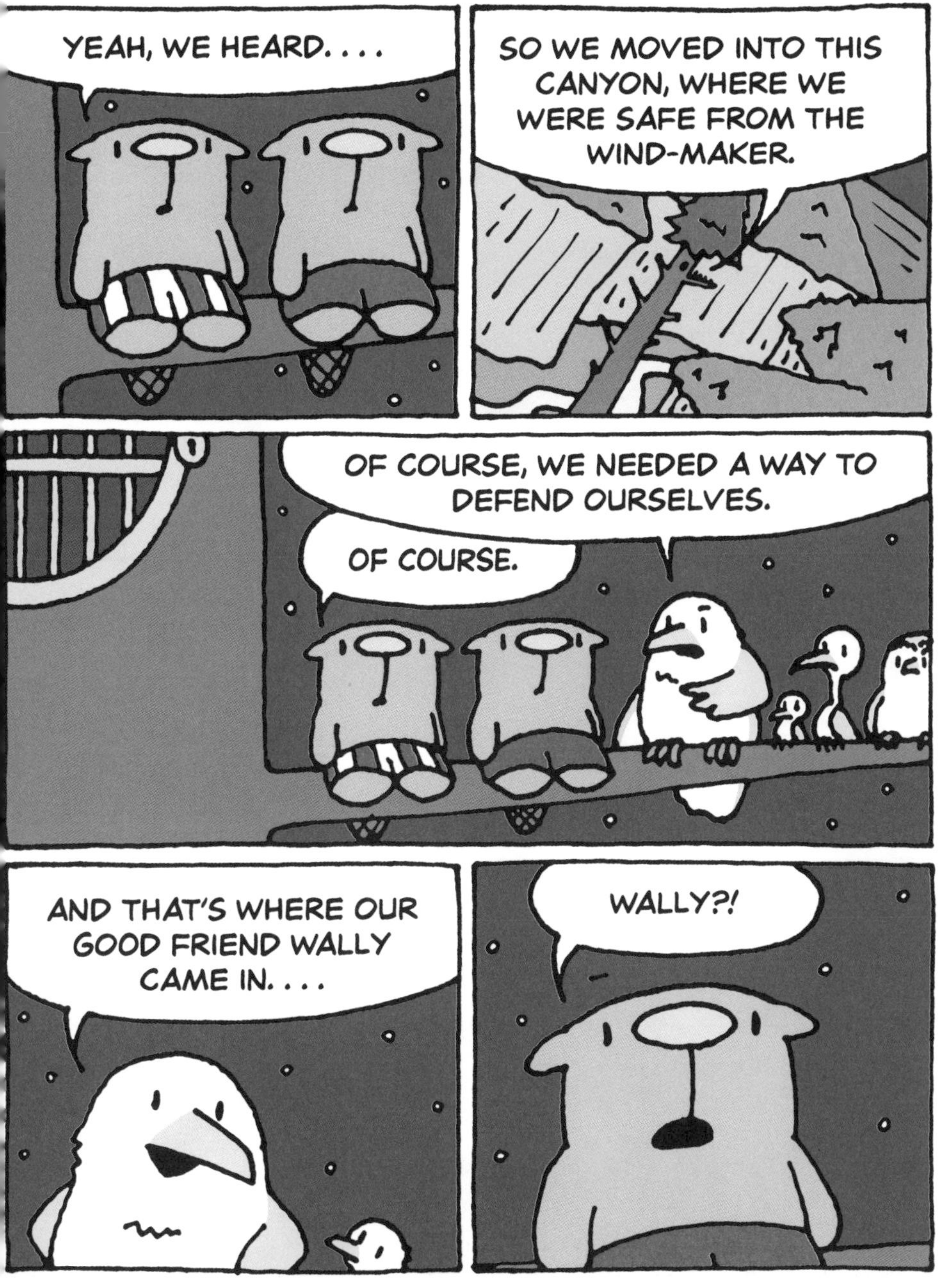
YEAH, WE HEARD. . . .
SO WE MOVED INTO THIS CANYON, WHERE WE WERE SAFE FROM THE WIND-MAKER.
OF COURSE, WE NEEDED A WAY TO DEFEND OURSELVES.
OF COURSE.
AND THAT'S WHERE OUR GOOD FRIEND WALLY CAME IN. . . .
WALLY?!

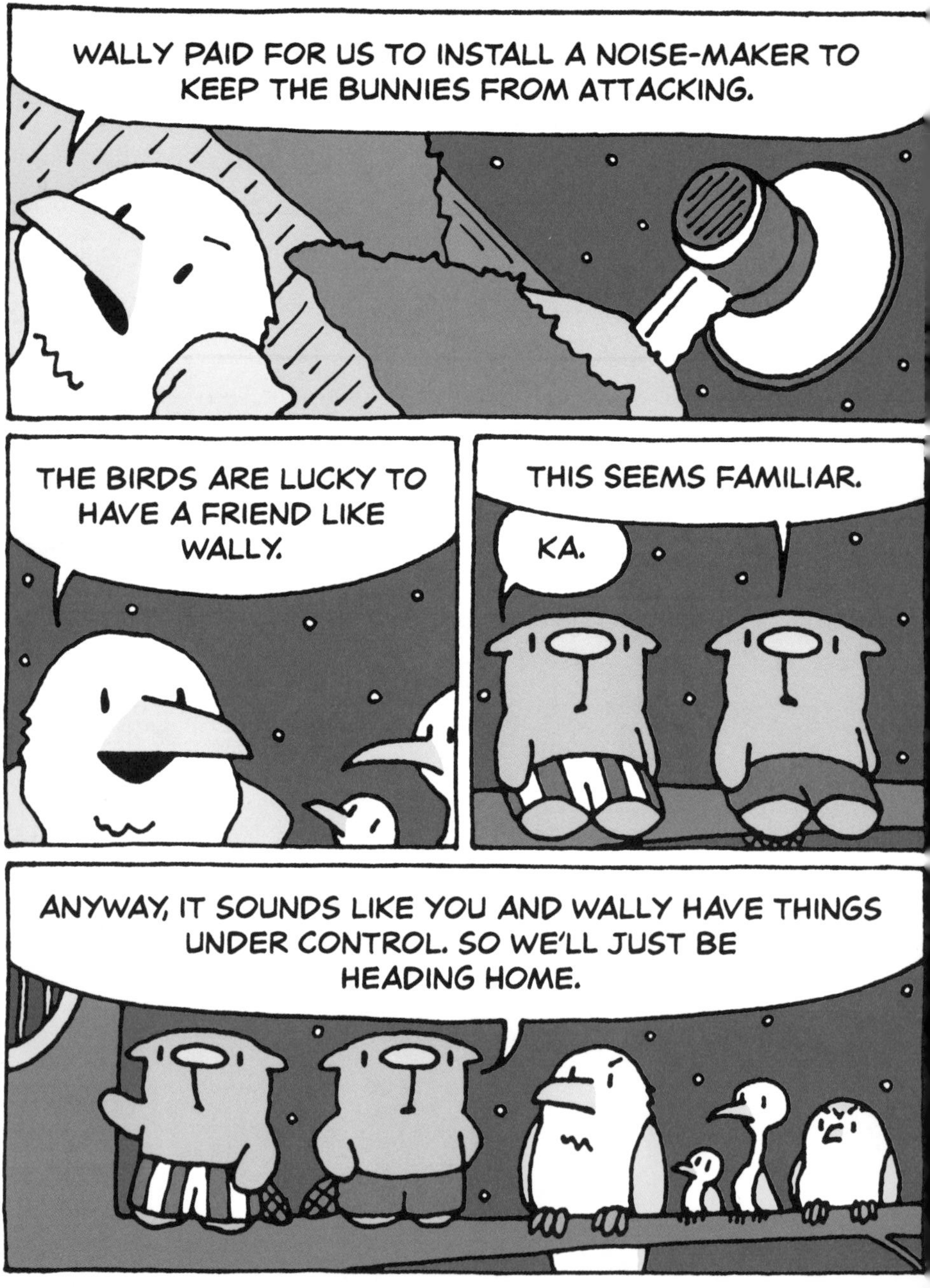
WALLY PAID FOR US TO INSTALL A NOISE-MAKER TO KEEP THE BUNNIES FROM ATTACKING.
THE BIRDS ARE LUCKY TO HAVE A FRIEND LIKE WALLY.
THIS SEEMS FAMILIAR.
KA.
ANYWAY, IT SOUNDS LIKE YOU AND WALLY HAVE THINGS UNDER CONTROL. SO WE'LL JUST BE HEADING HOME.

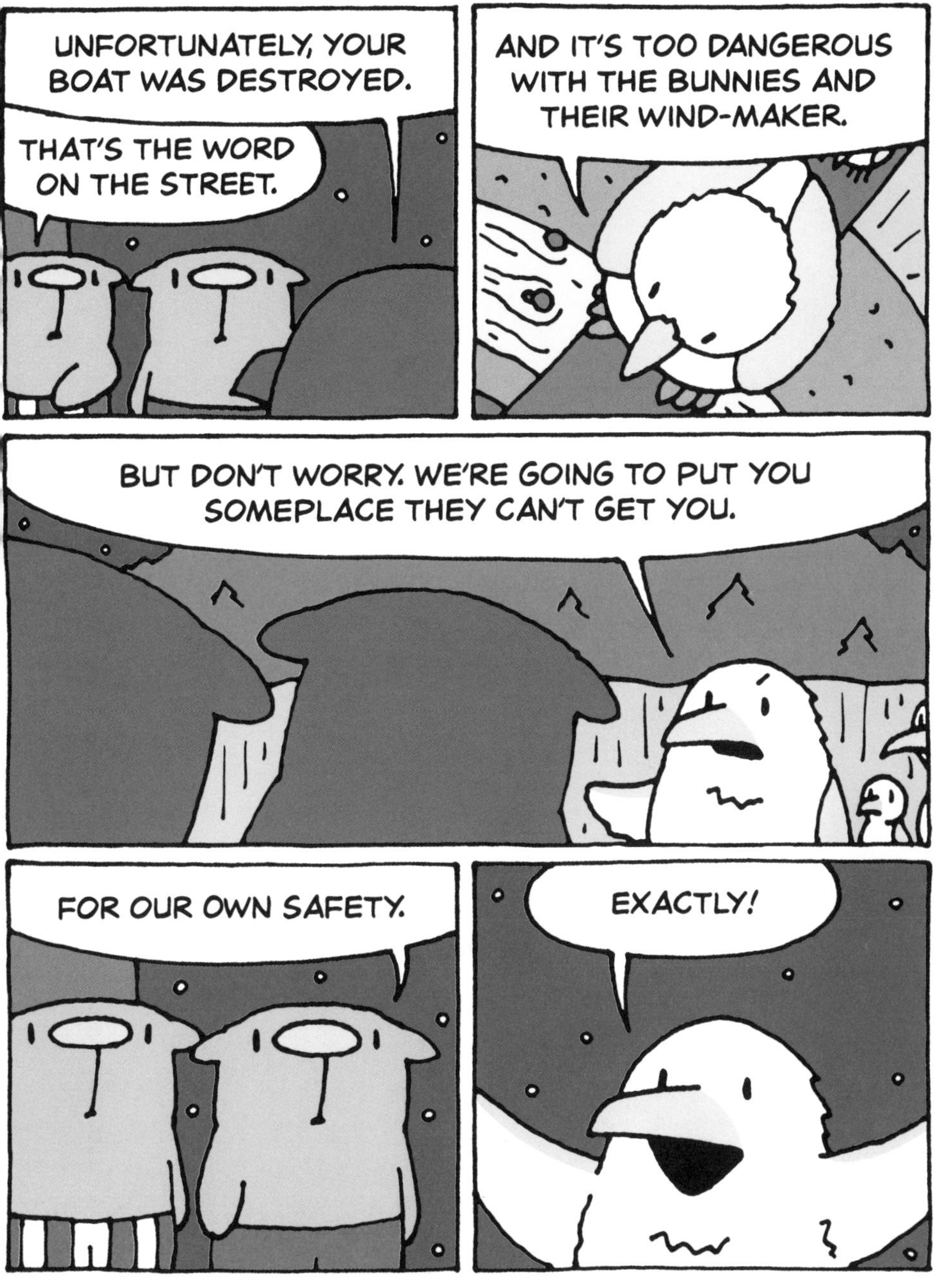
UNFORTUNATELY, YOUR BOAT WAS DESTROYED.
THAT'S THE WORD ON THE STREET.
AND IT'S TOO DANGEROUS WITH THE BUNNIES AND THEIR WIND-MAKER.
BUT DON'T WORRY. WE'RE GOING TO PUT YOU SOMEPLACE THEY CAN'T GET YOU.
FOR OUR OWN SAFETY.
EXACTLY!

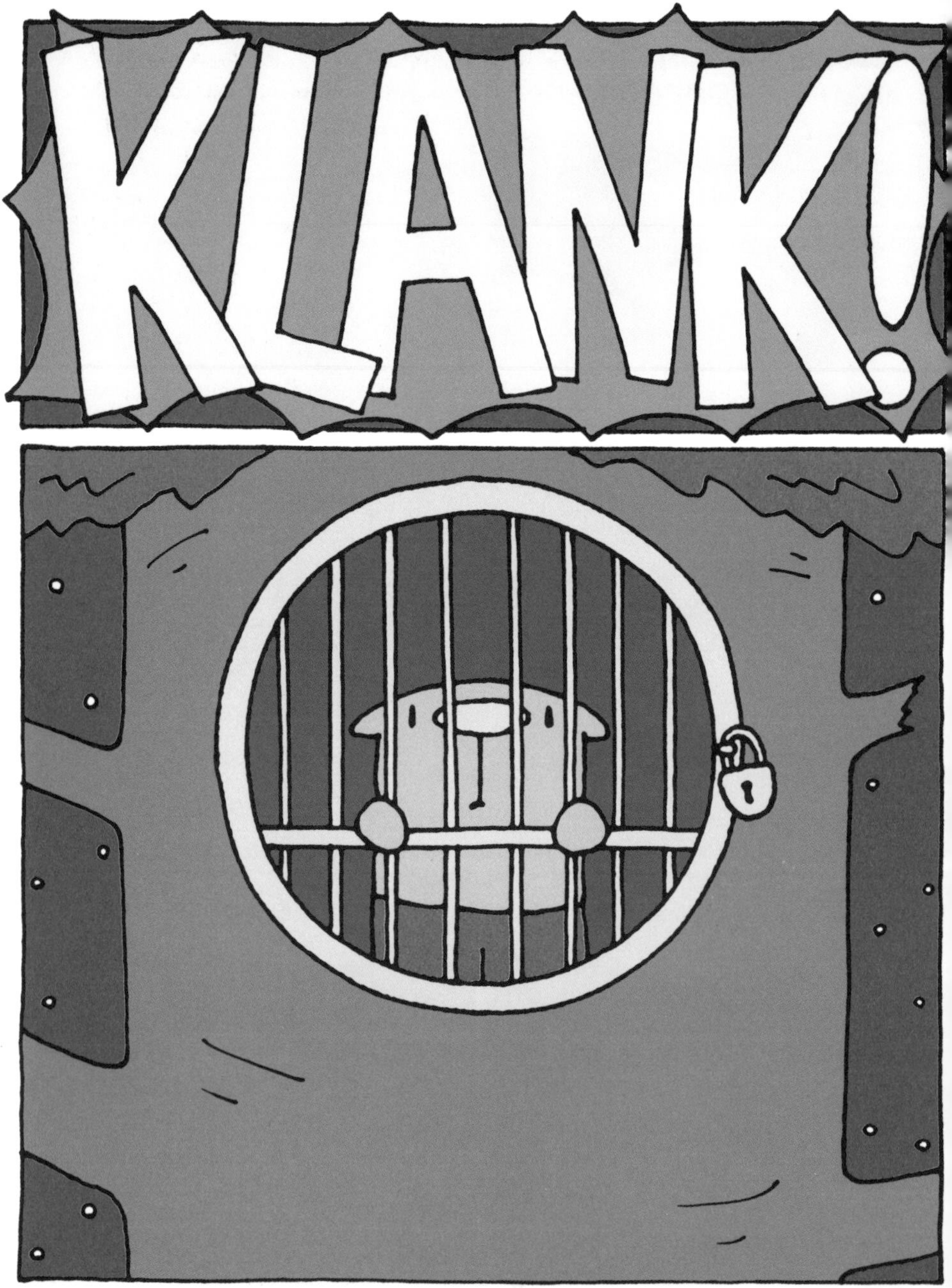
KLANK!

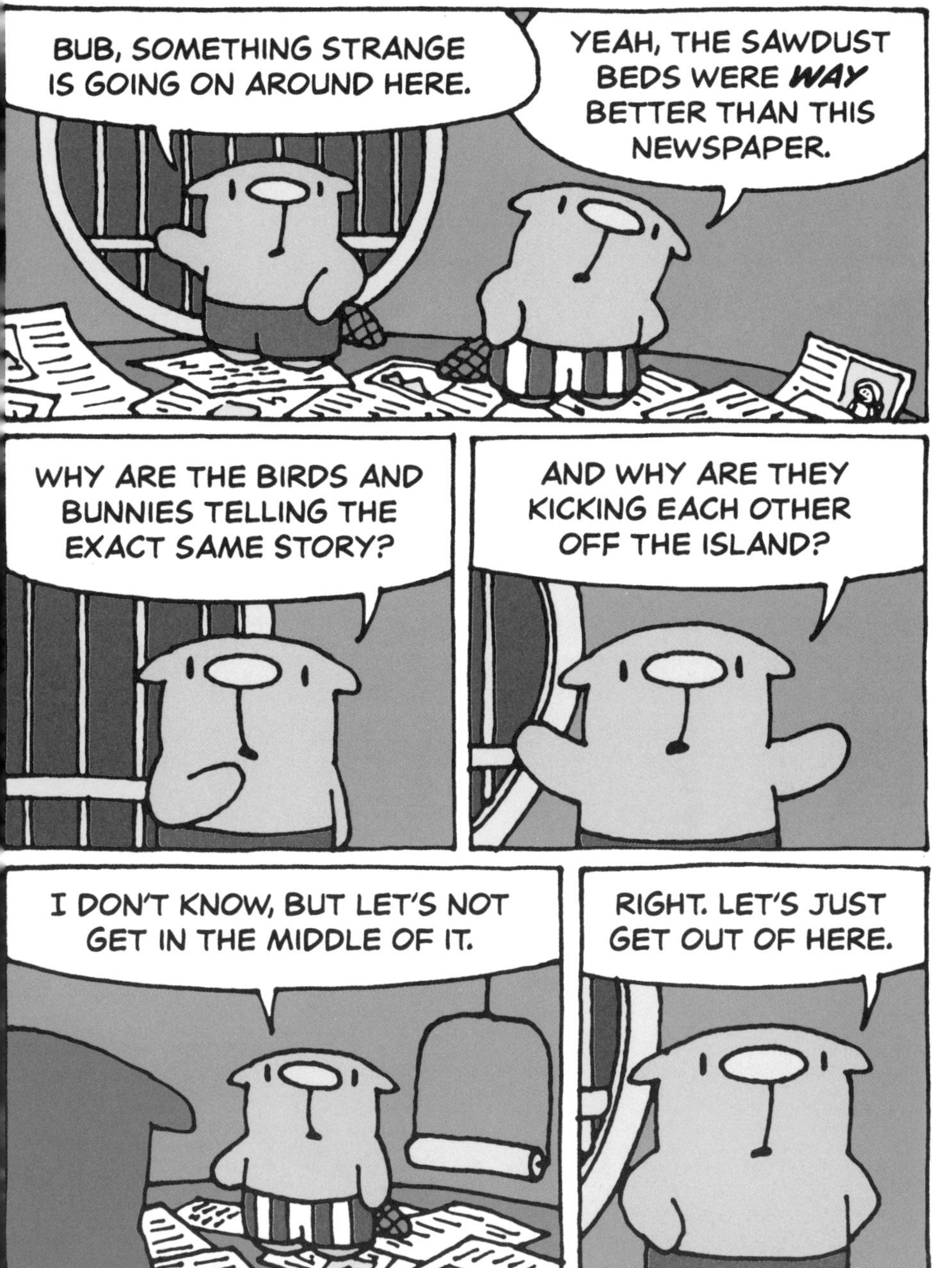
BUB, SOMETHING STRANGE IS GOING ON AROUND HERE.
YEAH, THE SAWDUST BEDS WERE *WAY* BETTER THAN THIS NEWSPAPER.
WHY ARE THE BIRDS AND BUNNIES TELLING THE EXACT SAME STORY?
AND WHY ARE THEY KICKING EACH OTHER OFF THE ISLAND?
I DON'T KNOW, BUT LET'S NOT GET IN THE MIDDLE OF IT.
RIGHT. LET'S JUST GET OUT OF HERE.

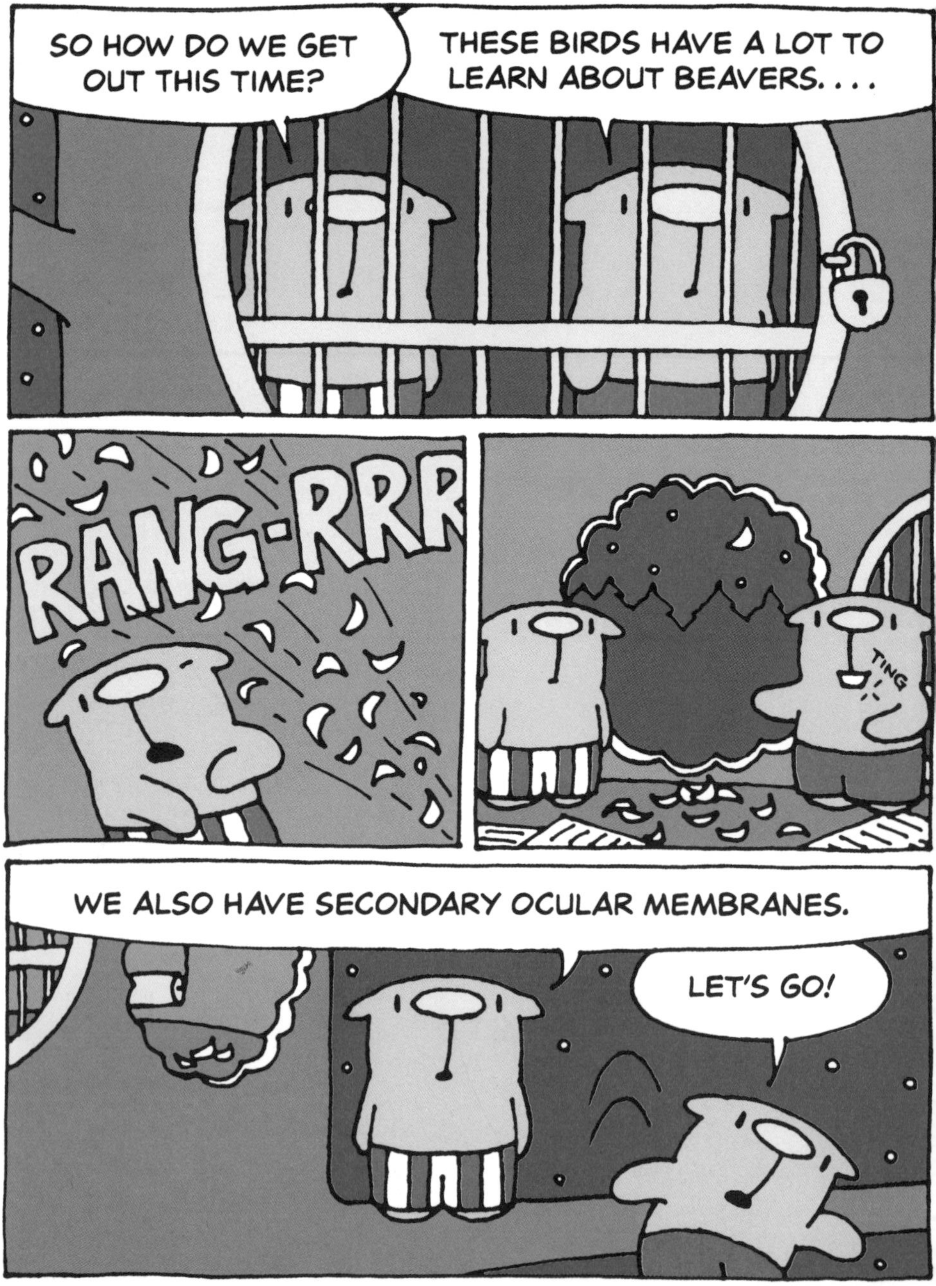
SO HOW DO WE GET OUT THIS TIME?
THESE BIRDS HAVE A LOT TO LEARN ABOUT BEAVERS. . . .
RANG-RRR
TING
WE ALSO HAVE SECONDARY OCULAR MEMBRANES.
LET'S GO!

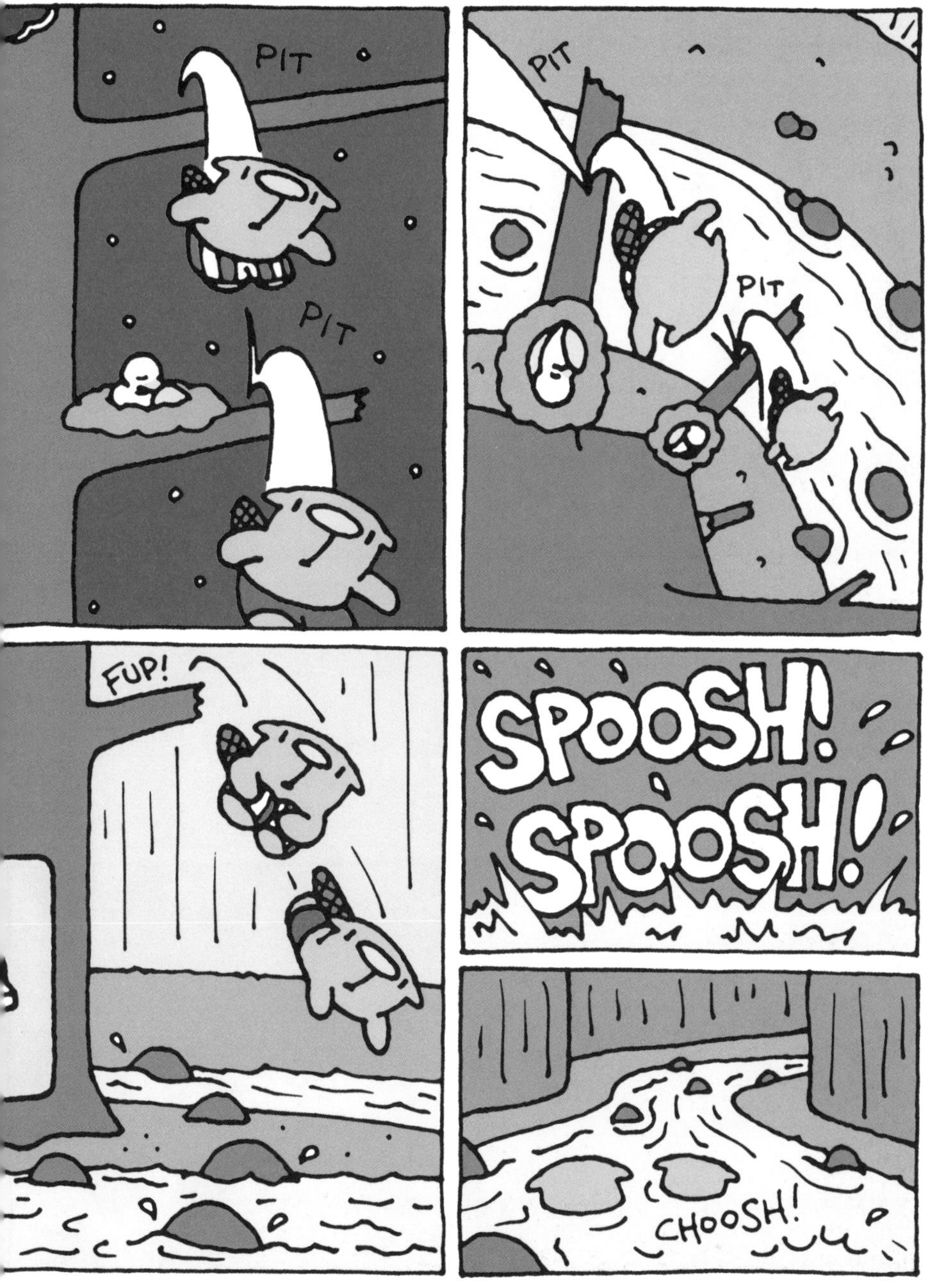
PIT
PIT
PIT
PIT
FUP!
SPOOSH! SPOOSH!
CHOOSH!

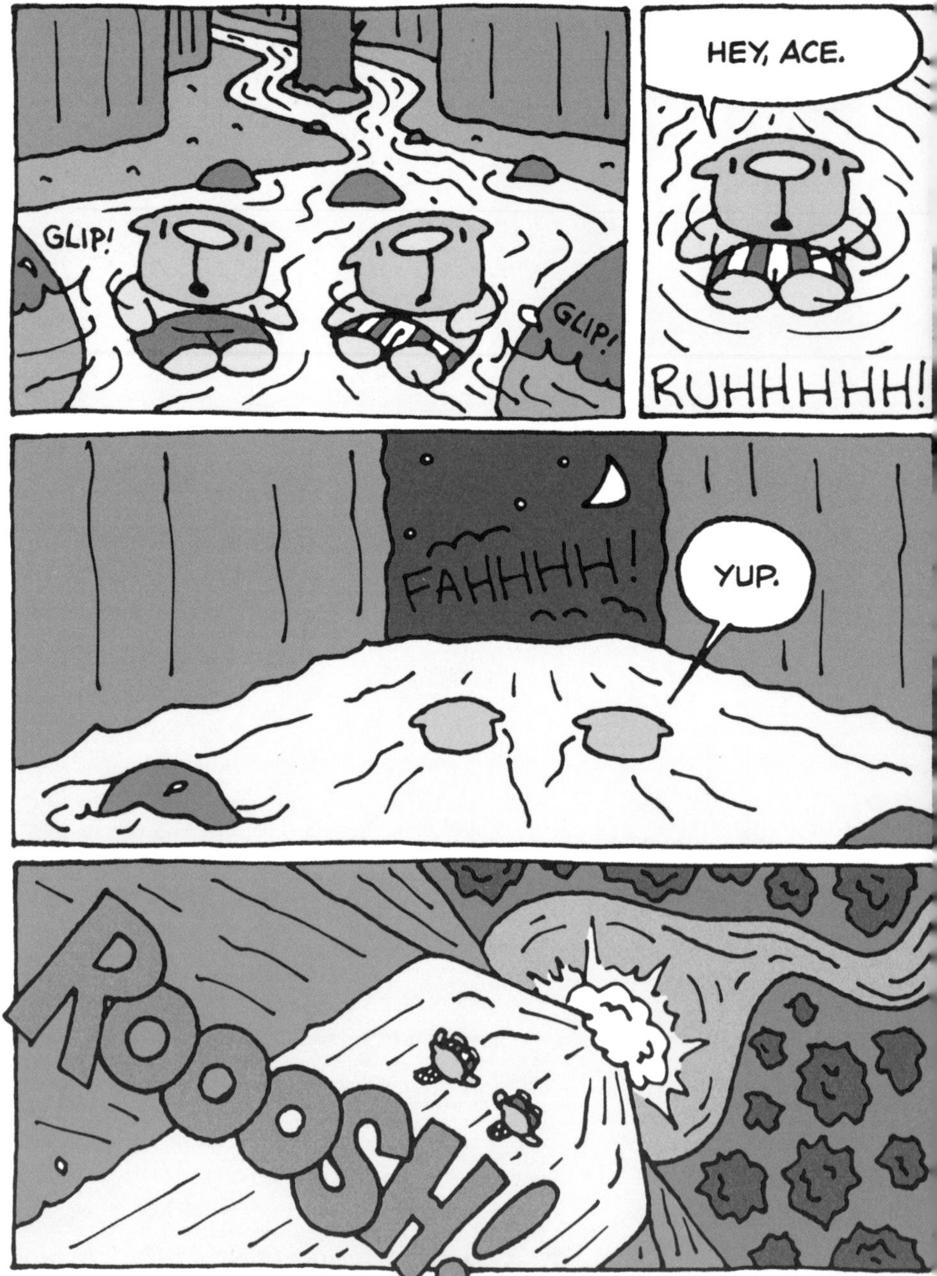
GLIP!
GLIP!
HEY, ACE.
RUHHHHH!
FAHHHH!
YUP.
ROOOOSH!

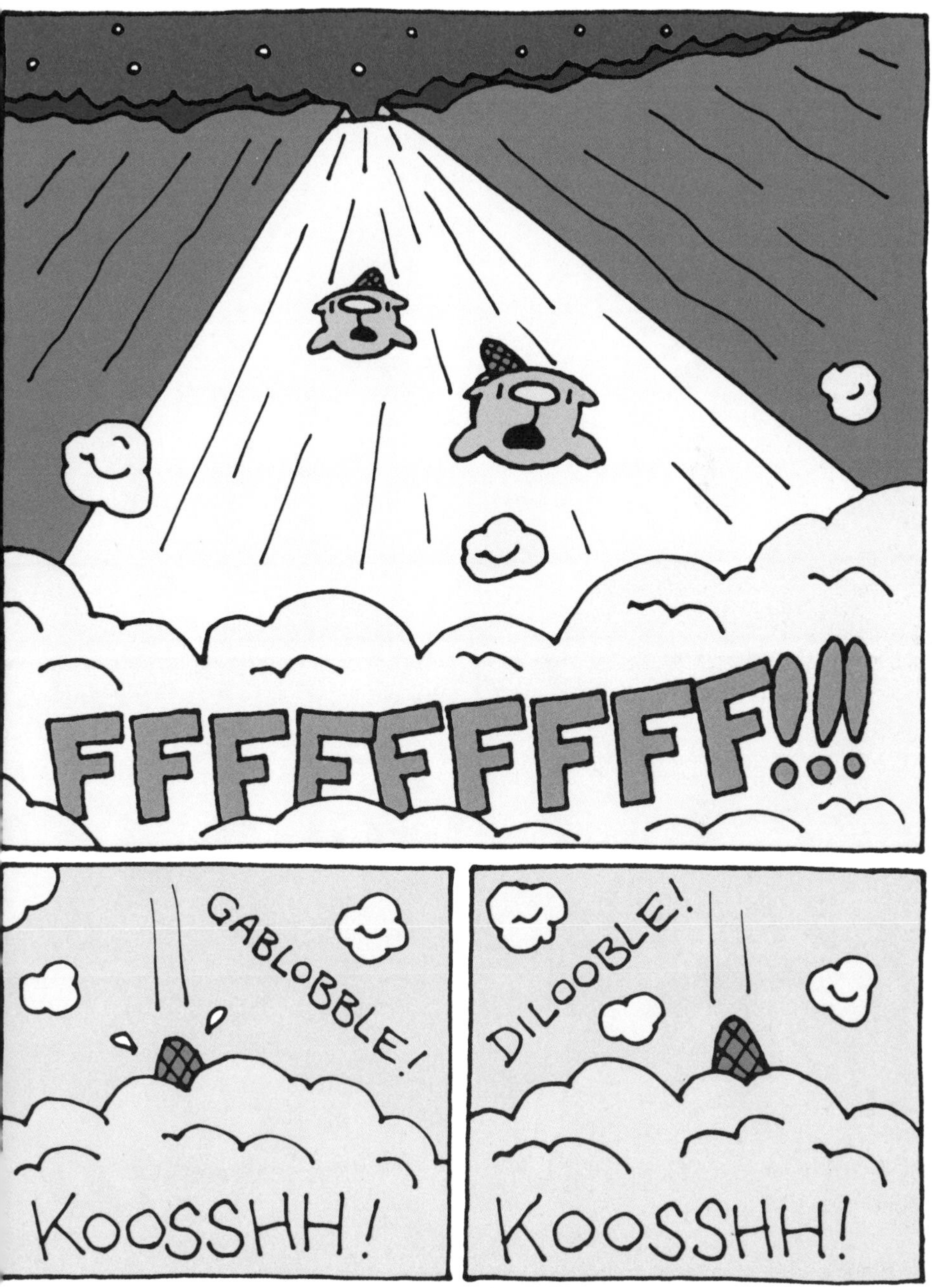
FFFFFFFFF!!!
GABLOBBLE!
KOOSSHH!
DILOOBLE!
KOOSSHH!

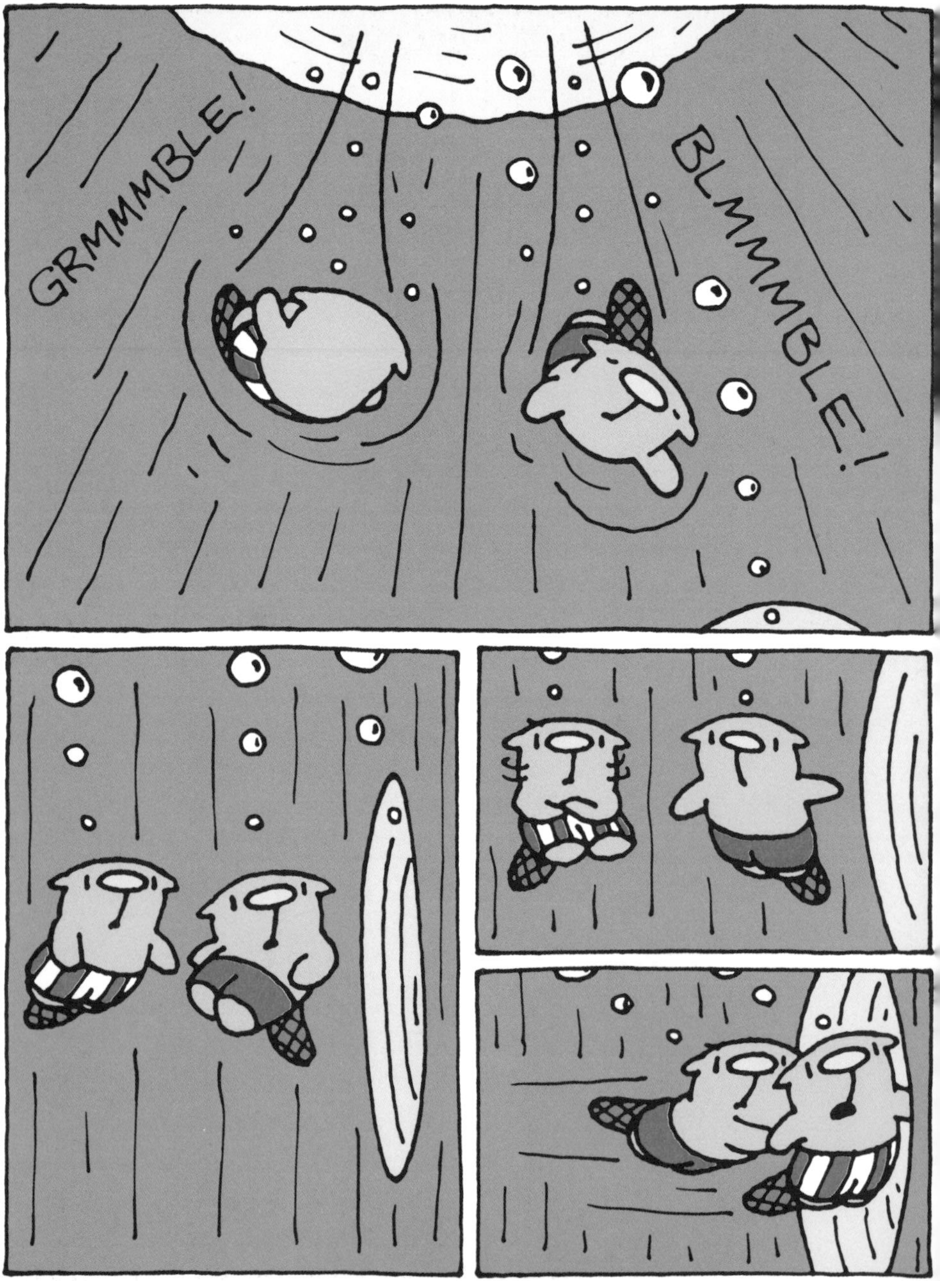
GRMMMBLE!
BLMMMBLE!

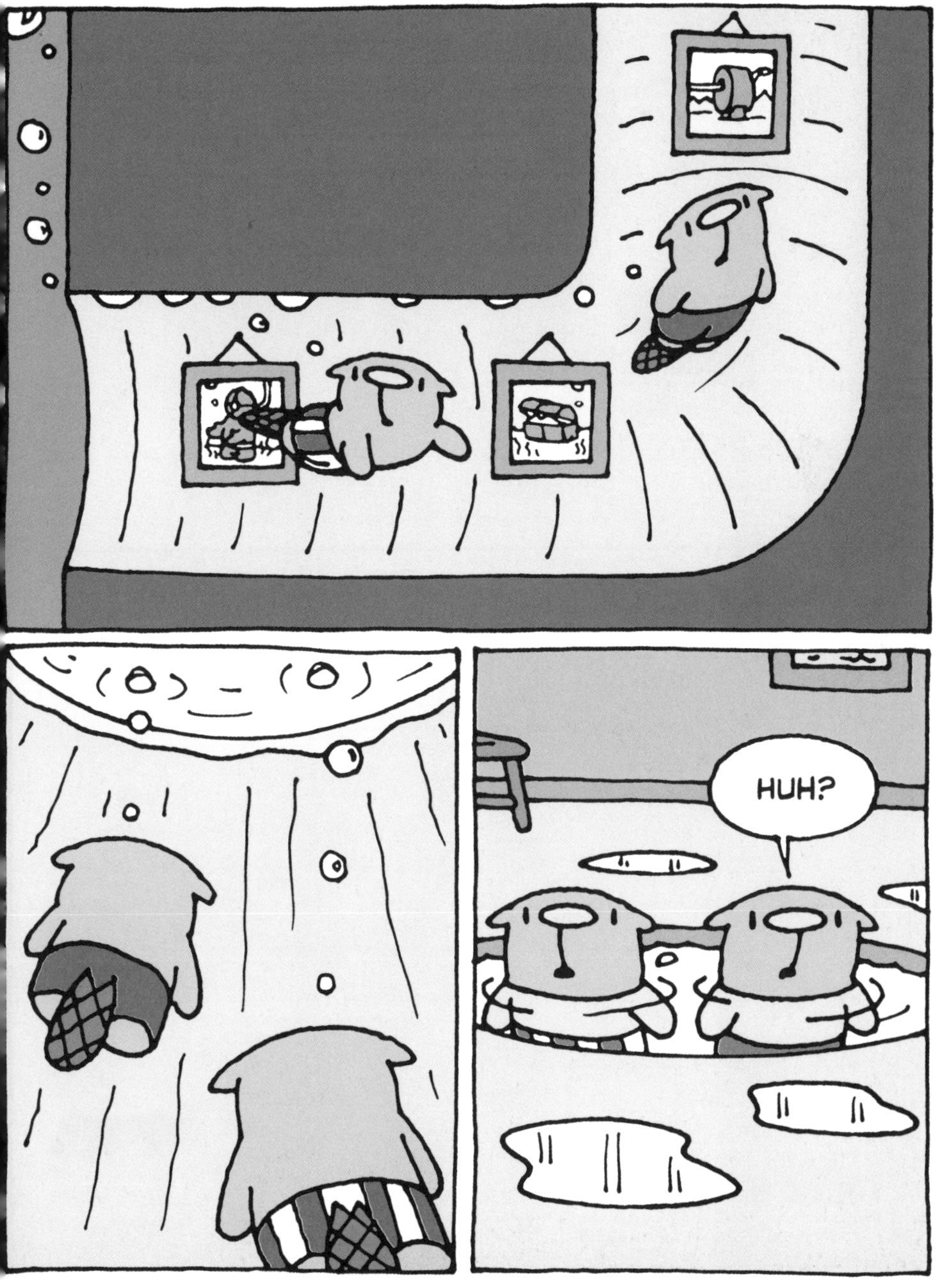
HUH?

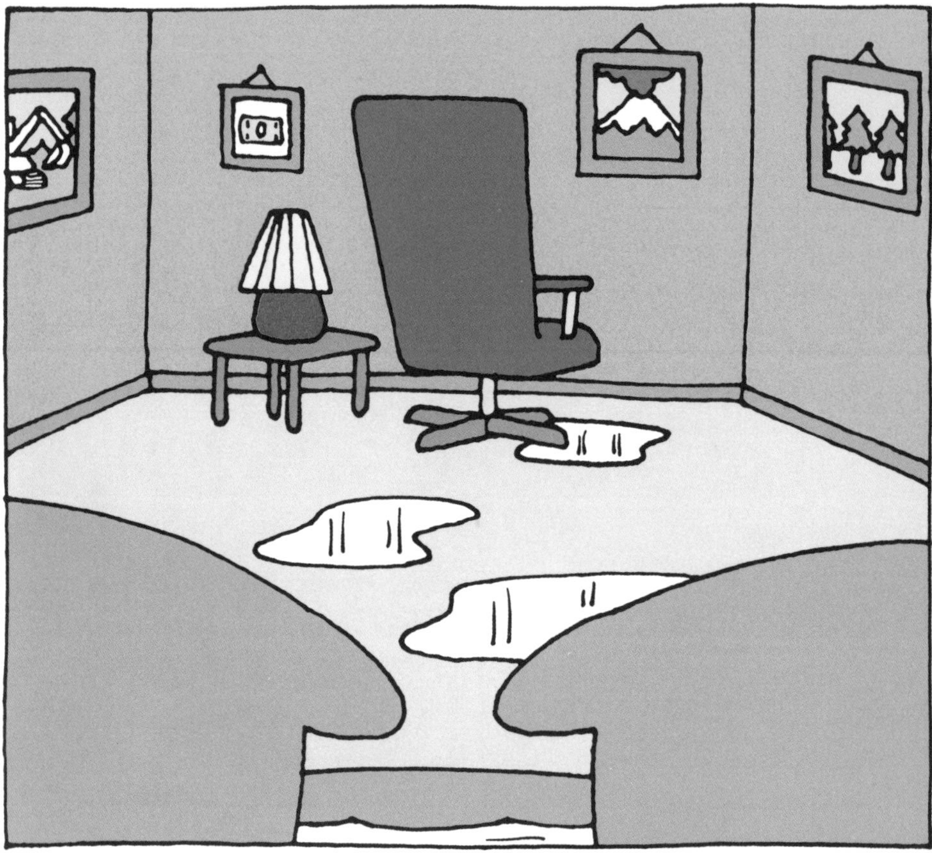

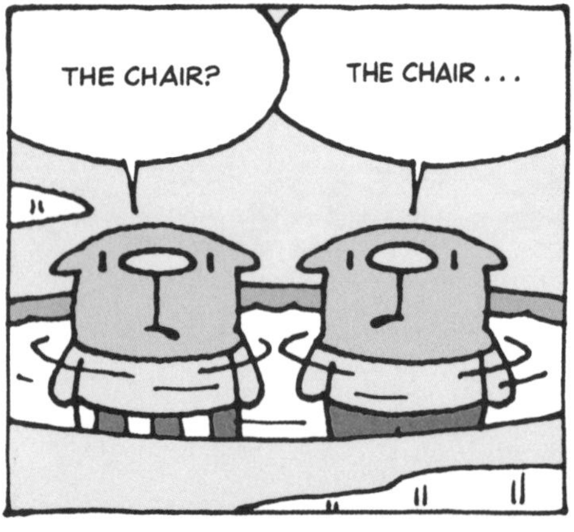
THE CHAIR?
THE CHAIR . . .

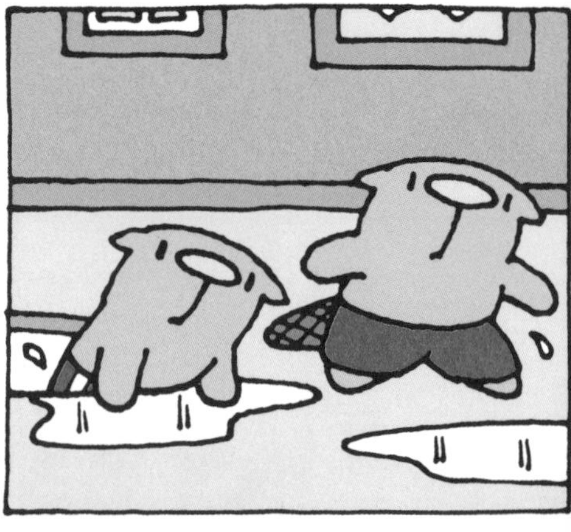

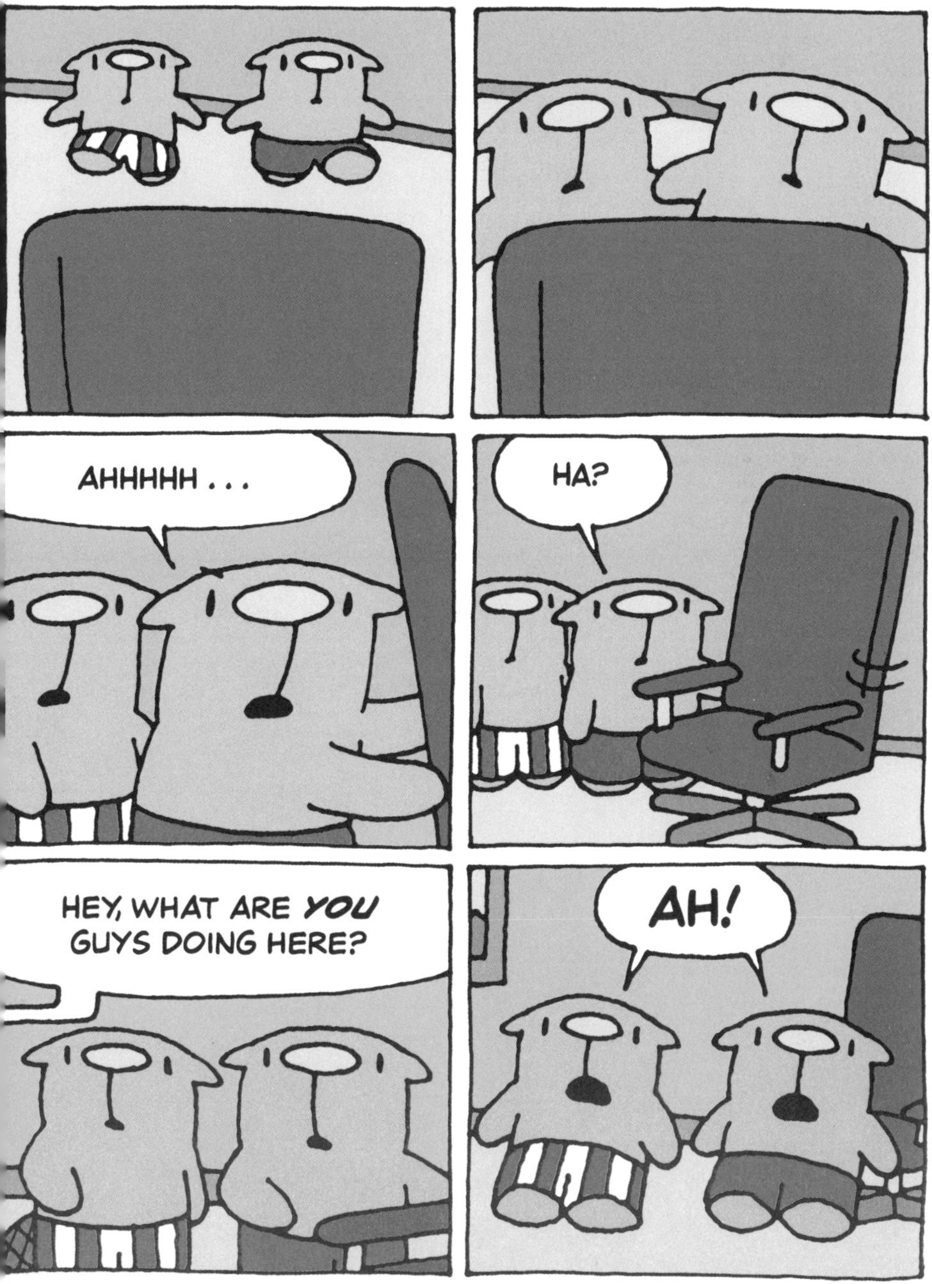
AHHHHH . . .
HA?
HEY, WHAT ARE *YOU* GUYS DOING HERE?
AH!

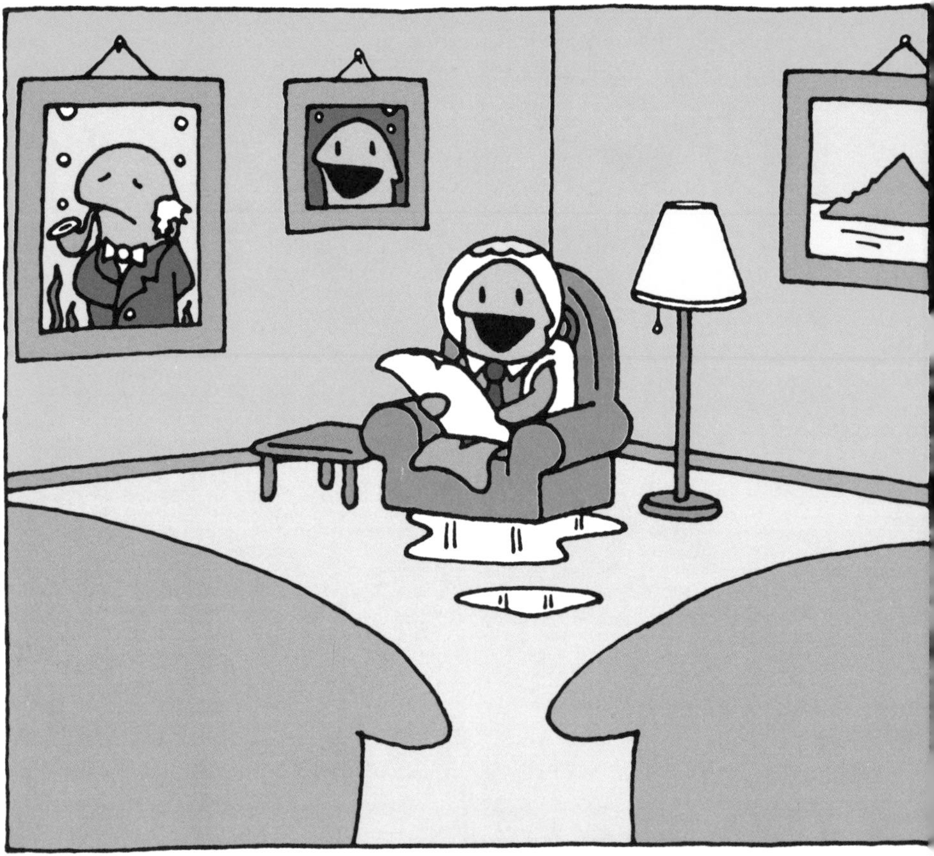

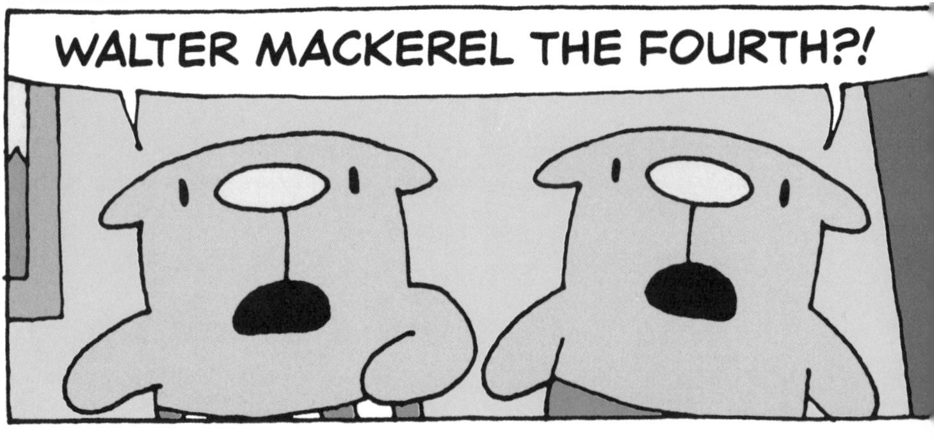
WALTER MACKEREL THE FOURTH?!

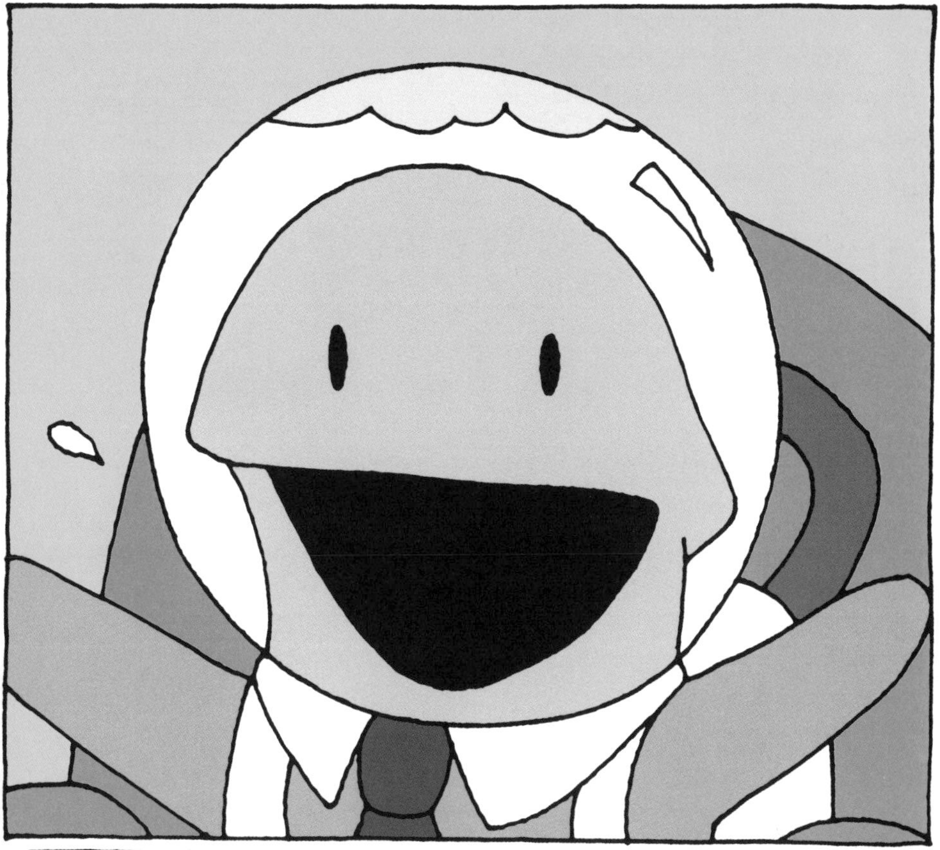
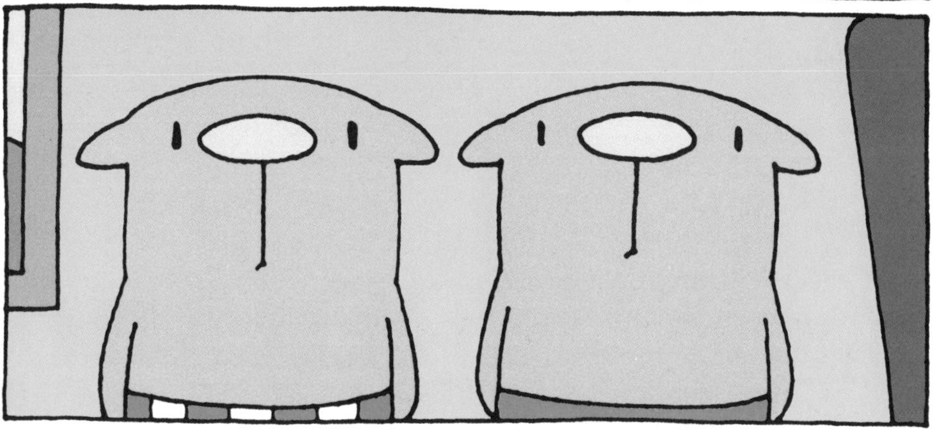

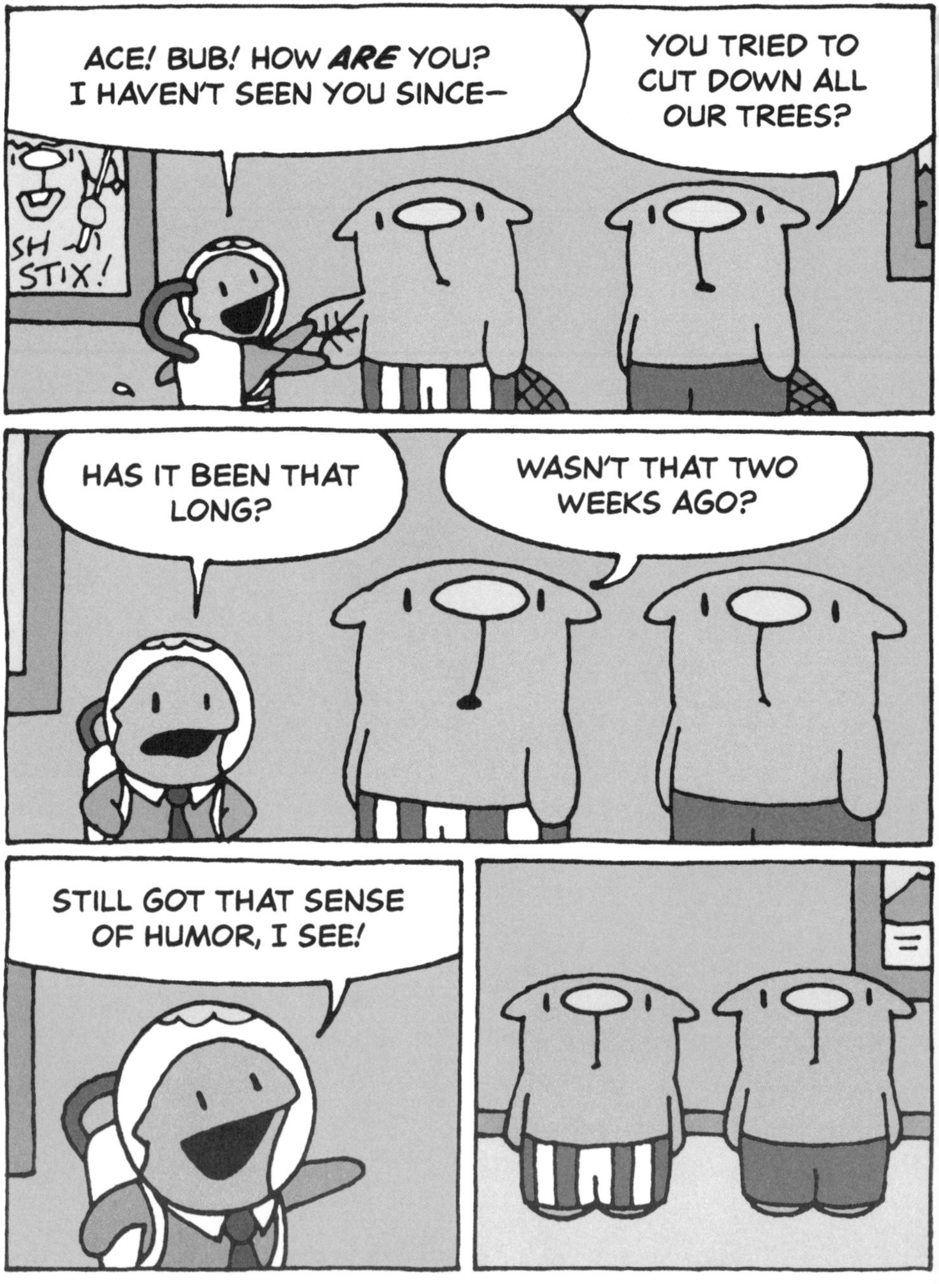
ACE! BUB! HOW ***ARE*** YOU? I HAVEN'T SEEN YOU SINCE–
YOU TRIED TO CUT DOWN ALL OUR TREES?
SH STIX!
HAS IT BEEN THAT LONG?
WASN'T THAT TWO WEEKS AGO?
STILL GOT THAT SENSE OF HUMOR, I SEE!

SO WHAT ARE YOU DOING HERE?

WELL, MY LAST BUSINESS RAN INTO SOME TROUBLE . . .

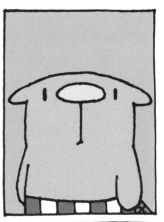

SO I CAME HERE TO DO SOME THINKING. SOME REFLECTING. TO GET AWAY FROM THE RAT RACE.

NO OFFENSE.

WE'RE ACTUALLY BEAVERS.

HUH.

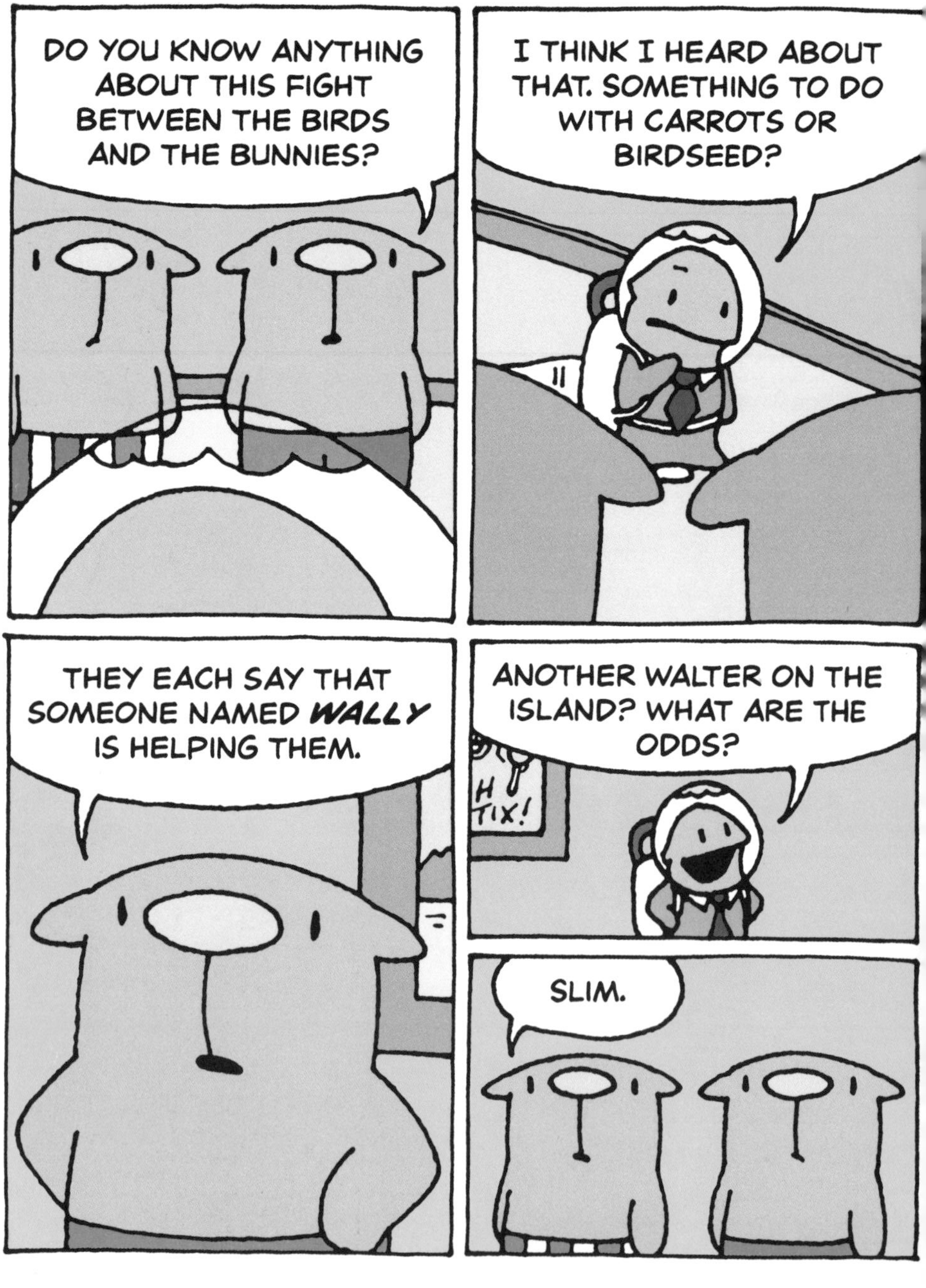
DO YOU KNOW ANYTHING ABOUT THIS FIGHT BETWEEN THE BIRDS AND THE BUNNIES?
I THINK I HEARD ABOUT THAT. SOMETHING TO DO WITH CARROTS OR BIRDSEED?
THEY EACH SAY THAT SOMEONE NAMED WALLY IS HELPING THEM.
ANOTHER WALTER ON THE ISLAND? WHAT ARE THE ODDS?
TIX!
SLIM.

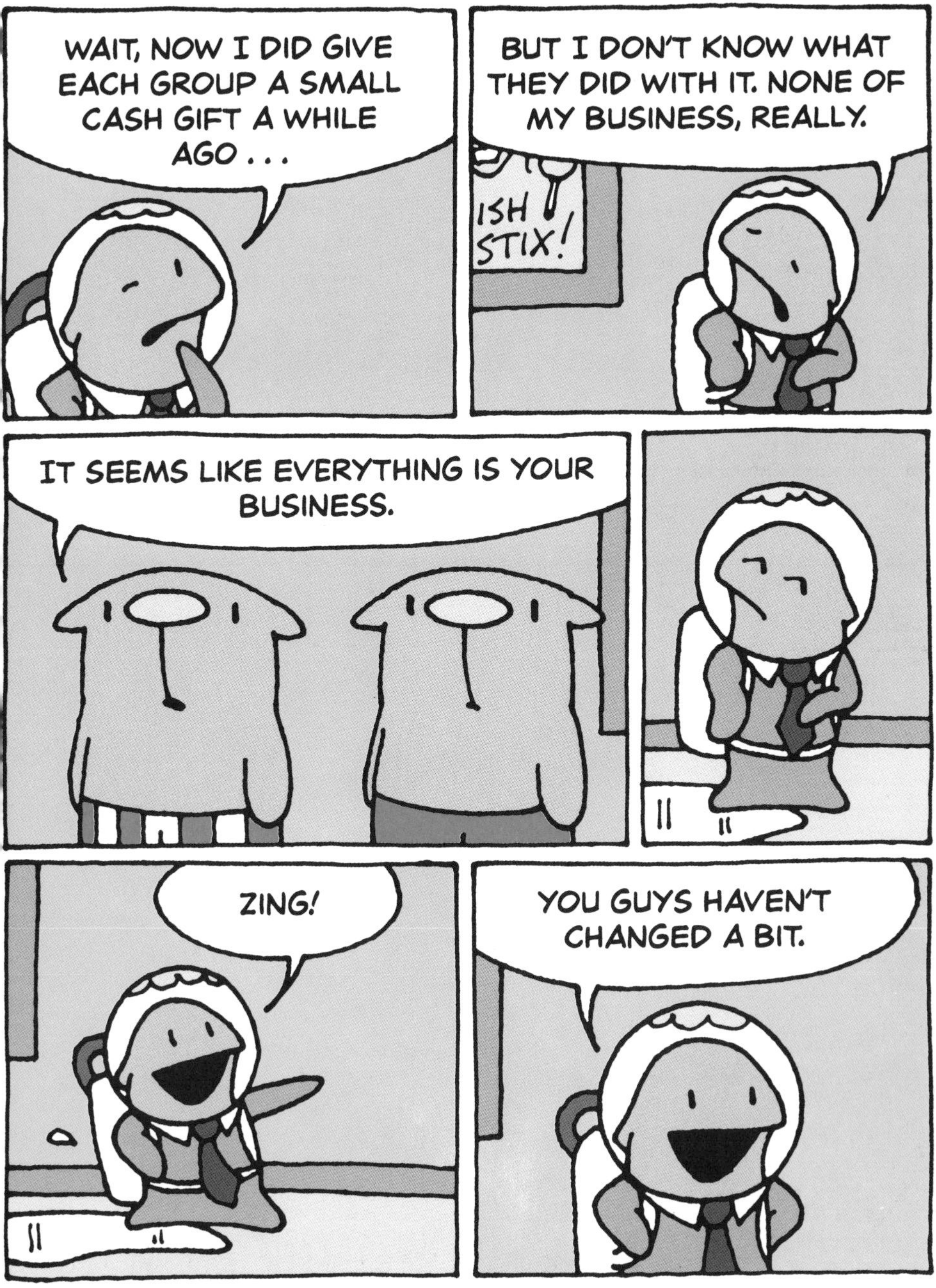
WAIT, NOW I DID GIVE EACH GROUP A SMALL CASH GIFT A WHILE AGO . . .
BUT I DON'T KNOW WHAT THEY DID WITH IT. NONE OF MY BUSINESS, REALLY.
ISH STIX!
IT SEEMS LIKE EVERYTHING IS YOUR BUSINESS.
ZING!
YOU GUYS HAVEN'T CHANGED A BIT.

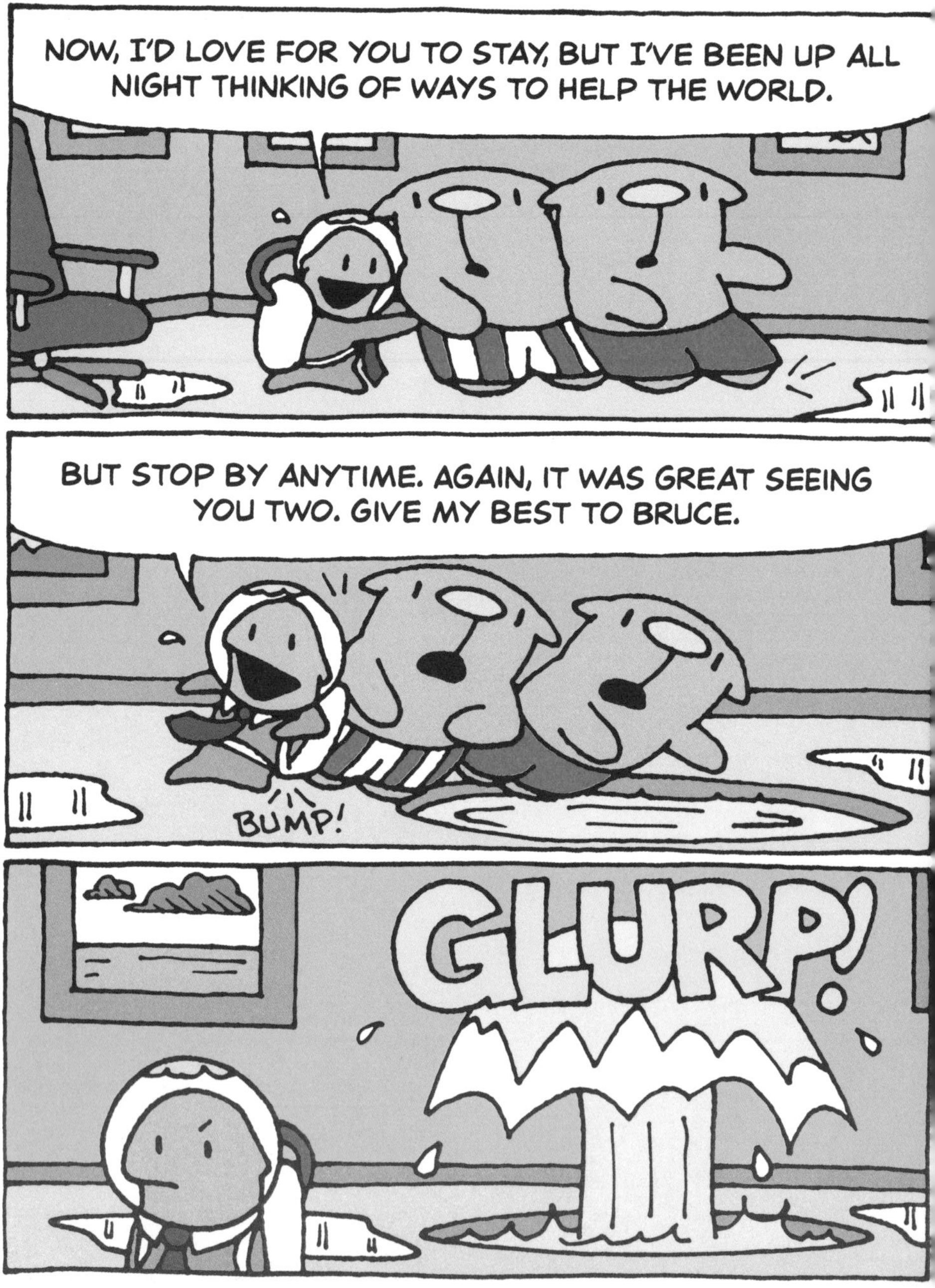
NOW, I'D LOVE FOR YOU TO STAY, BUT I'VE BEEN UP ALL NIGHT THINKING OF WAYS TO HELP THE WORLD.
BUT STOP BY ANYTIME. AGAIN, IT WAS GREAT SEEING YOU TWO. GIVE MY BEST TO BRUCE.
BUMP!
GLURP!

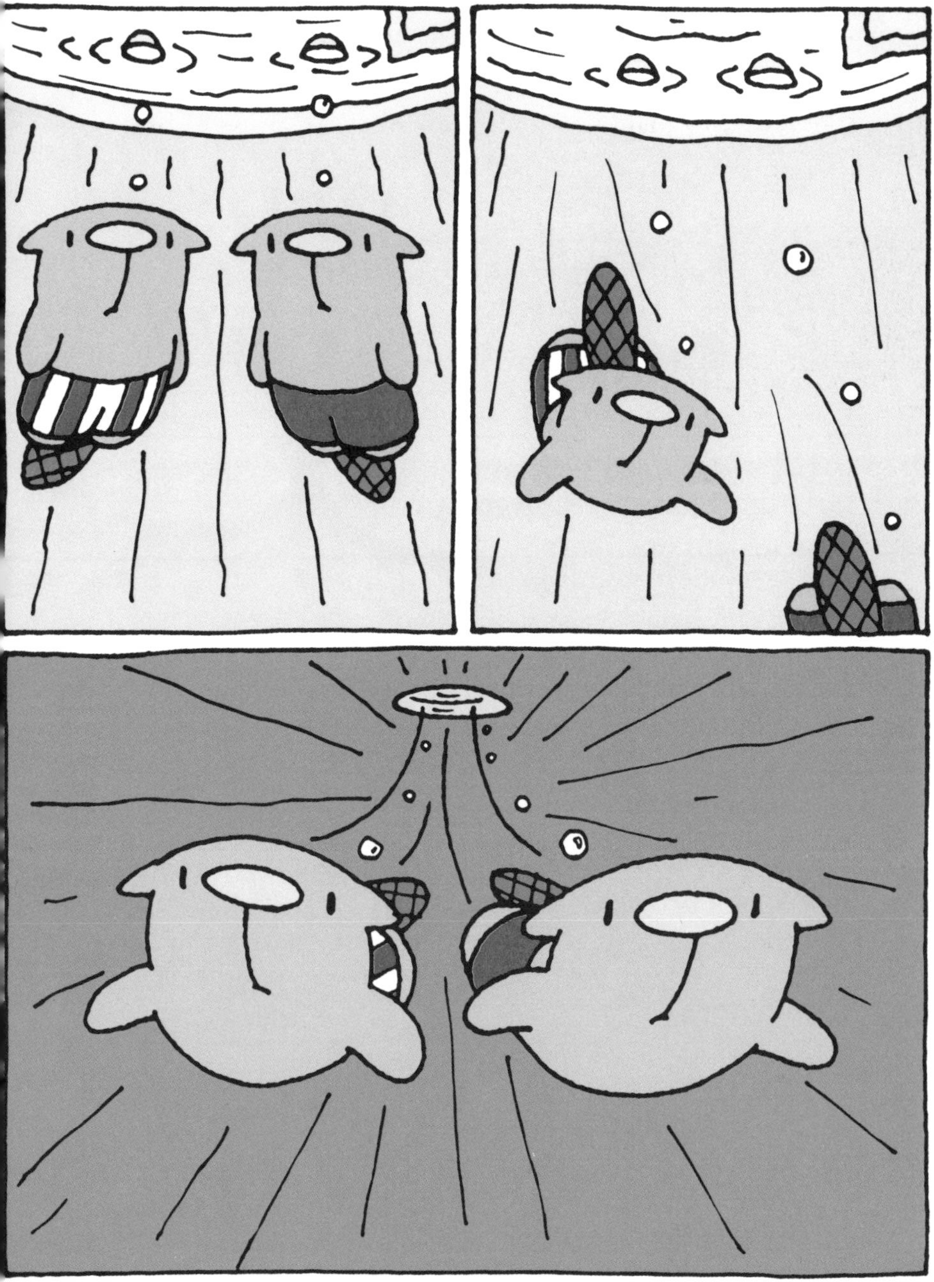

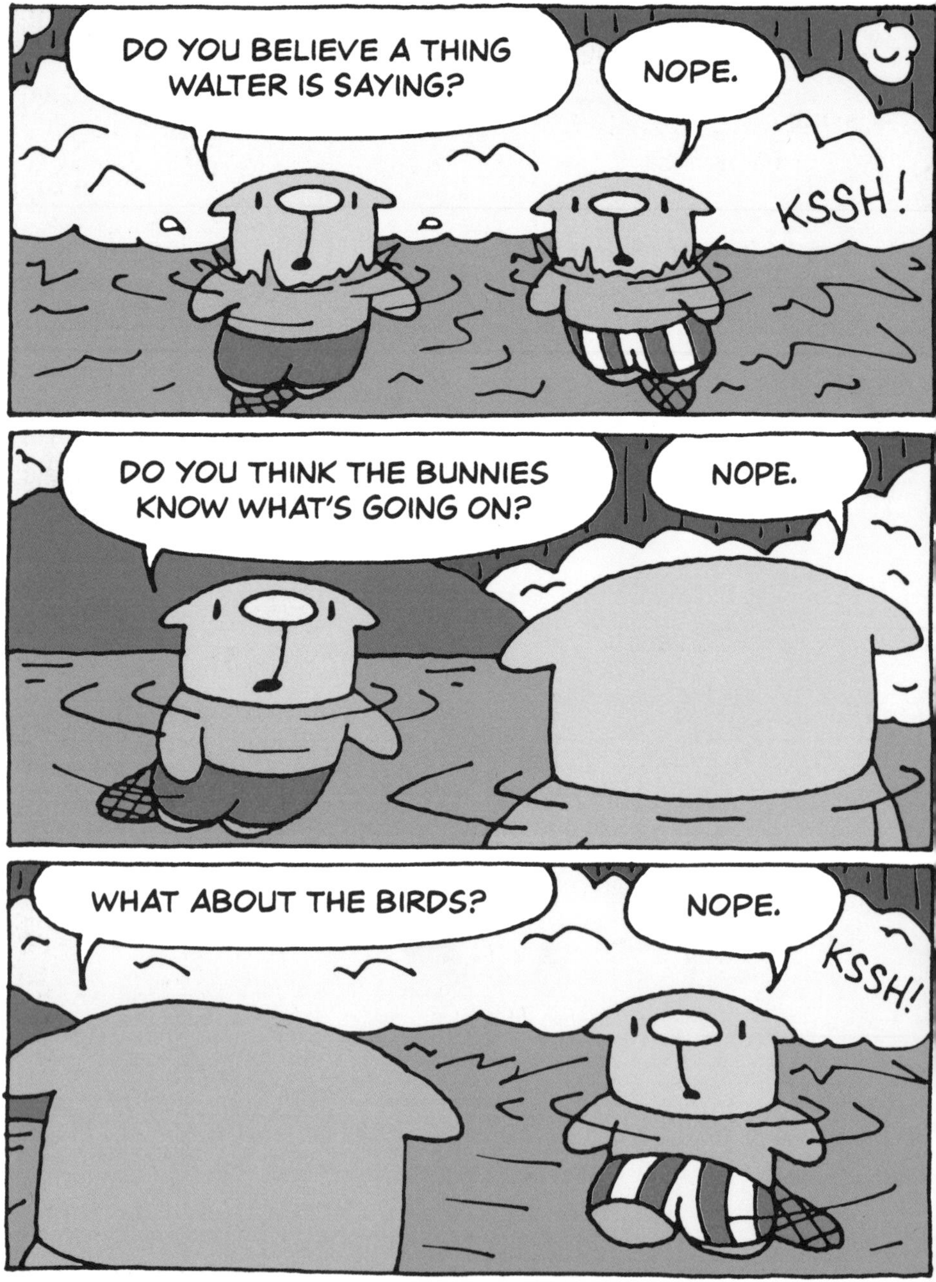
DO YOU BELIEVE A THING WALTER IS SAYING?
NOPE.
KSSH!
DO YOU THINK THE BUNNIES KNOW WHAT'S GOING ON?
NOPE.
WHAT ABOUT THE BIRDS?
NOPE.
KSSH!

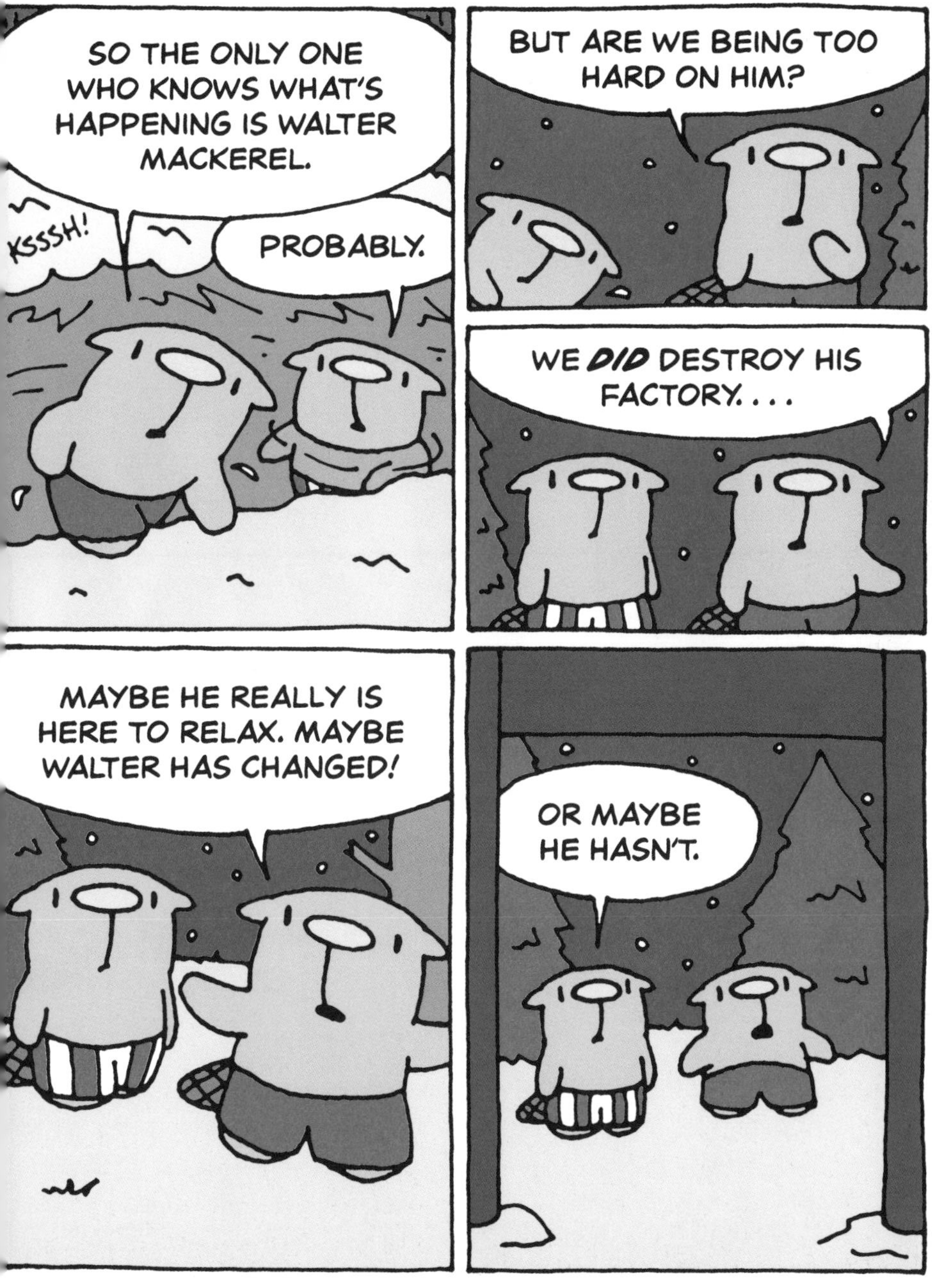
SO THE ONLY ONE WHO KNOWS WHAT'S HAPPENING IS WALTER MACKEREL.
KSSSH!
PROBABLY.
BUT ARE WE BEING TOO HARD ON HIM?
WE DID DESTROY HIS FACTORY. . . .
MAYBE HE REALLY IS HERE TO RELAX. MAYBE WALTER HAS CHANGED!
OR MAYBE HE HASN'T.

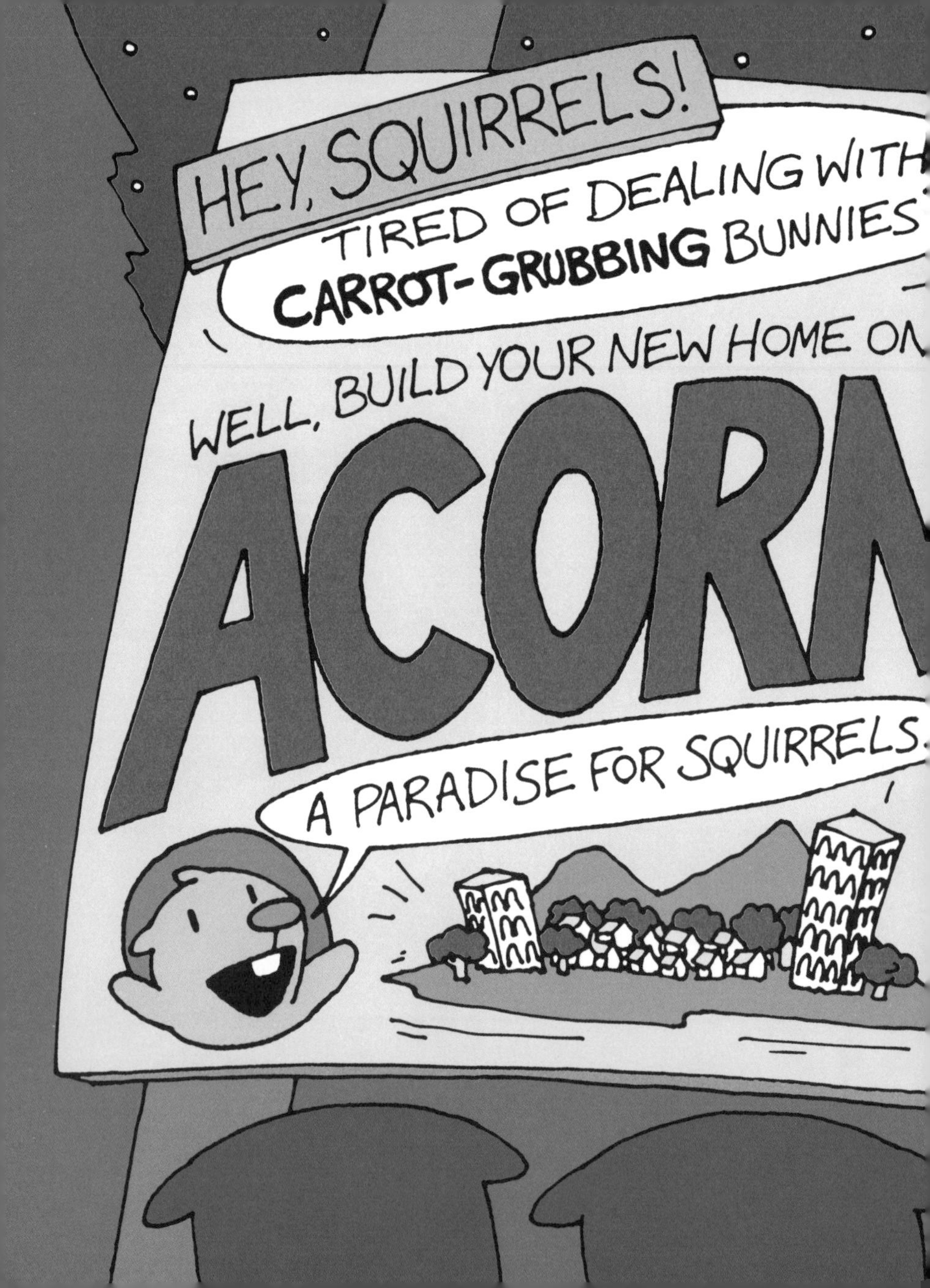
HEY, SQUIRRELS!
TIRED OF DEALING WITH CARROT-GRUBBING BUNNIES
WELL, BUILD YOUR NEW HOME ON
ACORN
A PARADISE FOR SQUIRRELS

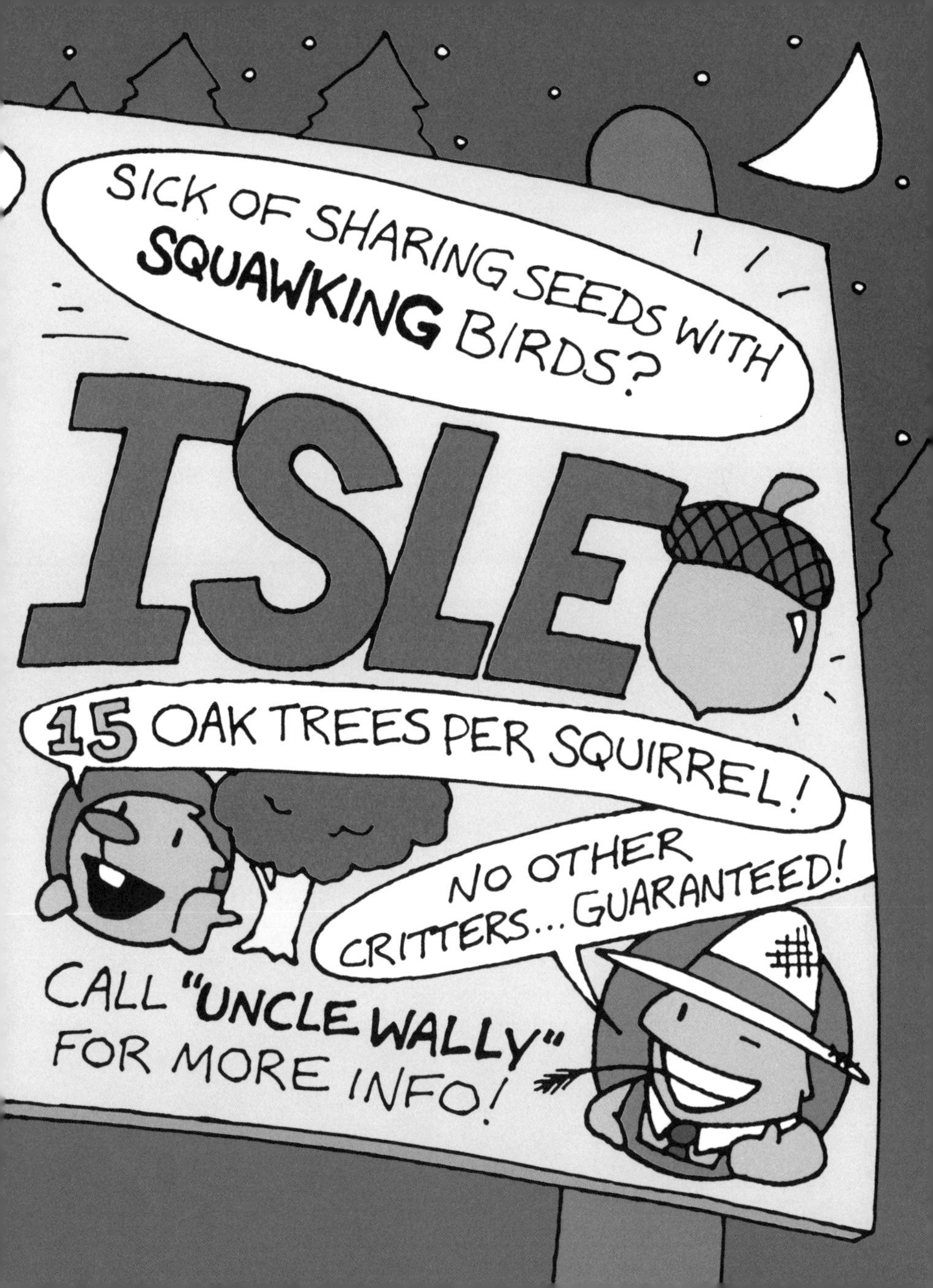
SICK OF SHARING SEEDS WITH SQUAWKING BIRDS?
ISLE
15 OAK TREES PER SQUIRREL!
NO OTHER CRITTERS... GUARANTEED!
CALL "UNCLE WALLY" FOR MORE INFO!

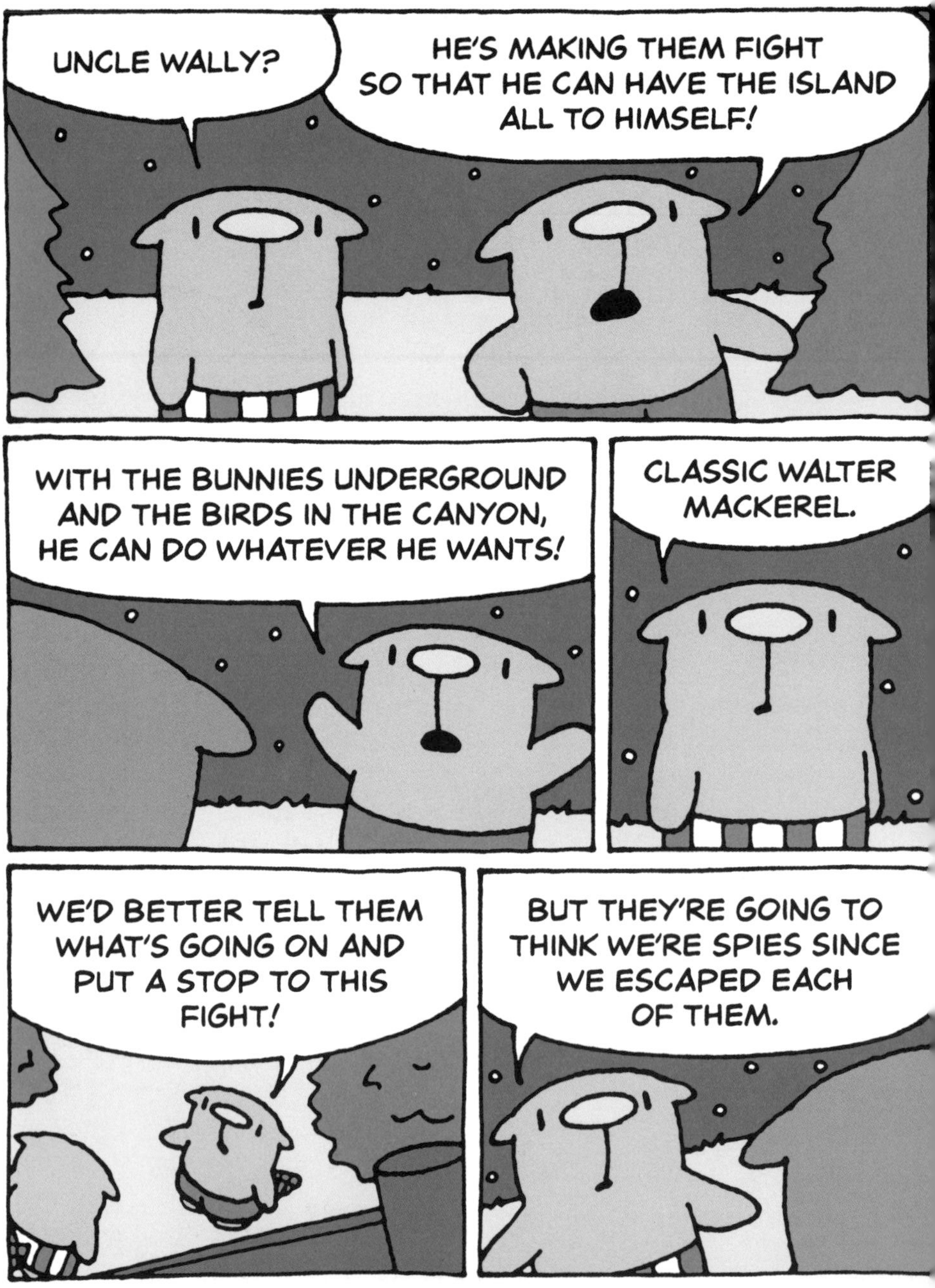
UNCLE WALLY?
HE'S MAKING THEM FIGHT SO THAT HE CAN HAVE THE ISLAND ALL TO HIMSELF!
WITH THE BUNNIES UNDERGROUND AND THE BIRDS IN THE CANYON, HE CAN DO WHATEVER HE WANTS!
CLASSIC WALTER MACKEREL.
WE'D BETTER TELL THEM WHAT'S GOING ON AND PUT A STOP TO THIS FIGHT!
BUT THEY'RE GOING TO THINK WE'RE SPIES SINCE WE ESCAPED EACH OF THEM.

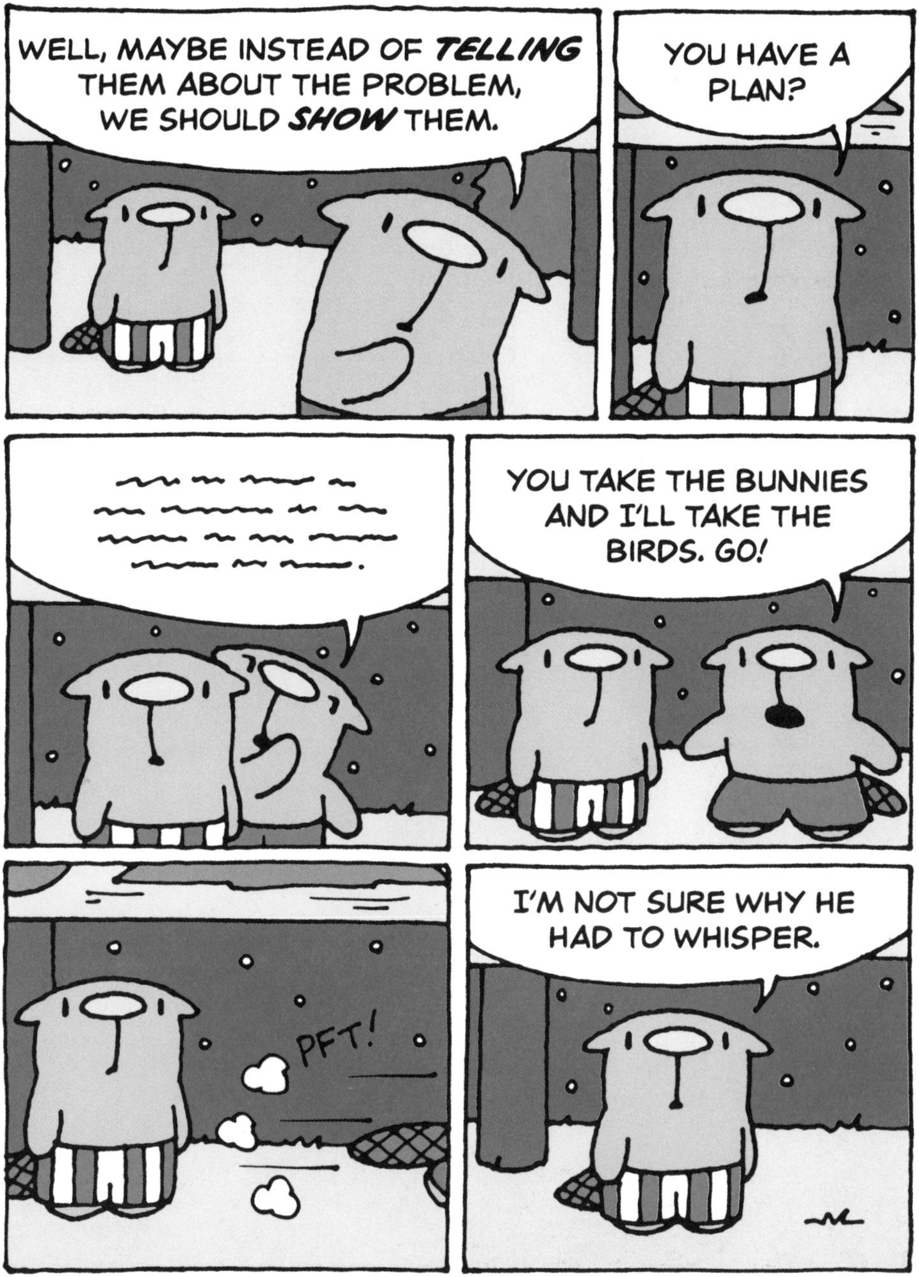
WELL, MAYBE INSTEAD OF TELLING THEM ABOUT THE PROBLEM, WE SHOULD SHOW THEM.
YOU HAVE A PLAN?
YOU TAKE THE BUNNIES AND I'LL TAKE THE BIRDS. GO!
PFT!
I'M NOT SURE WHY HE HAD TO WHISPER.

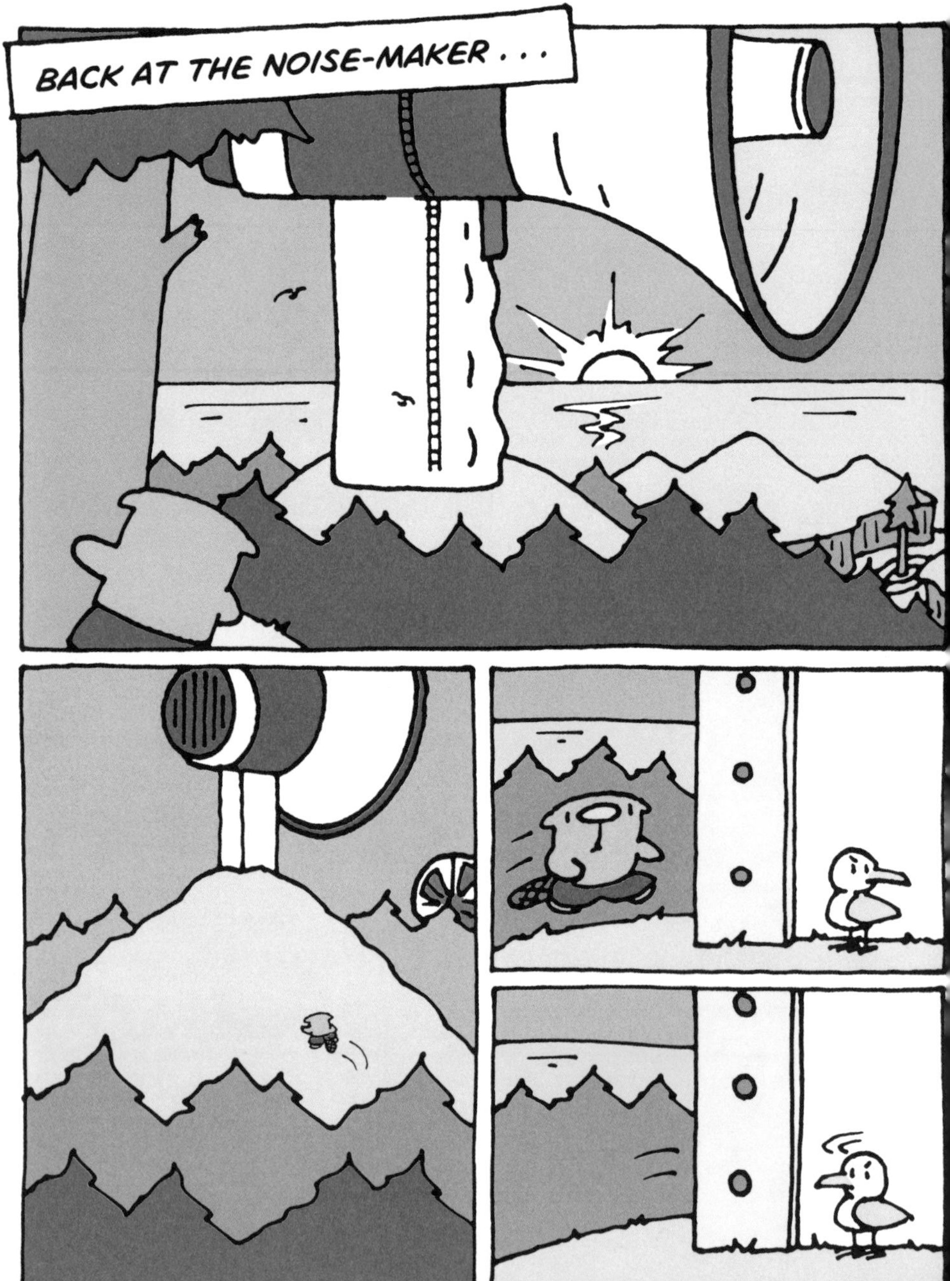
BACK AT THE NOISE-MAKER . . .

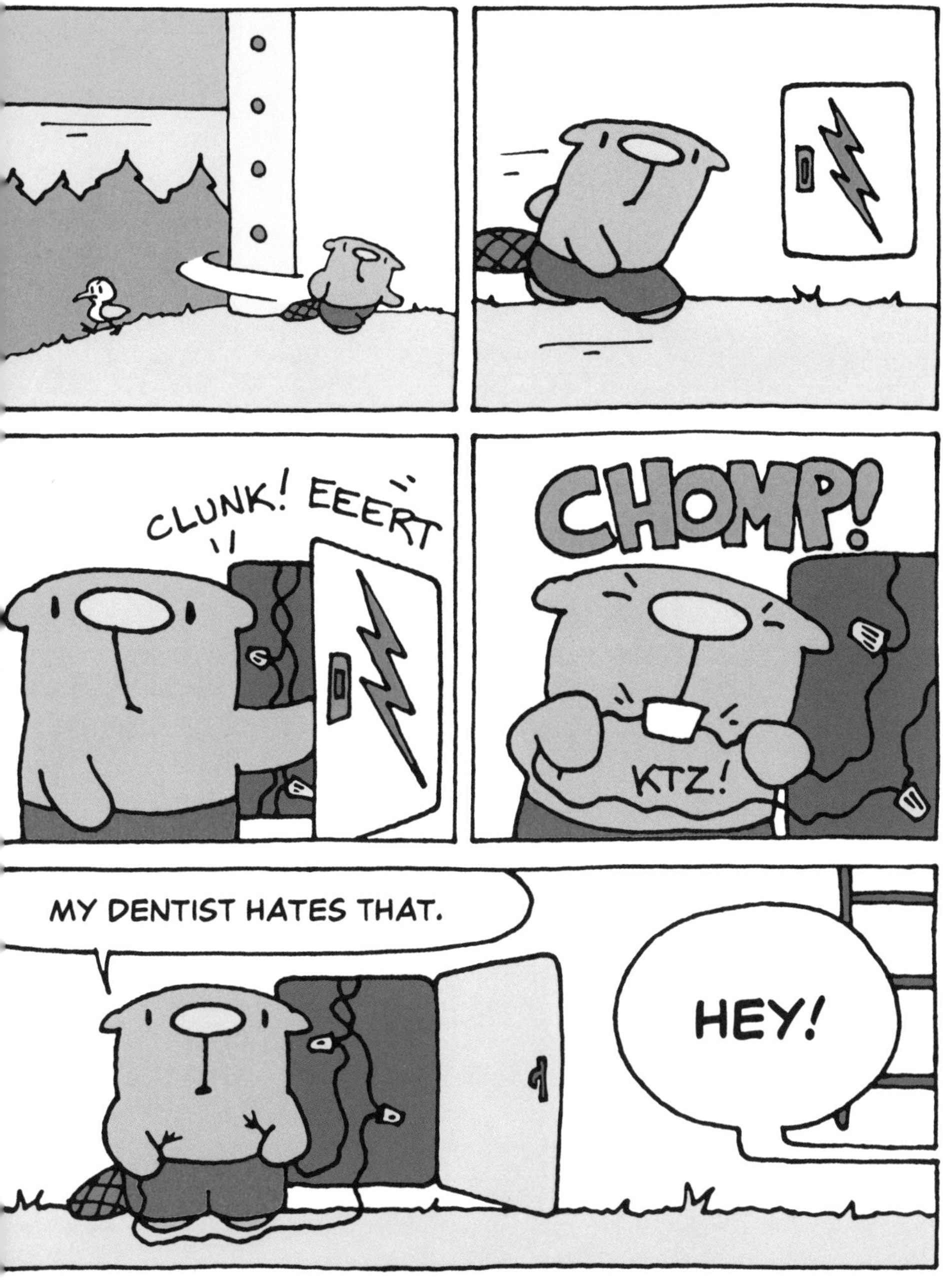
CLUNK! EEEERT
CHOMP!
KTZ!
MY DENTIST HATES THAT.
HEY!

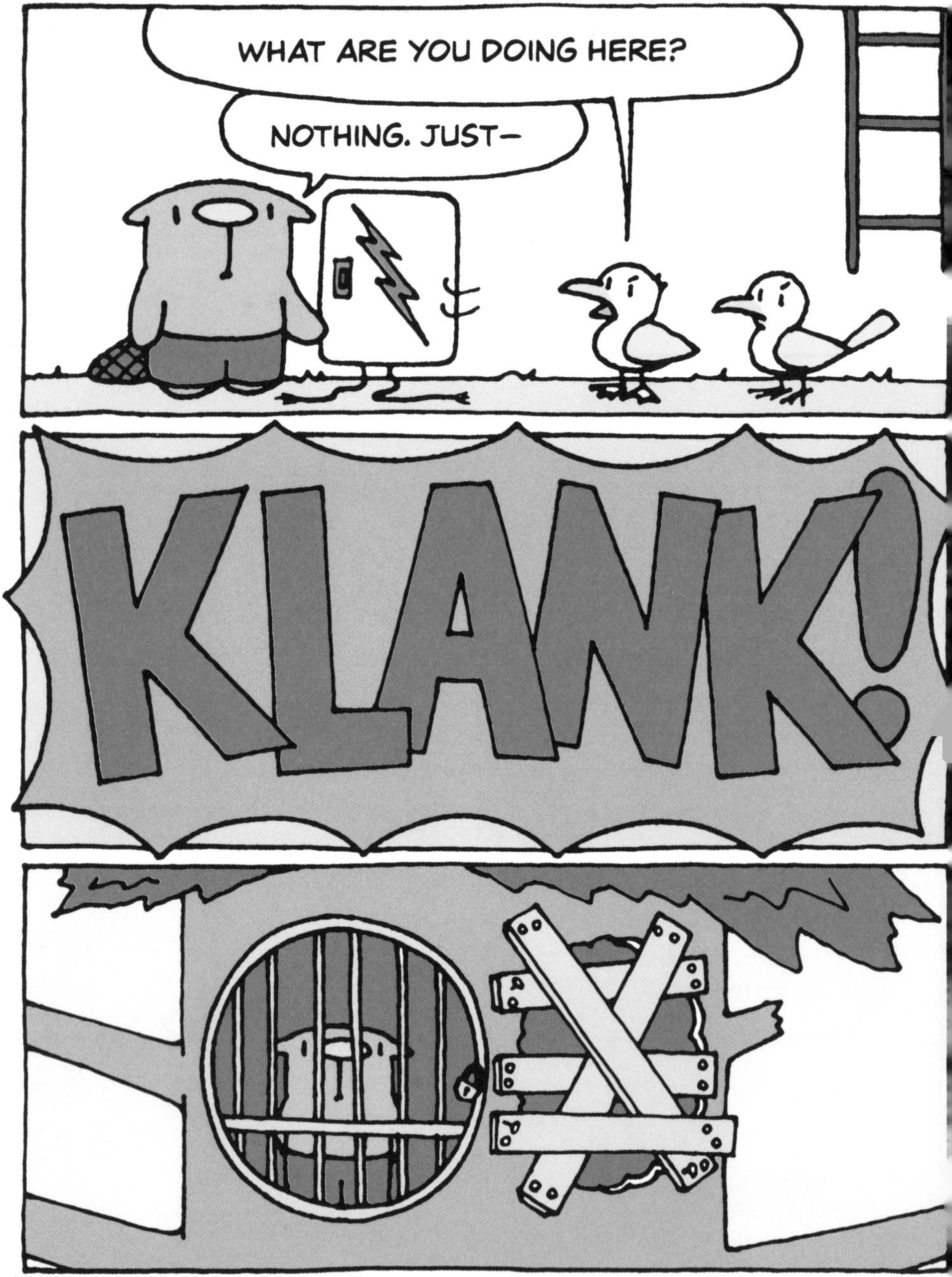
WHAT ARE YOU DOING HERE?
NOTHING. JUST—
KLANK!

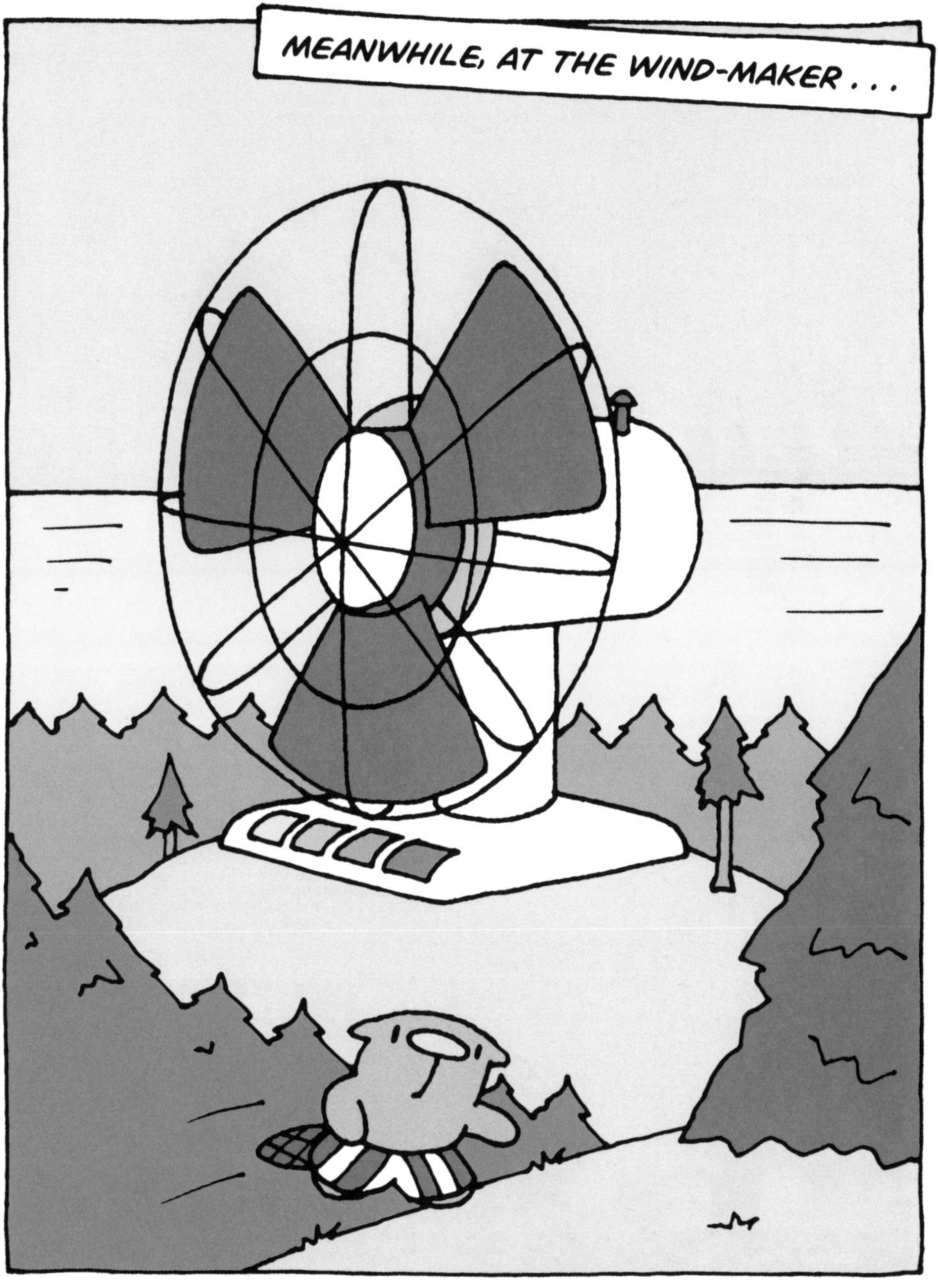
MEANWHILE, AT THE WIND-MAKER . . .

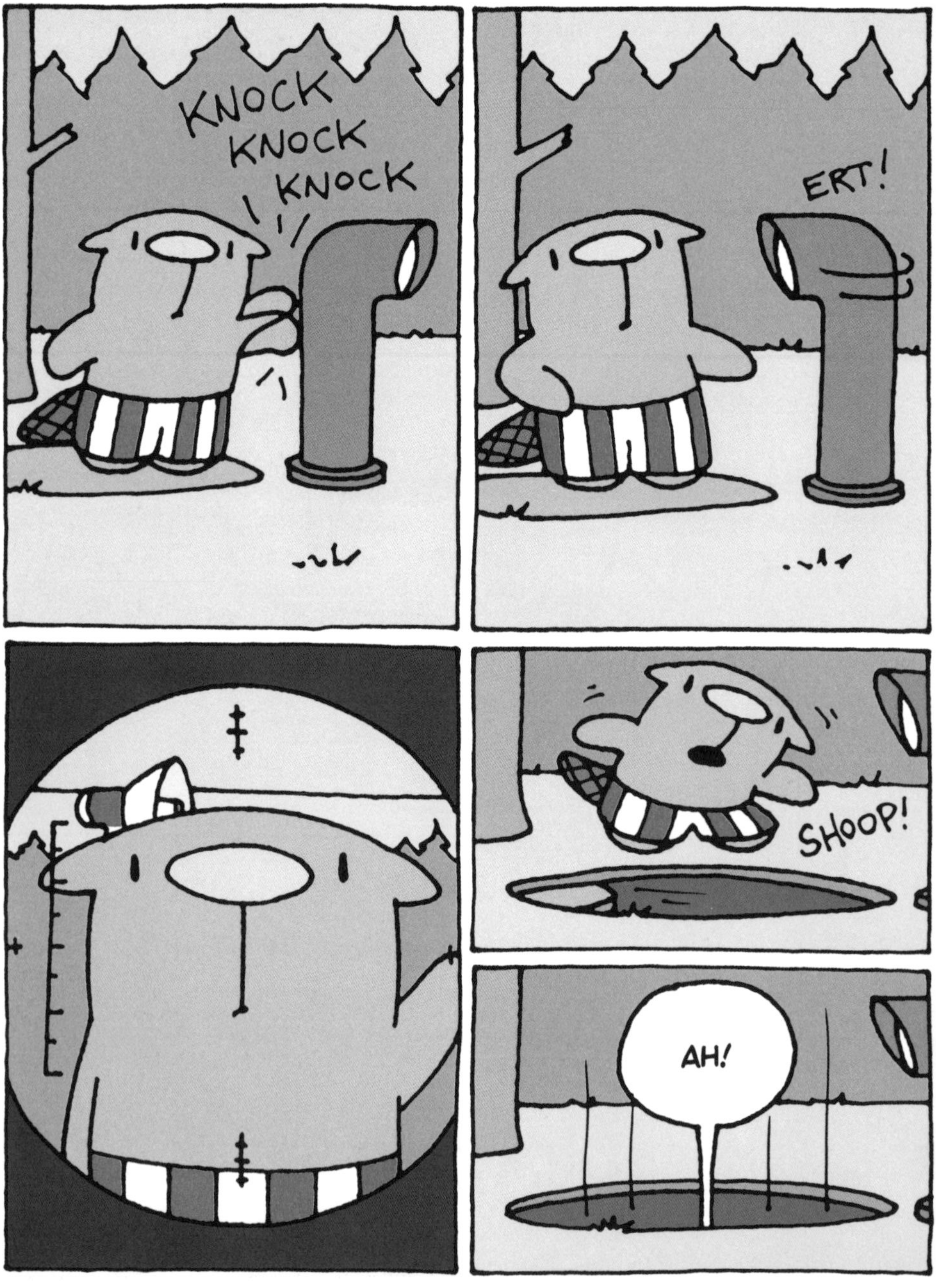
KNOCK
KNOCK
KNOCK
ERT!
SHOOP!
AH!

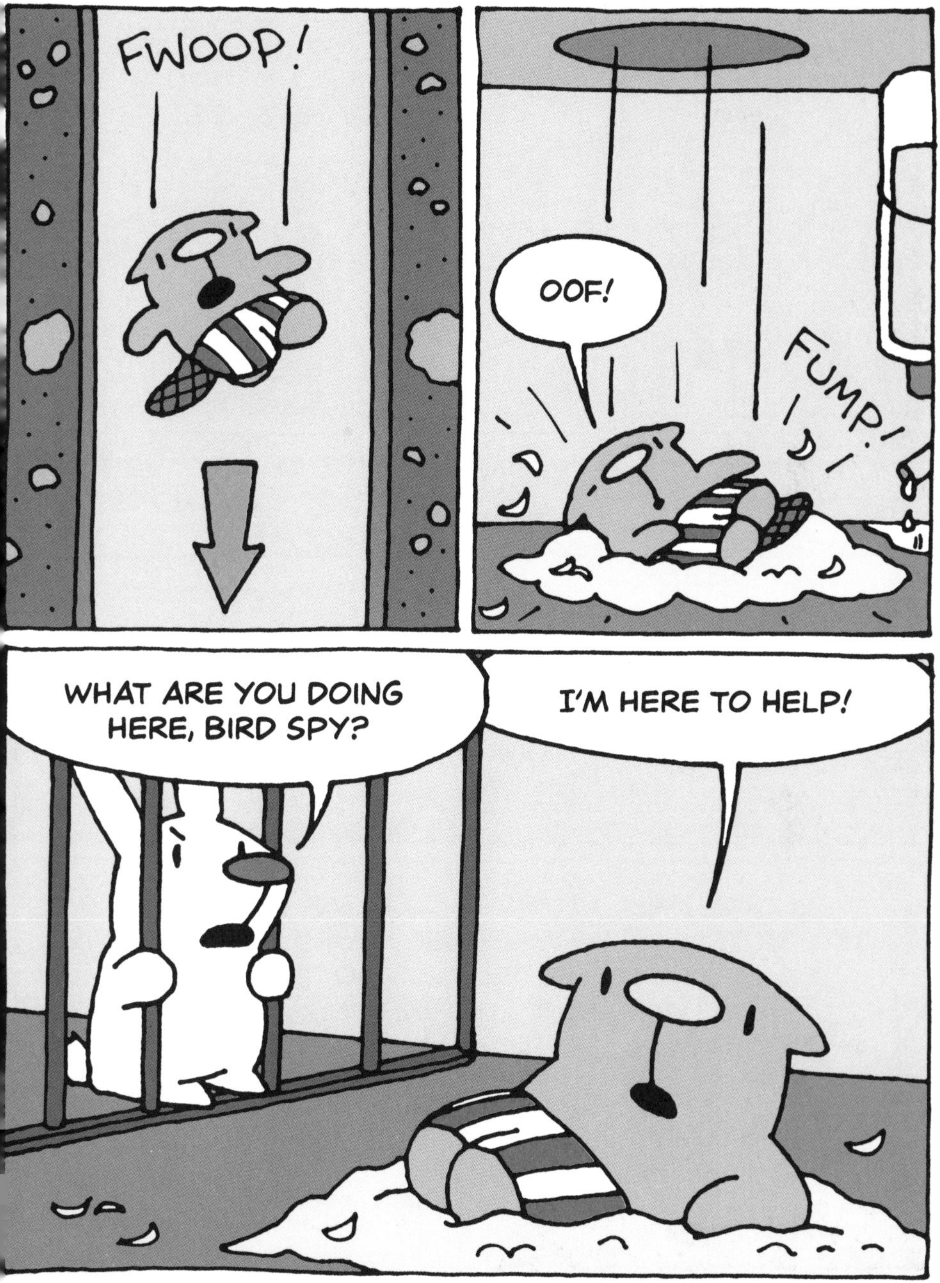
FWOOP!
OOF!
FUMP!
WHAT ARE YOU DOING HERE, BIRD SPY?
I'M HERE TO HELP!

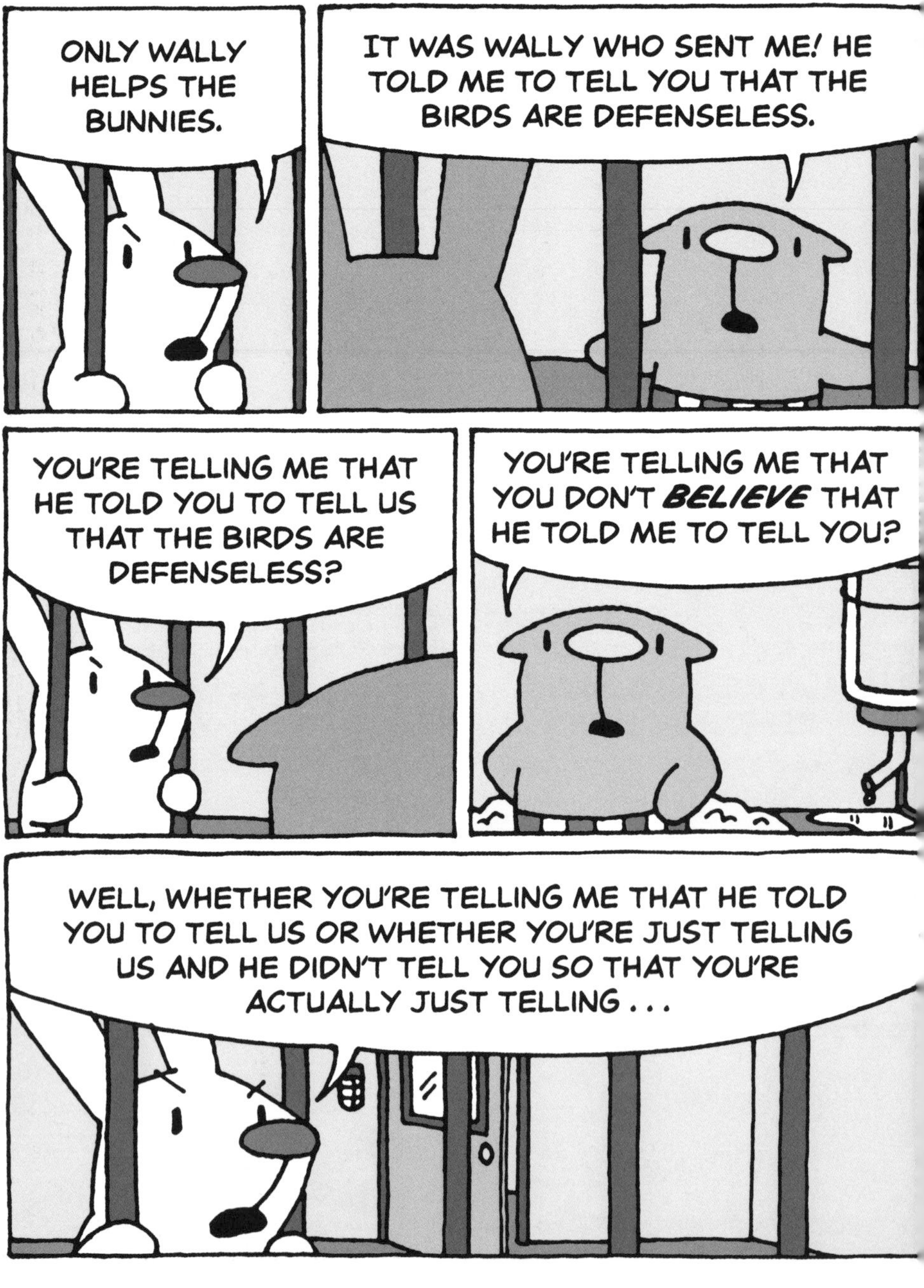

ONLY WALLY HELPS THE BUNNIES.
IT WAS WALLY WHO SENT ME! HE TOLD ME TO TELL *YOU* THAT THE BIRDS ARE DEFENSELESS.
YOU'RE TELLING ME THAT HE TOLD YOU TO TELL US THAT THE BIRDS ARE DEFENSELESS?
YOU'RE TELLING ME THAT YOU DON'T ***BELIEVE*** THAT HE TOLD ME TO TELL YOU?
WELL, WHETHER YOU'RE TELLING ME THAT HE TOLD YOU TO TELL US OR WHETHER YOU'RE JUST TELLING US AND HE DIDN'T TELL YOU SO THAT YOU'RE ACTUALLY JUST TELLING . . .

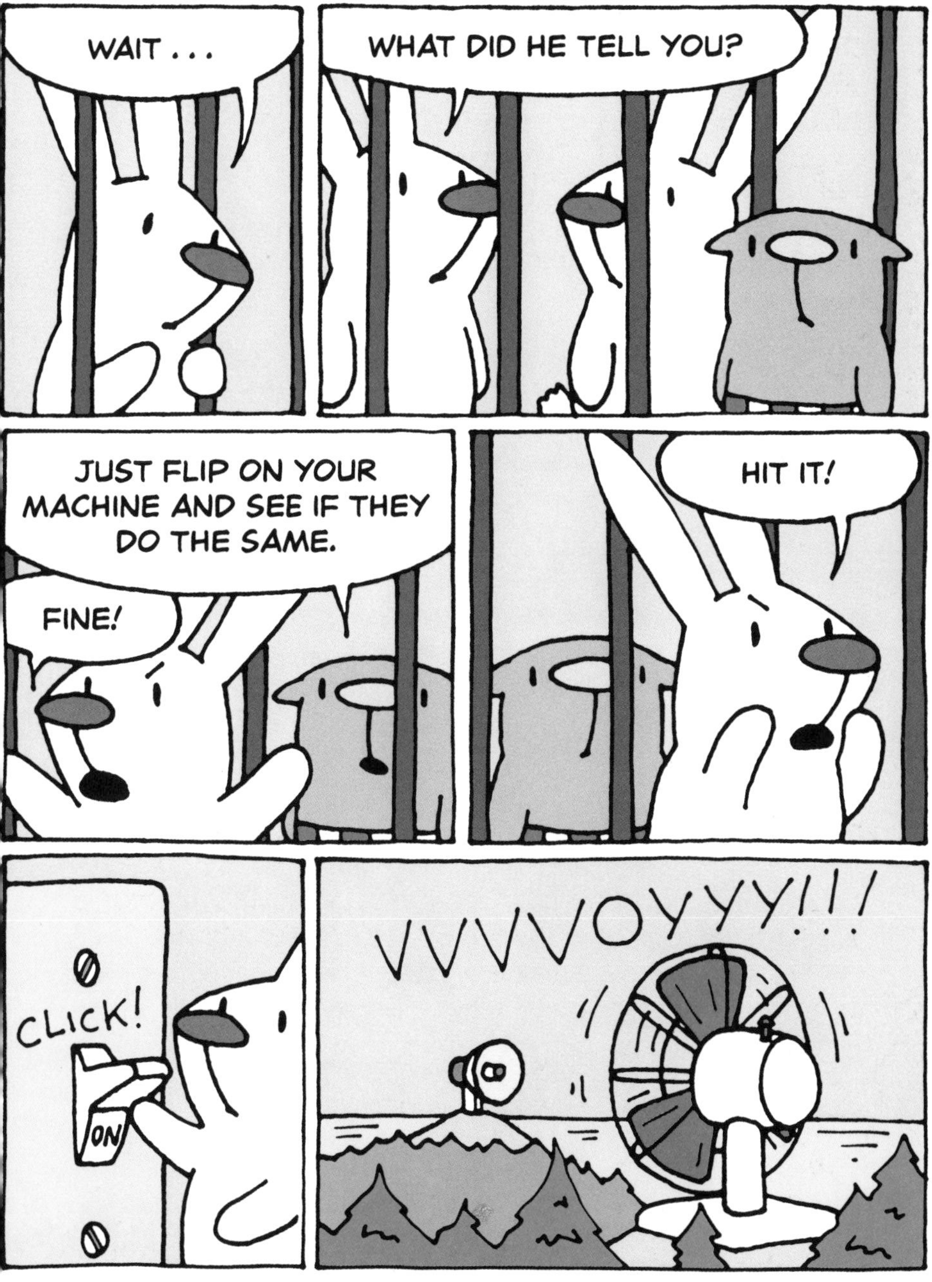
WAIT . . .
WHAT DID HE TELL YOU?
JUST FLIP ON YOUR MACHINE AND SEE IF THEY DO THE SAME.
FINE!
HIT IT!
CLICK!
ON
VVVVOYYYY!!!

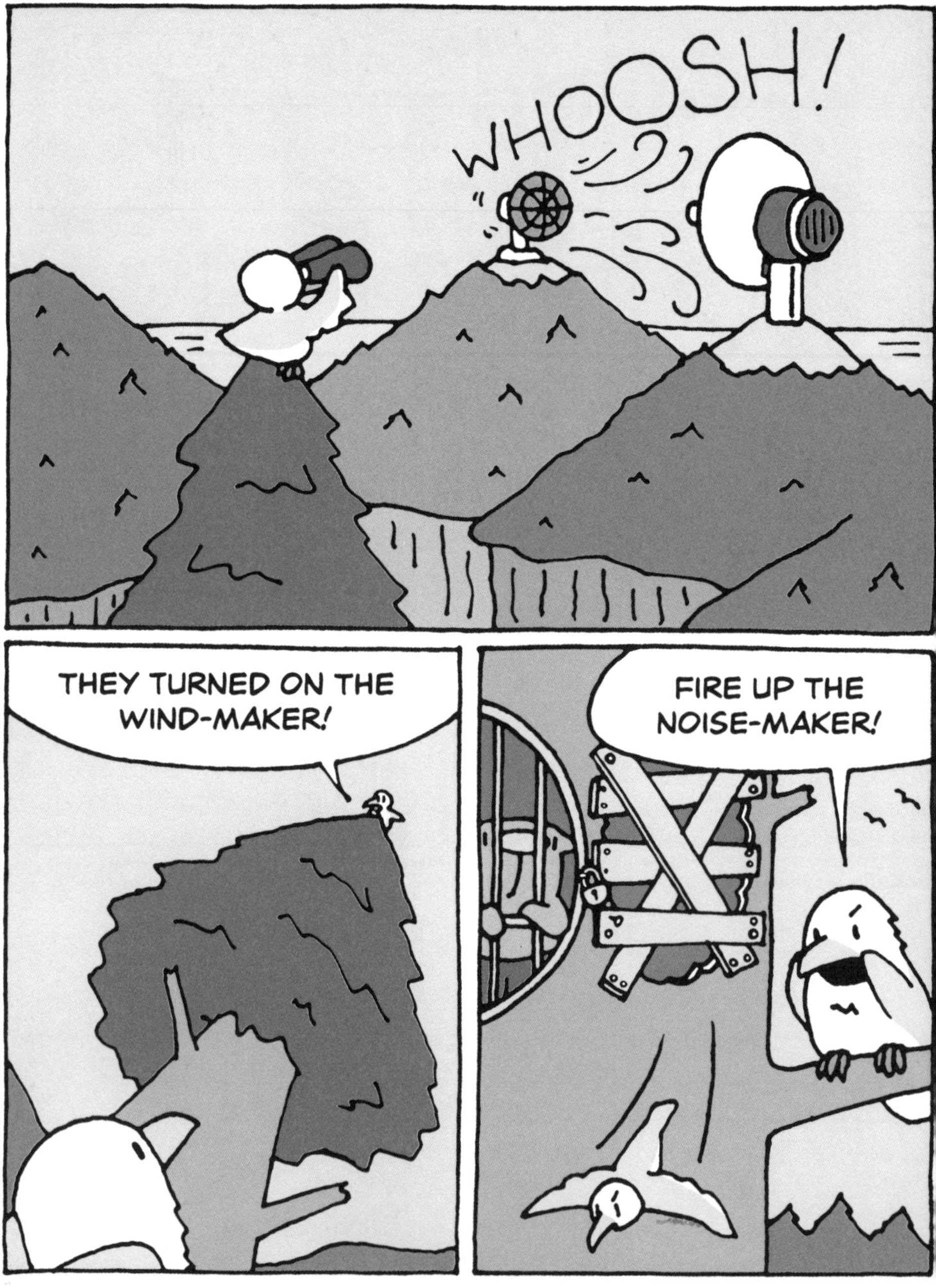
WHOOSH!
THEY TURNED ON THE WIND-MAKER!
FIRE UP THE NOISE-MAKER!

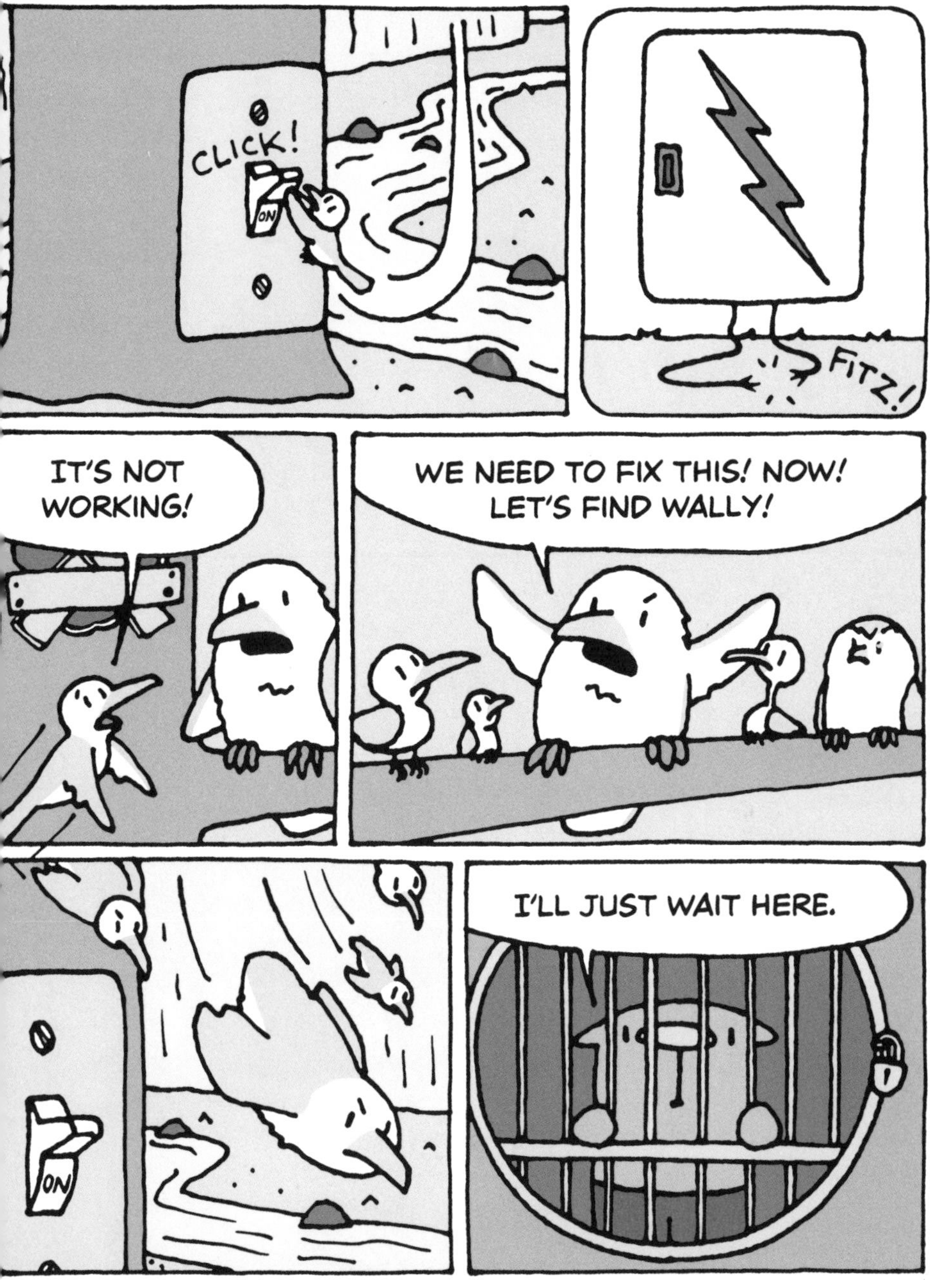
CLICK!
ON
FITZ!
IT'S NOT WORKING!
WE NEED TO FIX THIS! NOW! LET'S FIND WALLY!
ON
I'LL JUST WAIT HERE.

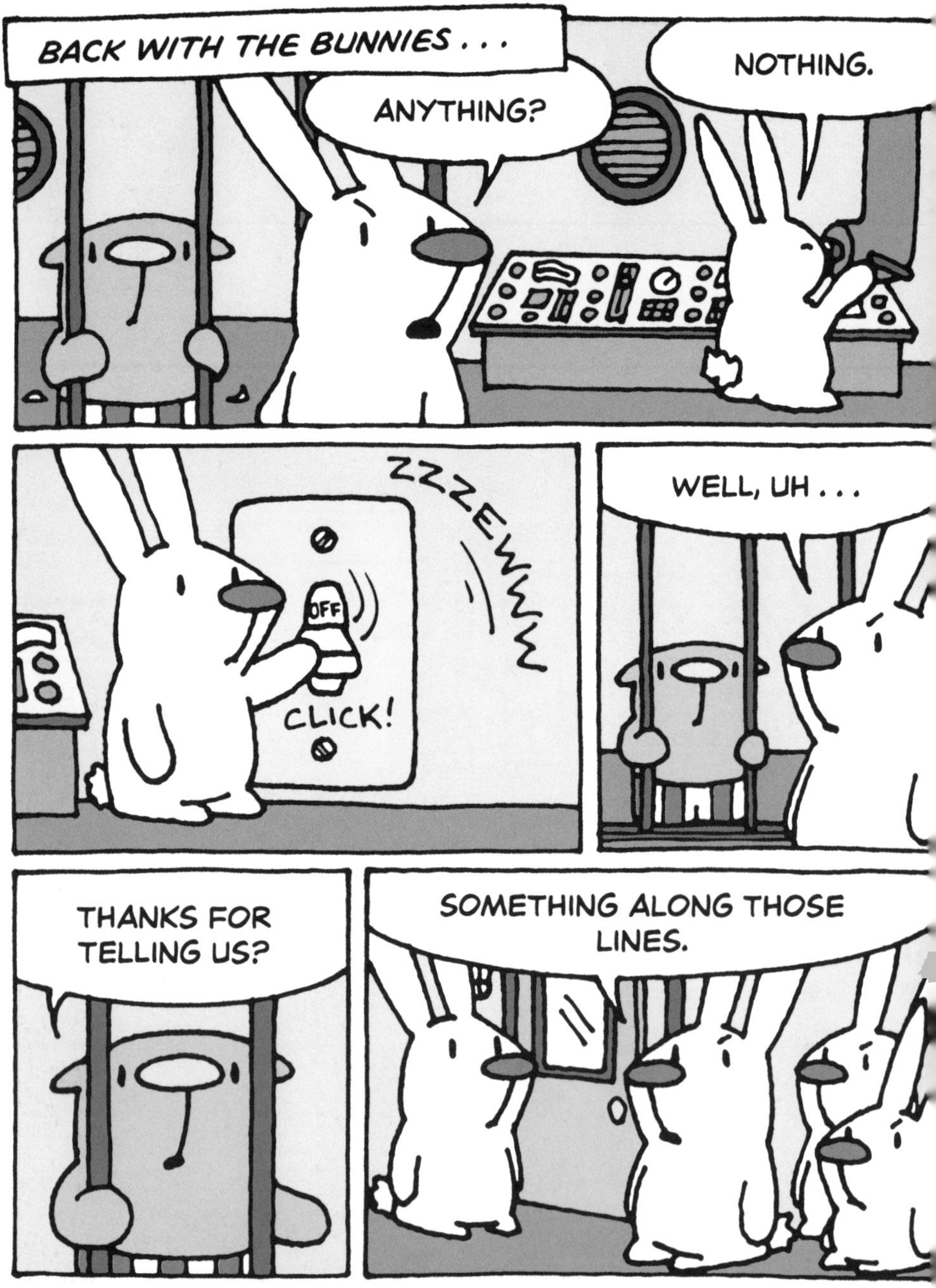
BACK WITH THE BUNNIES . . .
ANYTHING?
NOTHING.
ZZZEWWWW
OFF
CLICK!
WELL, UH . . .
THANKS FOR TELLING US?
SOMETHING ALONG THOSE LINES.

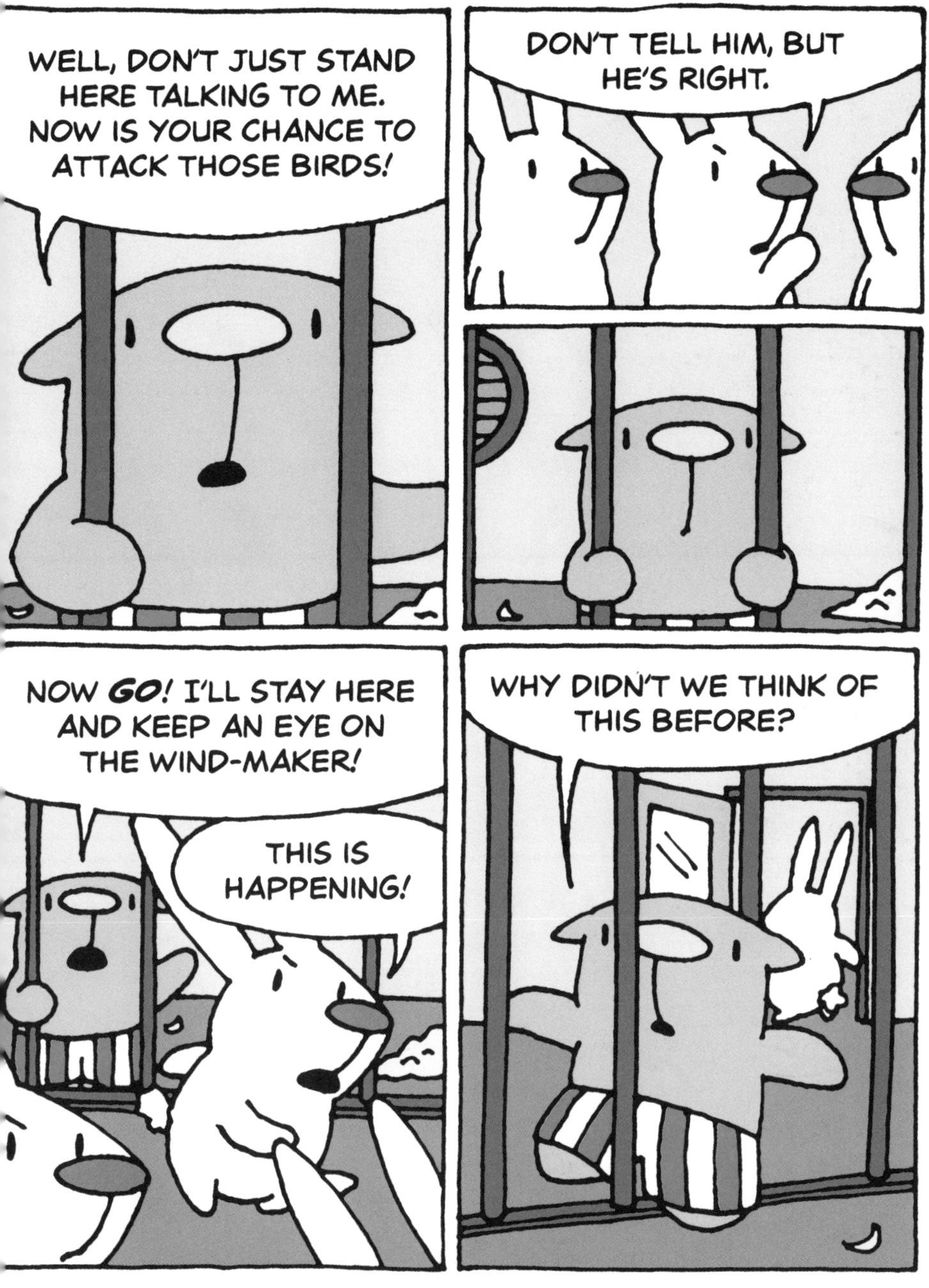
WELL, DON'T JUST STAND HERE TALKING TO ME. NOW IS YOUR CHANCE TO ATTACK THOSE BIRDS!
DON'T TELL HIM, BUT HE'S RIGHT.
NOW GO! I'LL STAY HERE AND KEEP AN EYE ON THE WIND-MAKER!
THIS IS HAPPENING!
WHY DIDN'T WE THINK OF THIS BEFORE?

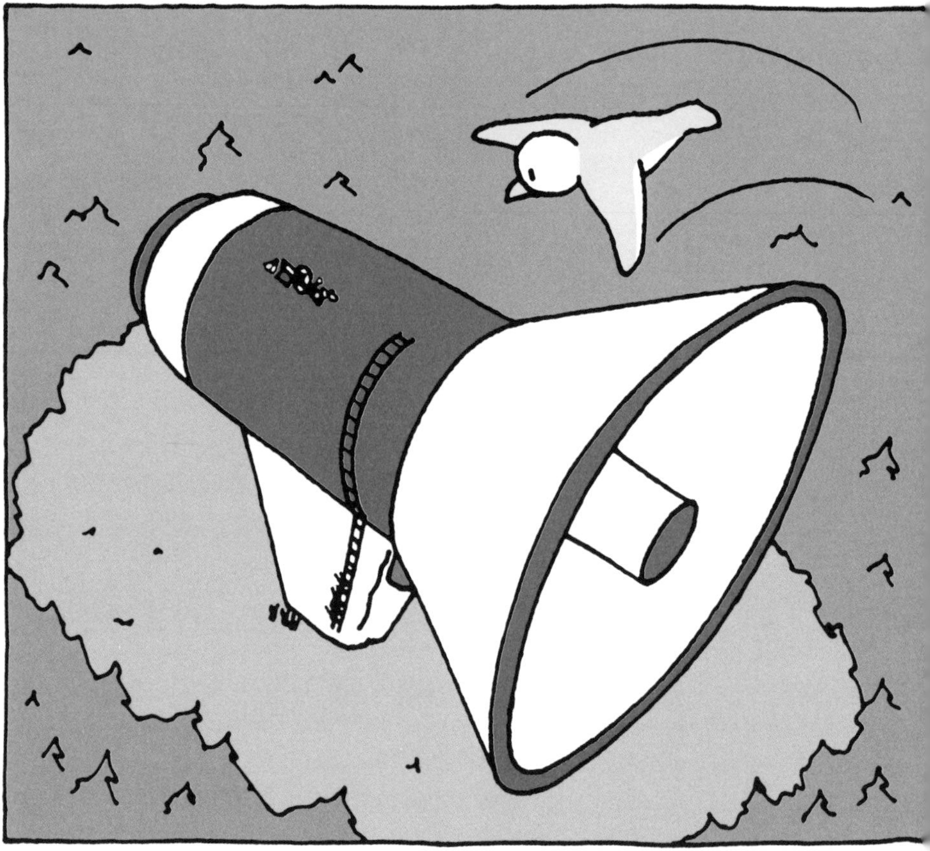

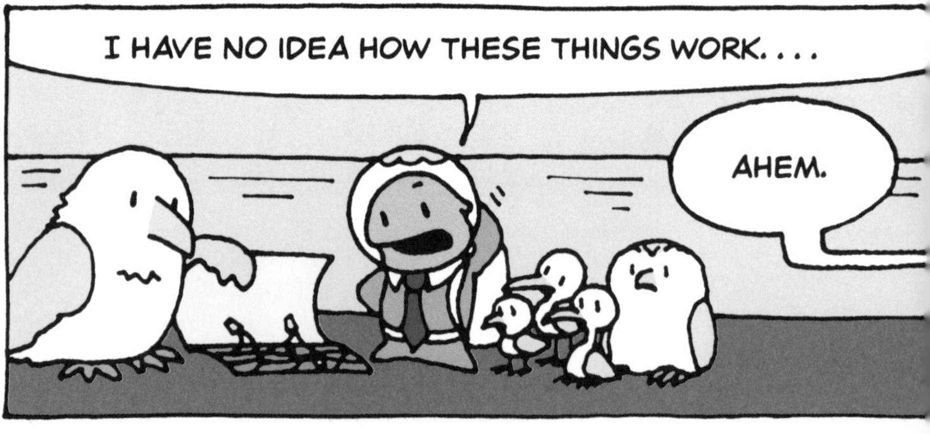
I HAVE NO IDEA HOW THESE THINGS WORK. . . .
AHEM.

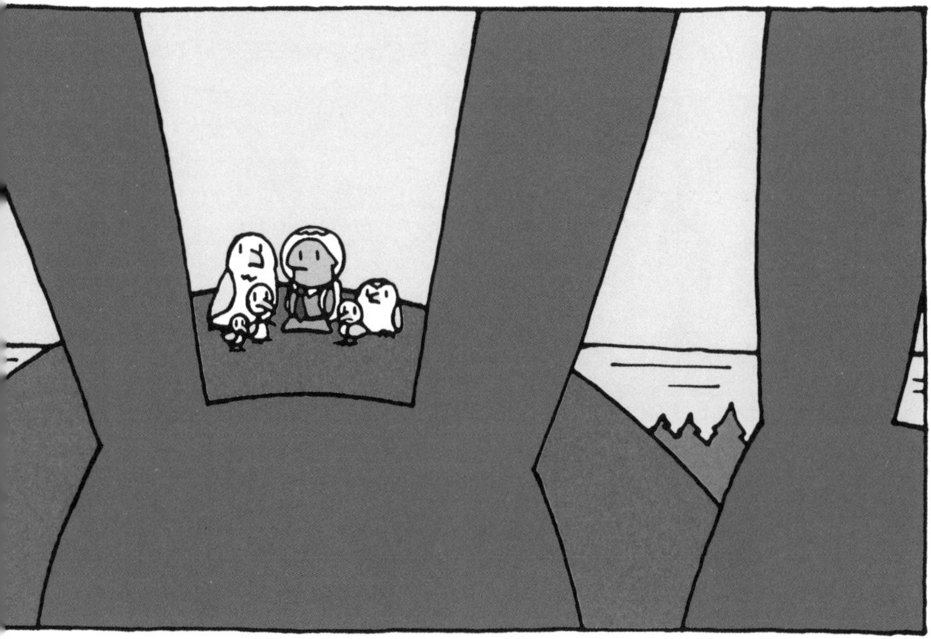

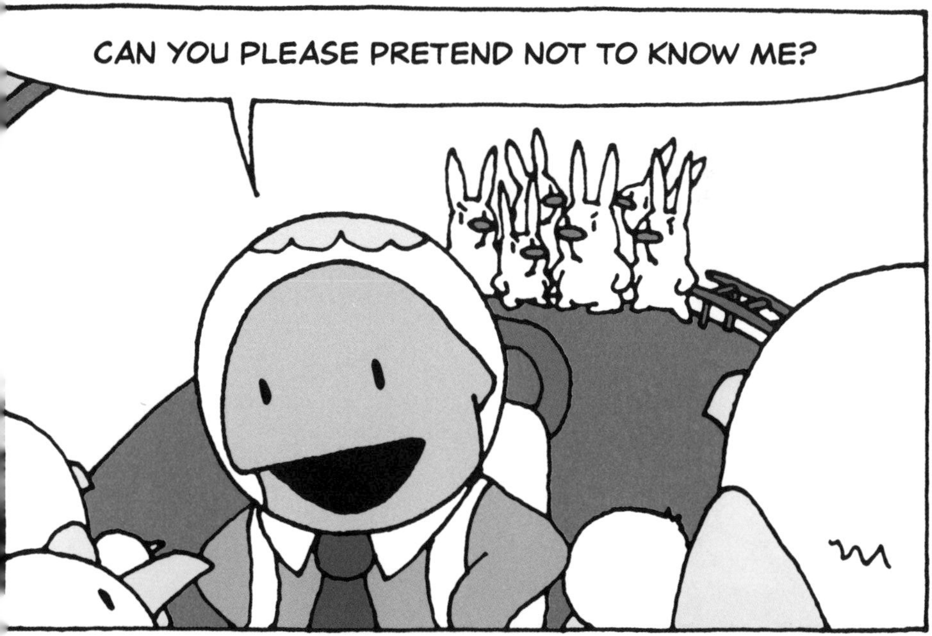
CAN YOU PLEASE PRETEND NOT TO KNOW ME?

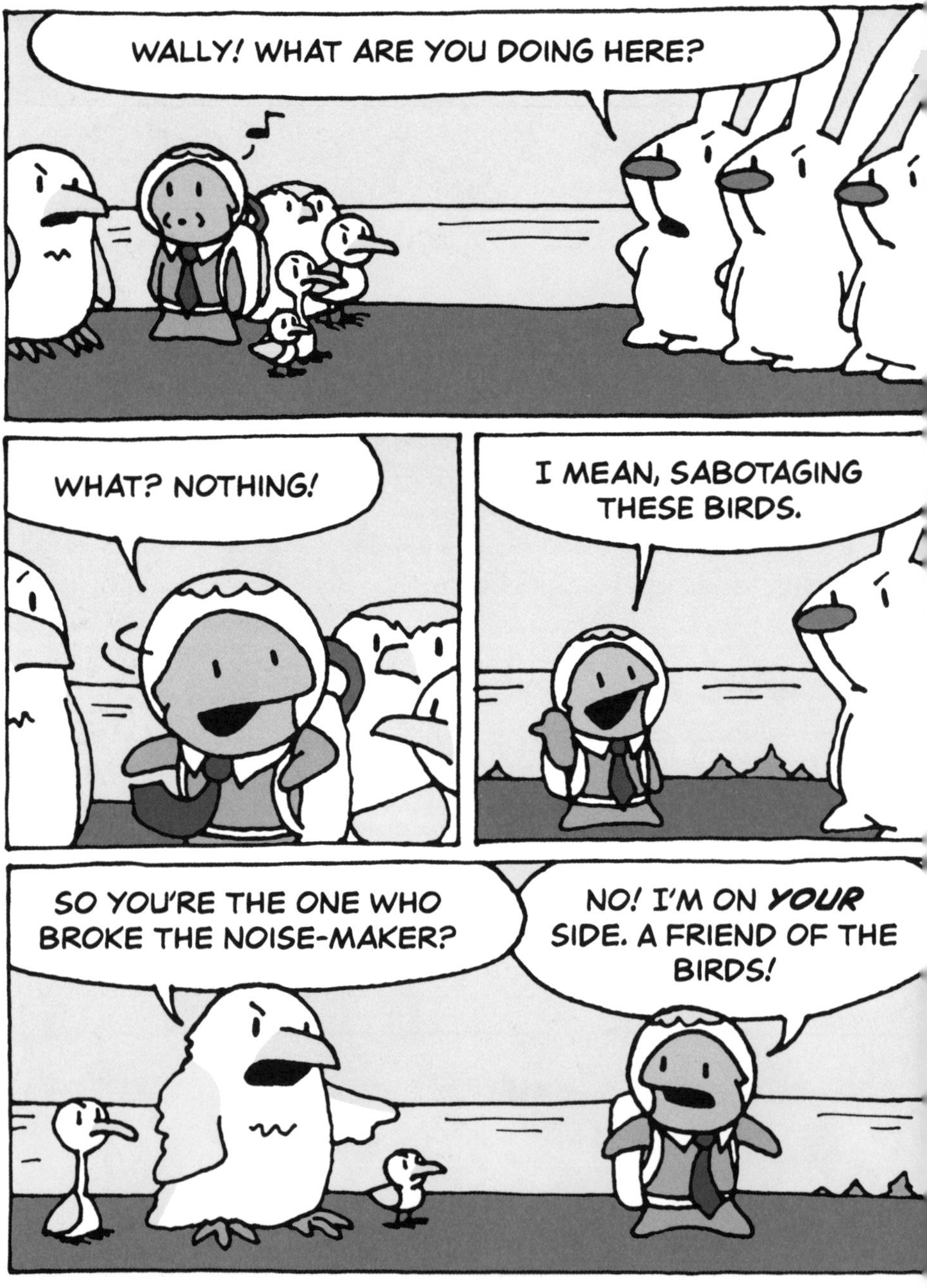
WALLY! WHAT ARE YOU DOING HERE?
WHAT? NOTHING!
I MEAN, SABOTAGING THESE BIRDS.
SO YOU'RE THE ONE WHO BROKE THE NOISE-MAKER?
NO! I'M ON *YOUR* SIDE. A FRIEND OF THE BIRDS!

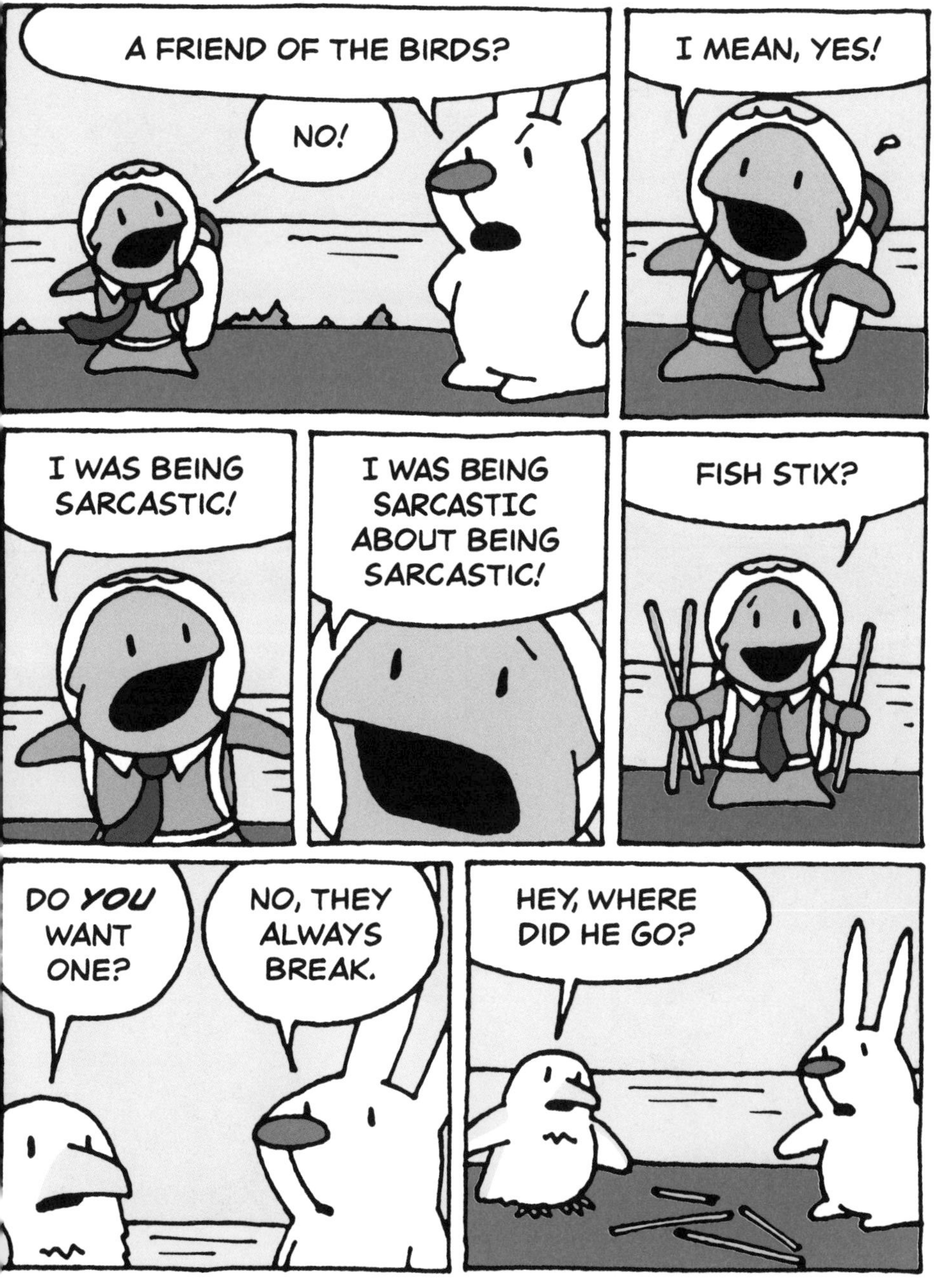
A FRIEND OF THE BIRDS?
NO!
I MEAN, YES!
I WAS BEING SARCASTIC!
I WAS BEING SARCASTIC ABOUT BEING SARCASTIC!
FISH STIX?
DO *YOU* WANT ONE?
NO, THEY ALWAYS BREAK.
HEY, WHERE DID HE GO?

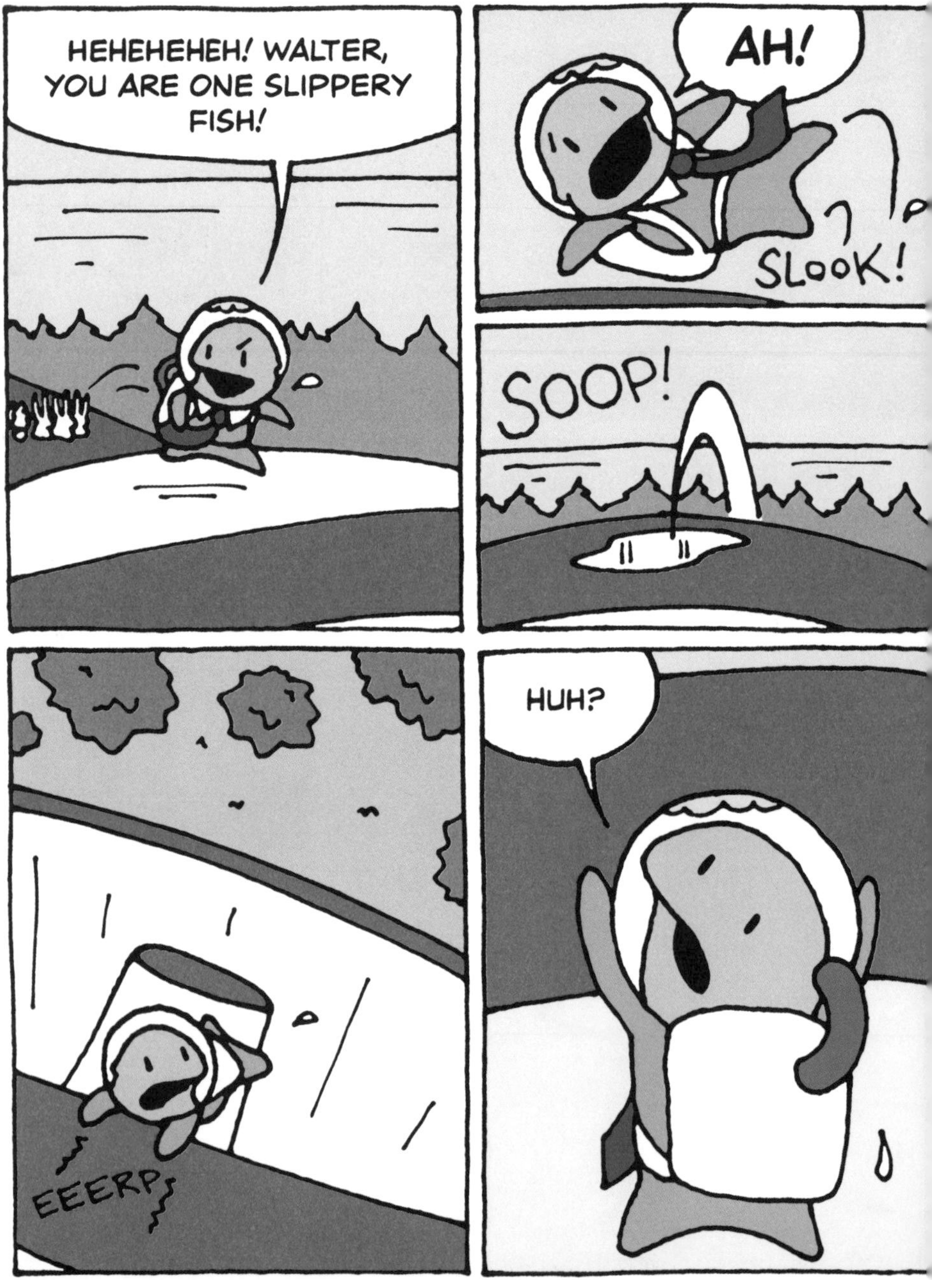
HEHEHEHEH! WALTER, YOU ARE ONE SLIPPERY FISH!
AH!
SLOOK!
SOOP!
EEERP
HUH?

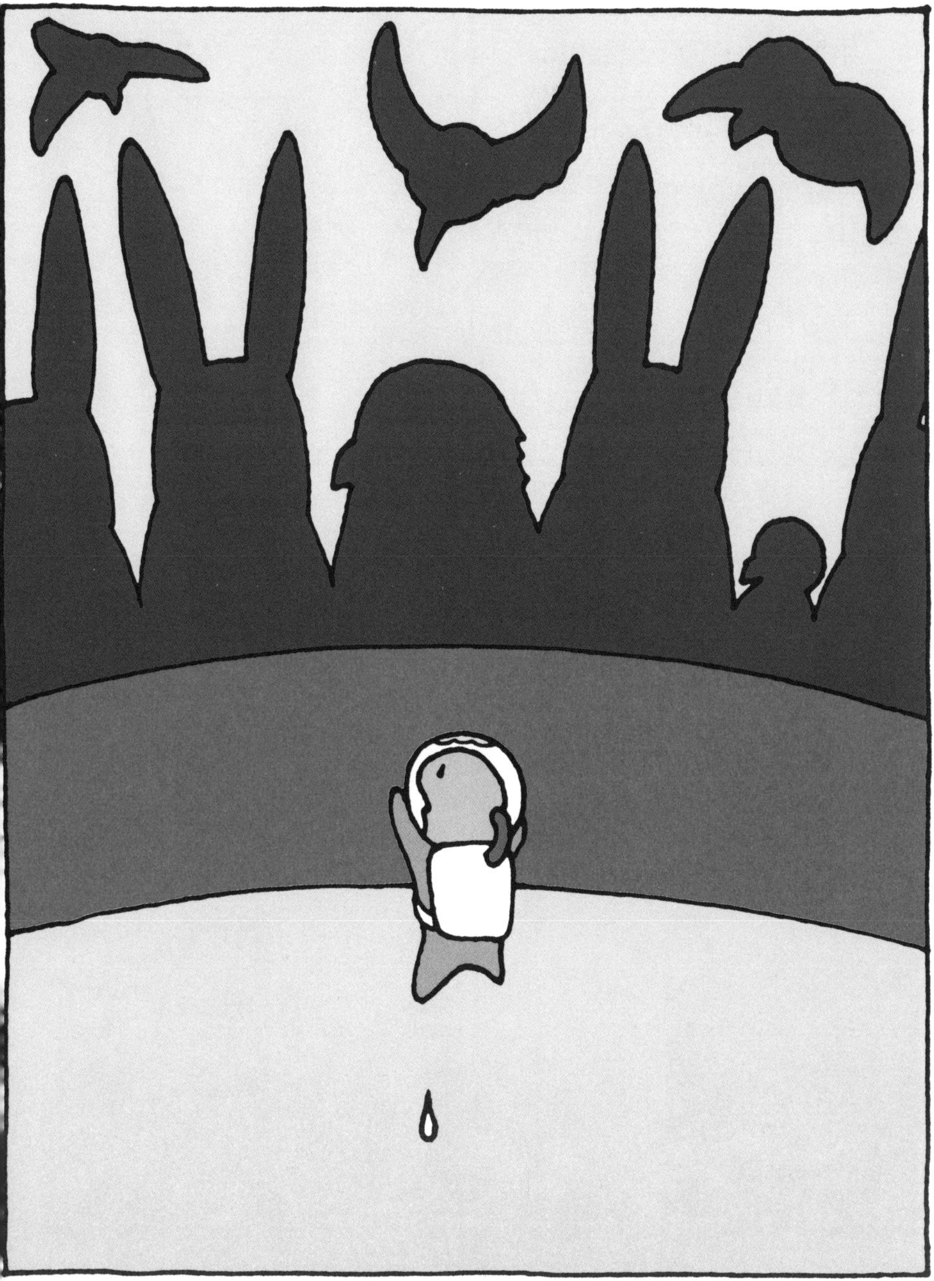

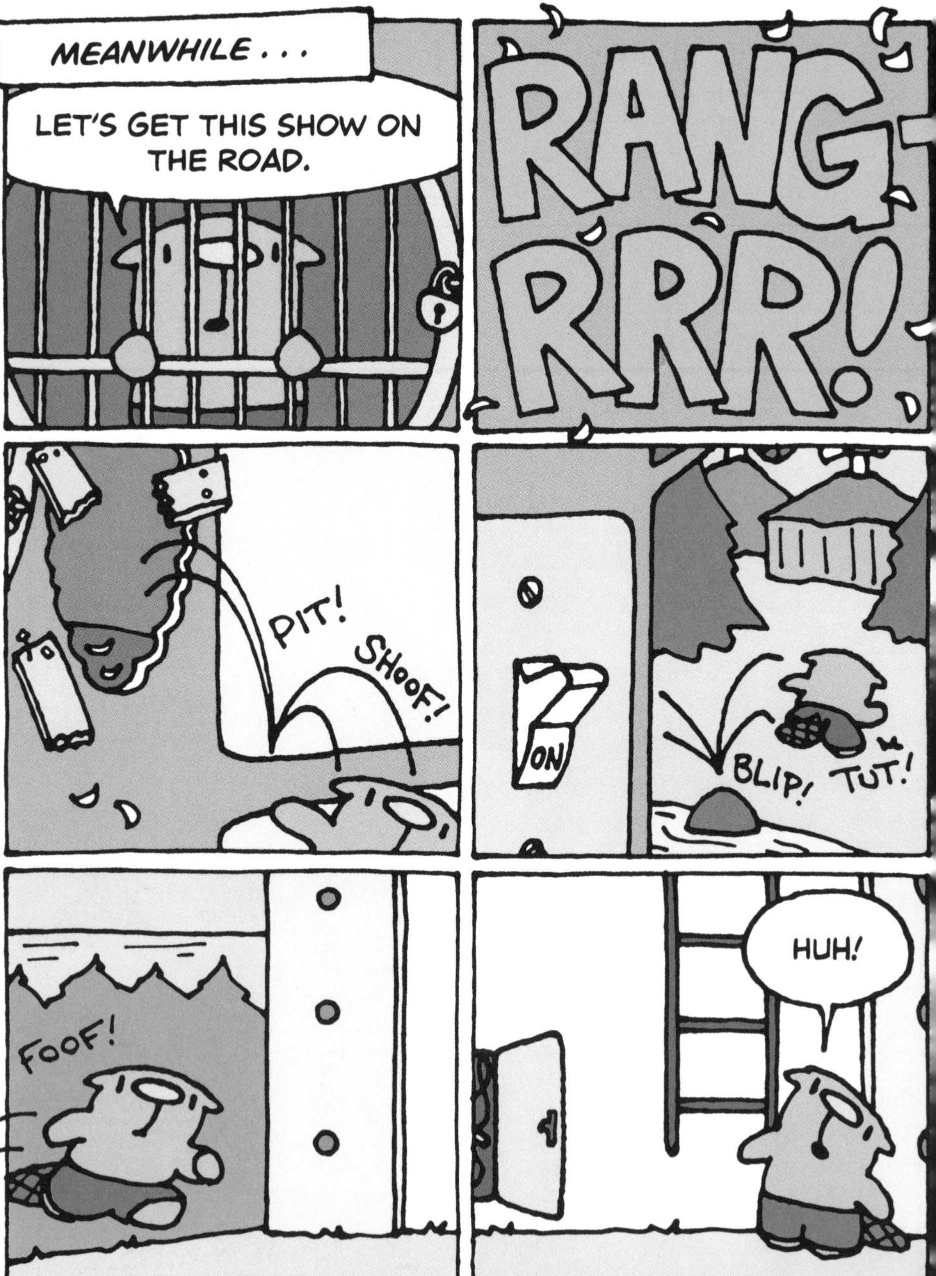
MEANWHILE . . .
LET'S GET THIS SHOW ON THE ROAD.
RANG-RRRR!
PIT!
SHOOF!
ON
BLIP!
TUT!
FOOF!
HUH!

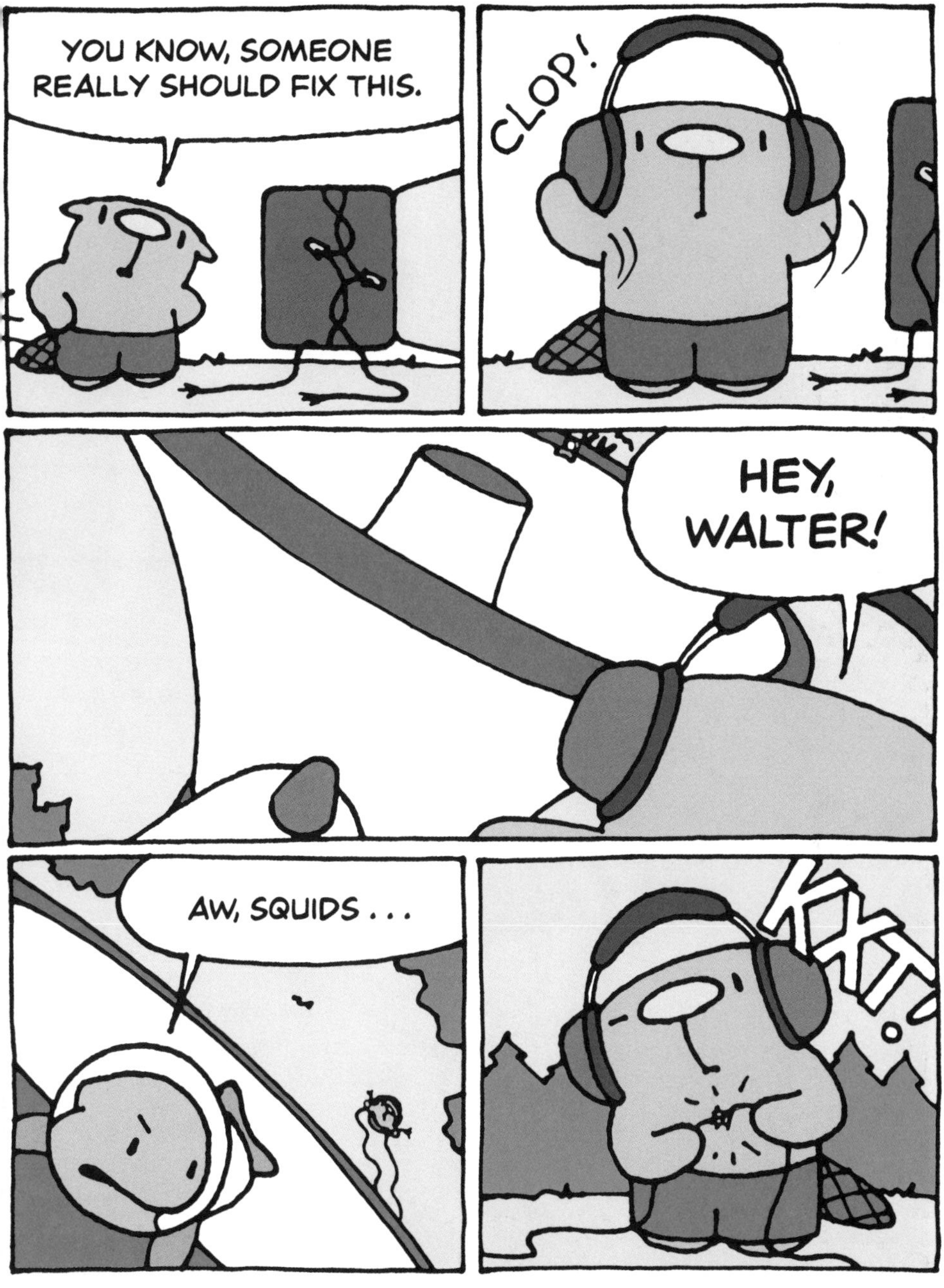
YOU KNOW, SOMEONE REALLY SHOULD FIX THIS.
CLOP!
HEY, WALTER!
AW, SQUIDS . . .
KXT!

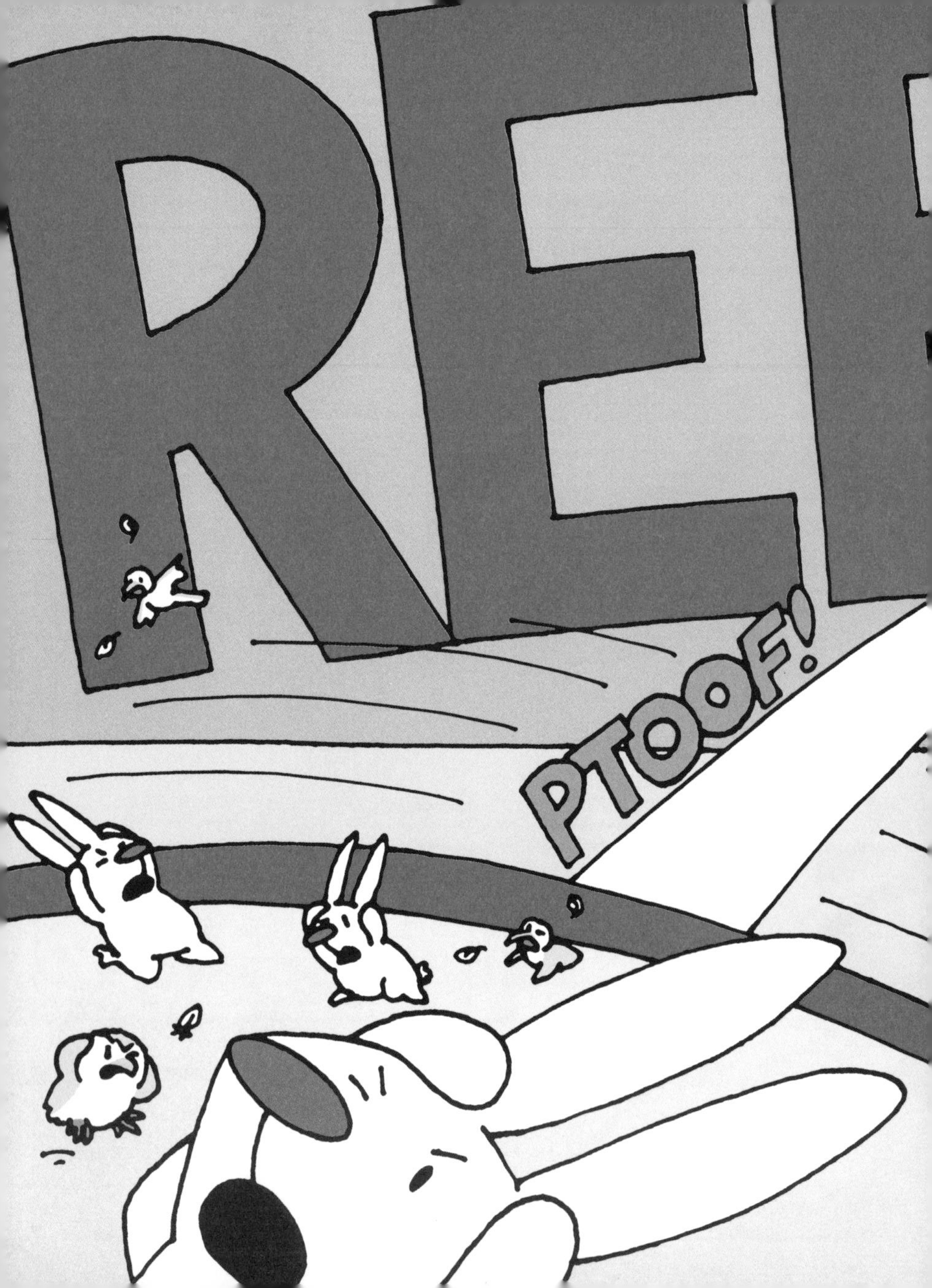
REE
PTOOF!

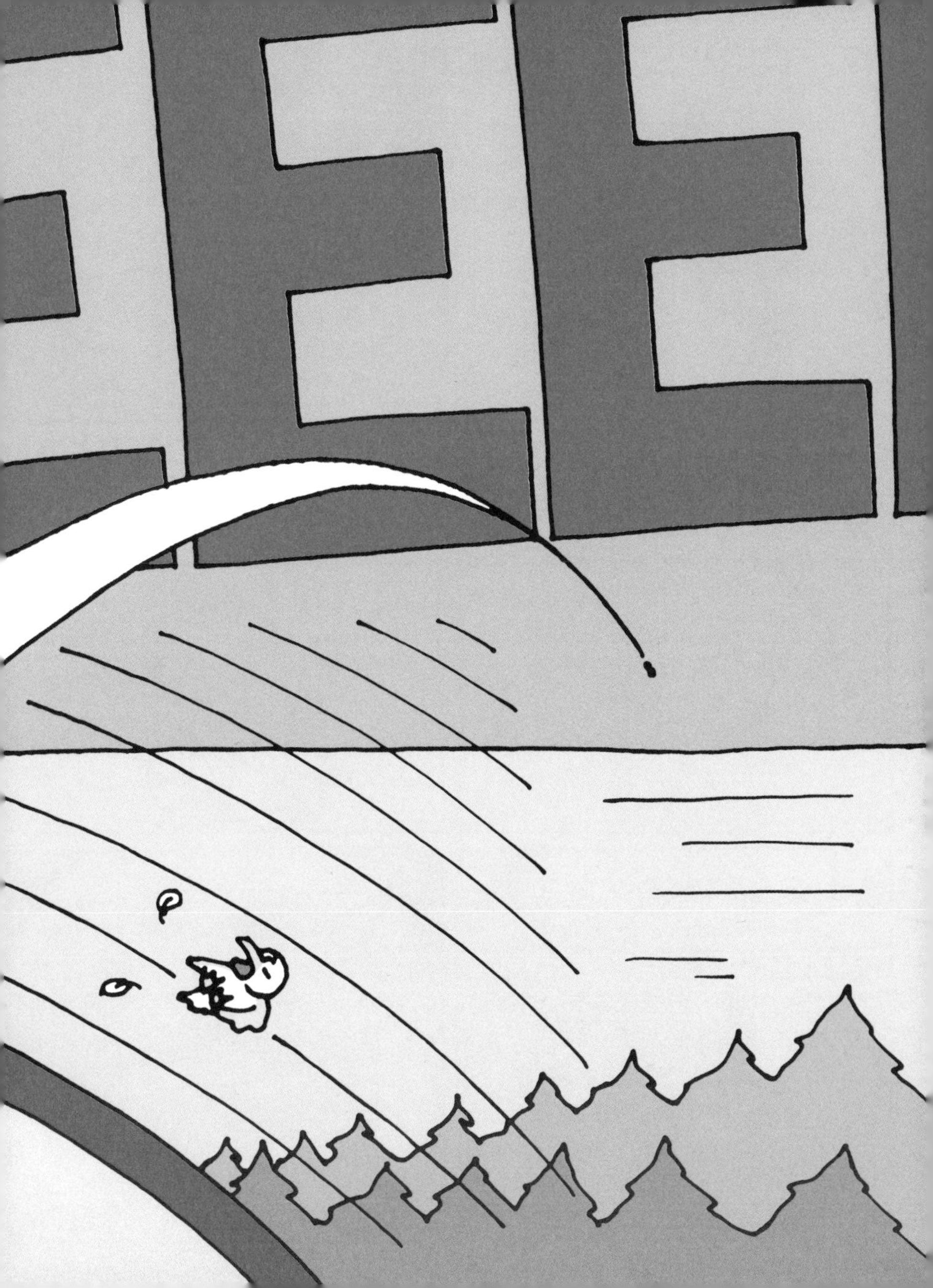

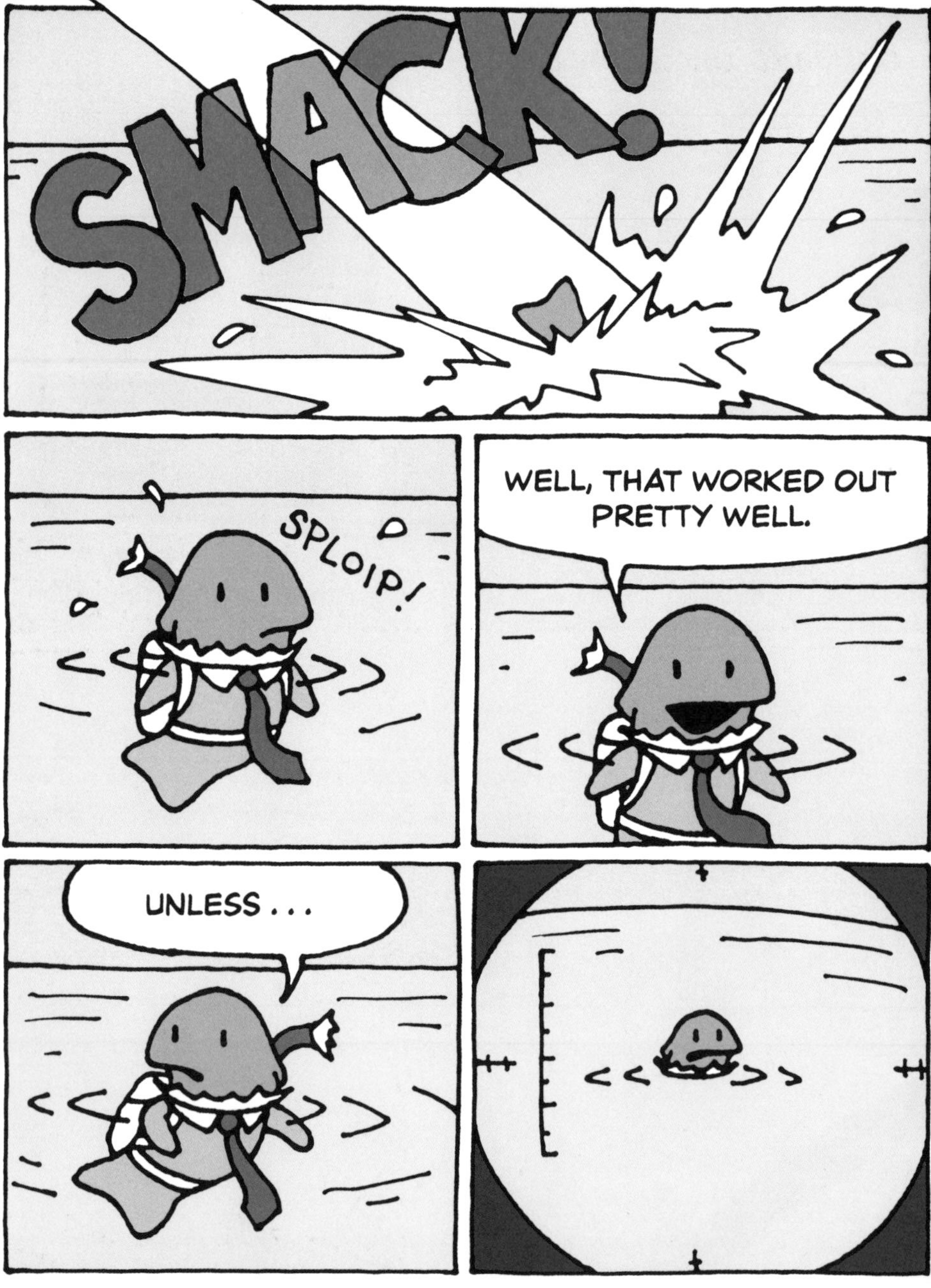
SMACK!
SPLOIP!
WELL, THAT WORKED OUT PRETTY WELL.
UNLESS . . .

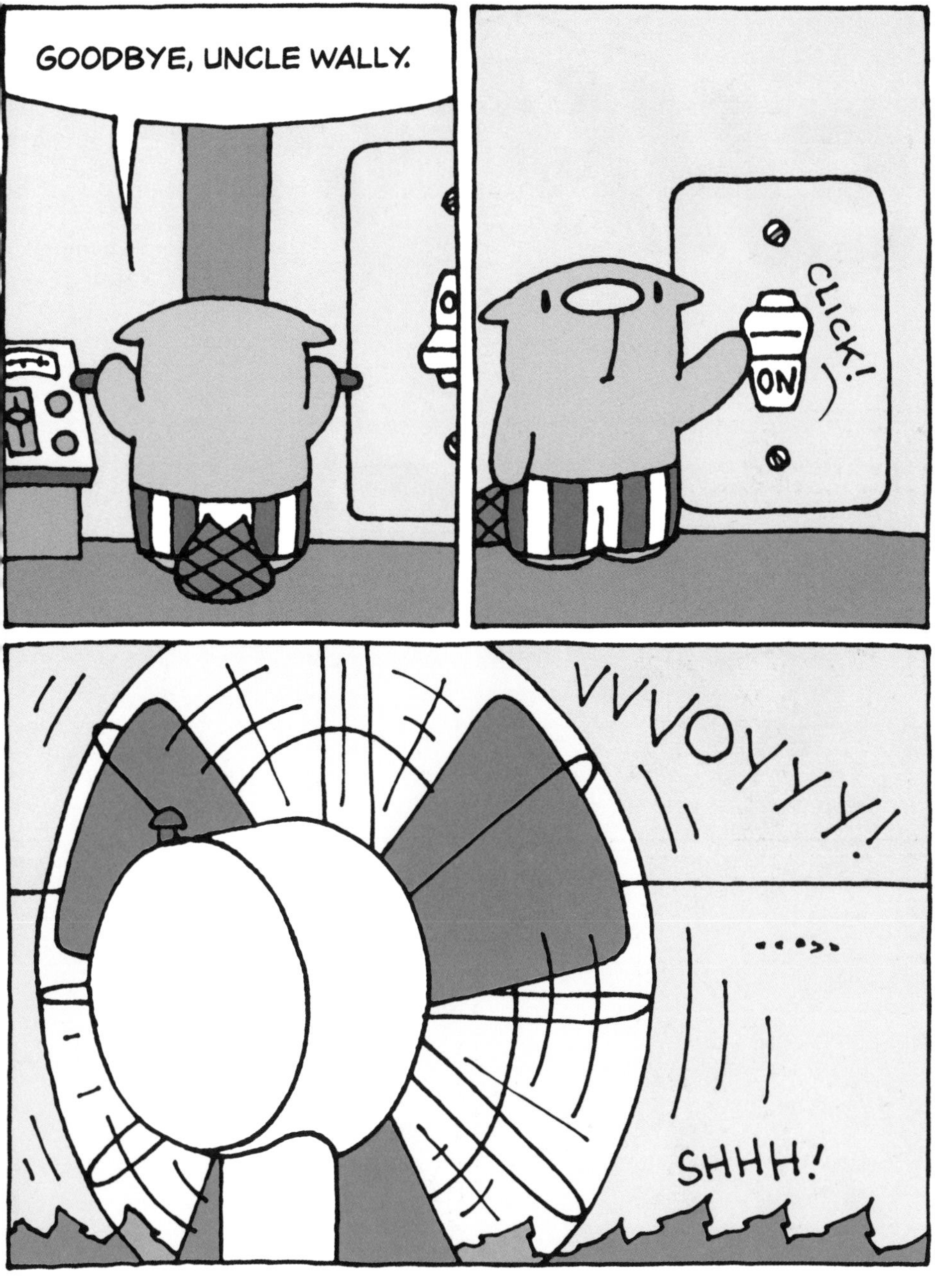
GOODBYE, UNCLE WALLY.
ON
CLICK!
VVVOYYY!
...
SHHH!

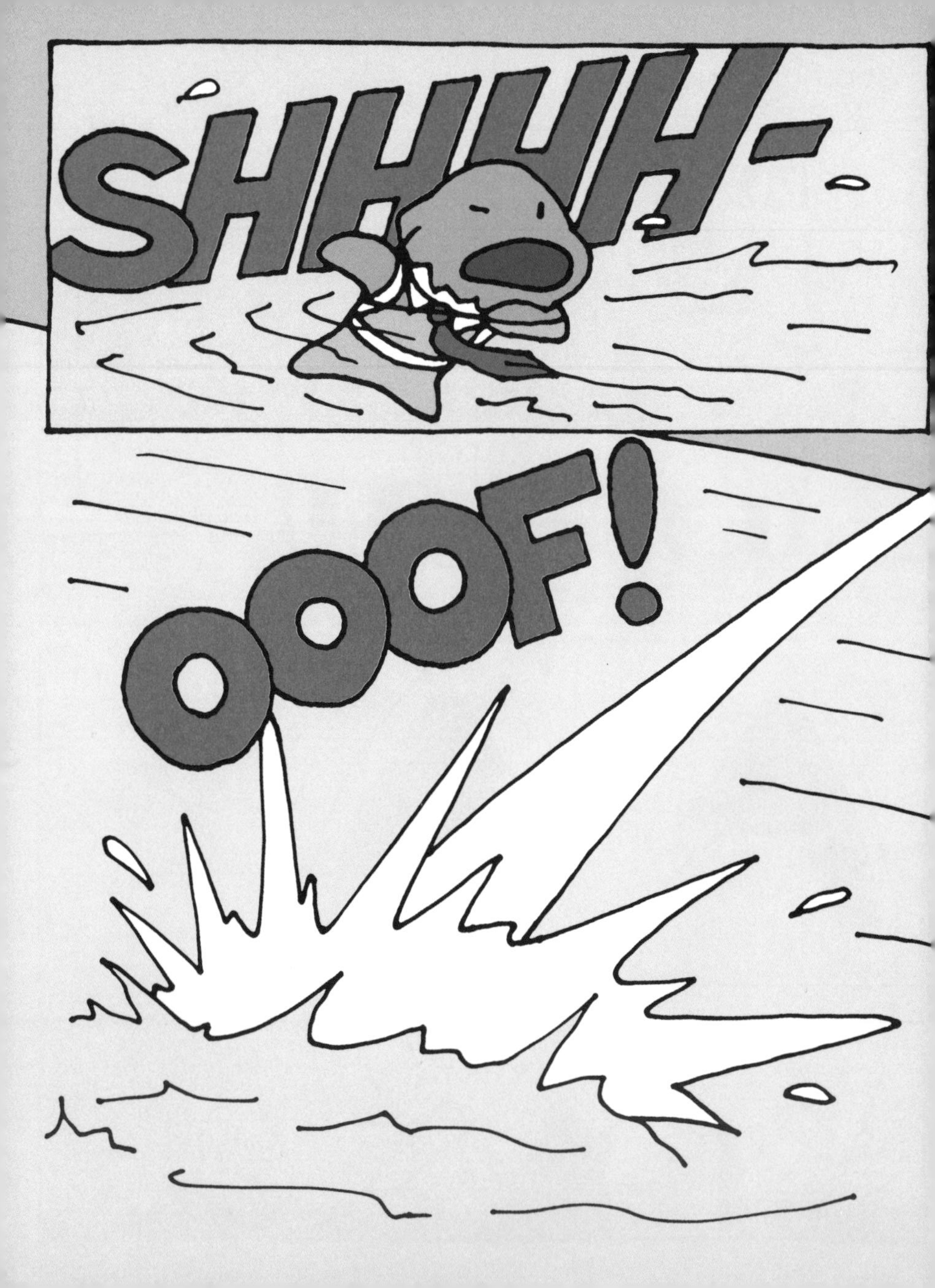
SHHHH-
OOOF!

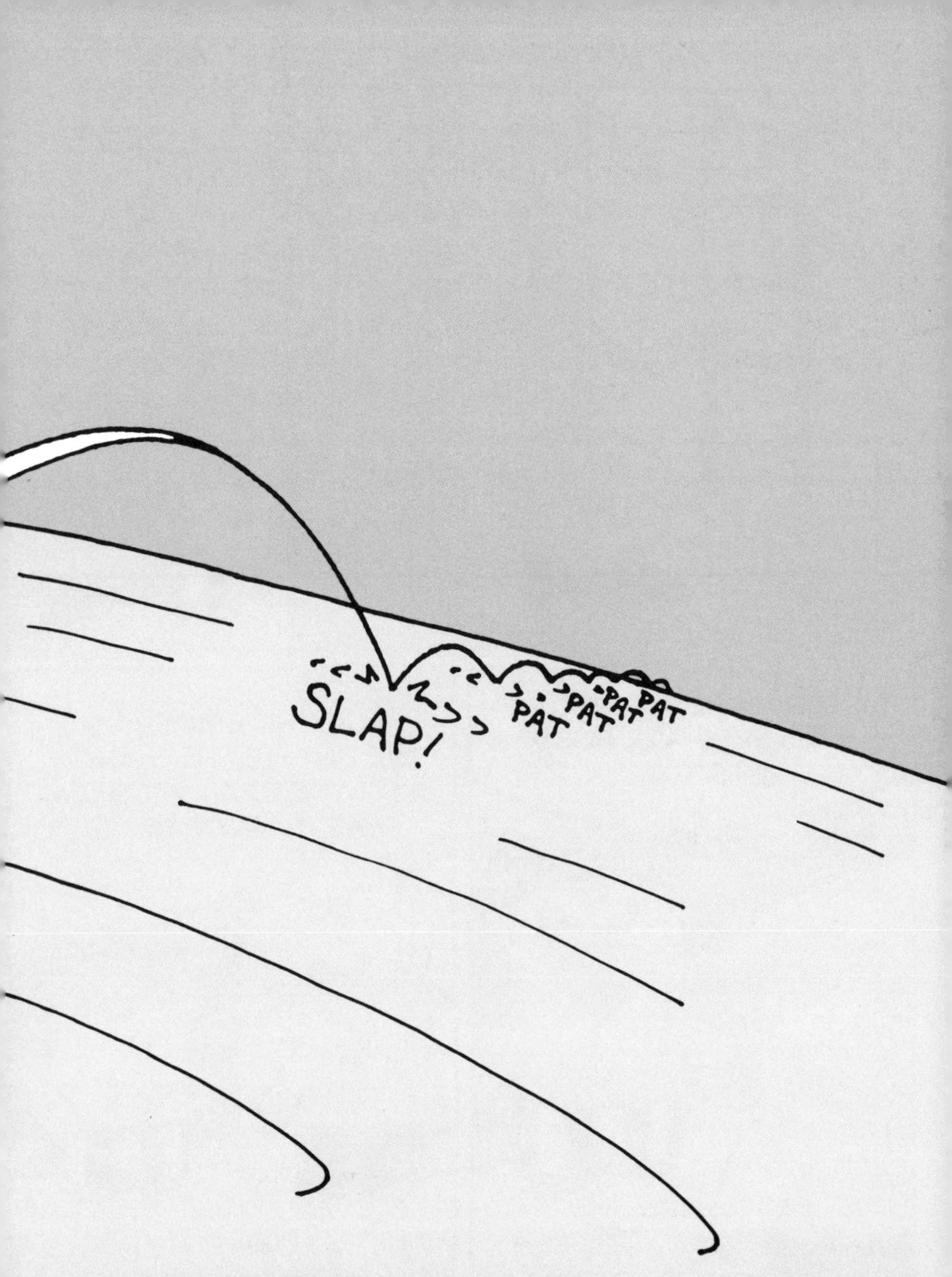
SLAP!
PAT
PAT
PAT
PAT

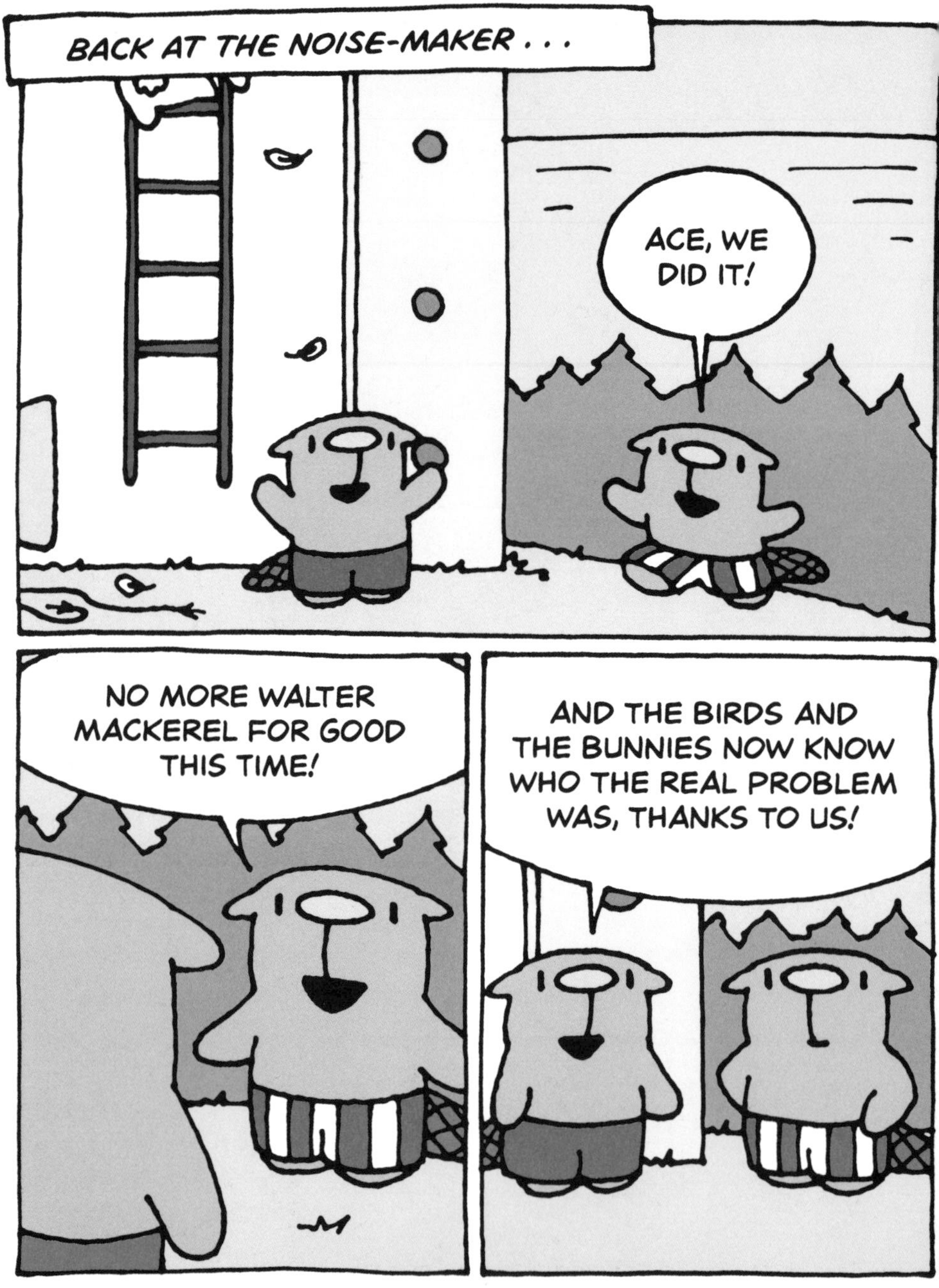
BACK AT THE NOISE-MAKER . . .
ACE, WE DID IT!
NO MORE WALTER MACKEREL FOR GOOD THIS TIME!
AND THE BIRDS AND THE BUNNIES NOW KNOW WHO THE REAL PROBLEM WAS, THANKS TO US!

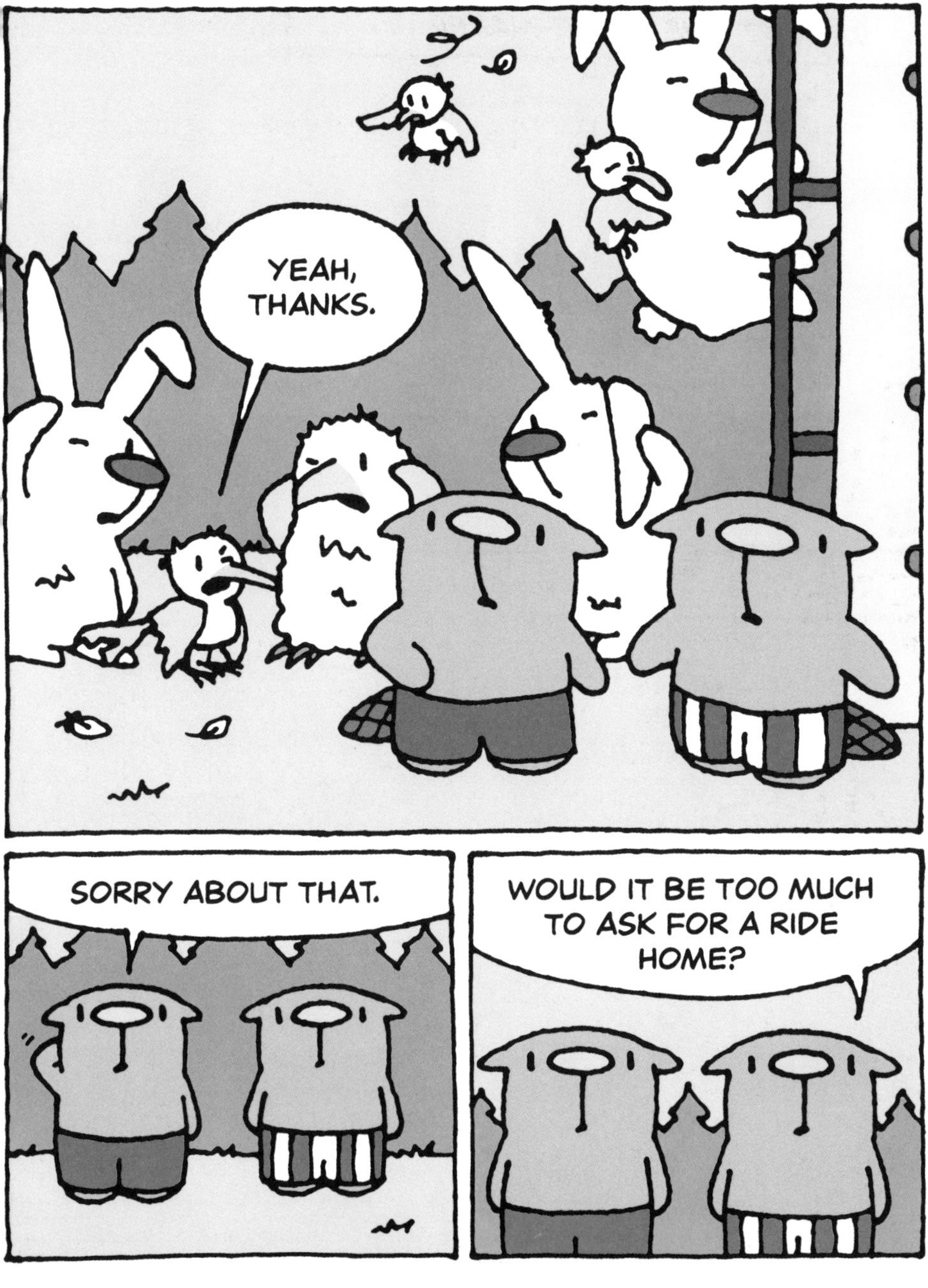
YEAH, THANKS.
SORRY ABOUT THAT.
WOULD IT BE TOO MUCH TO ASK FOR A RIDE HOME?

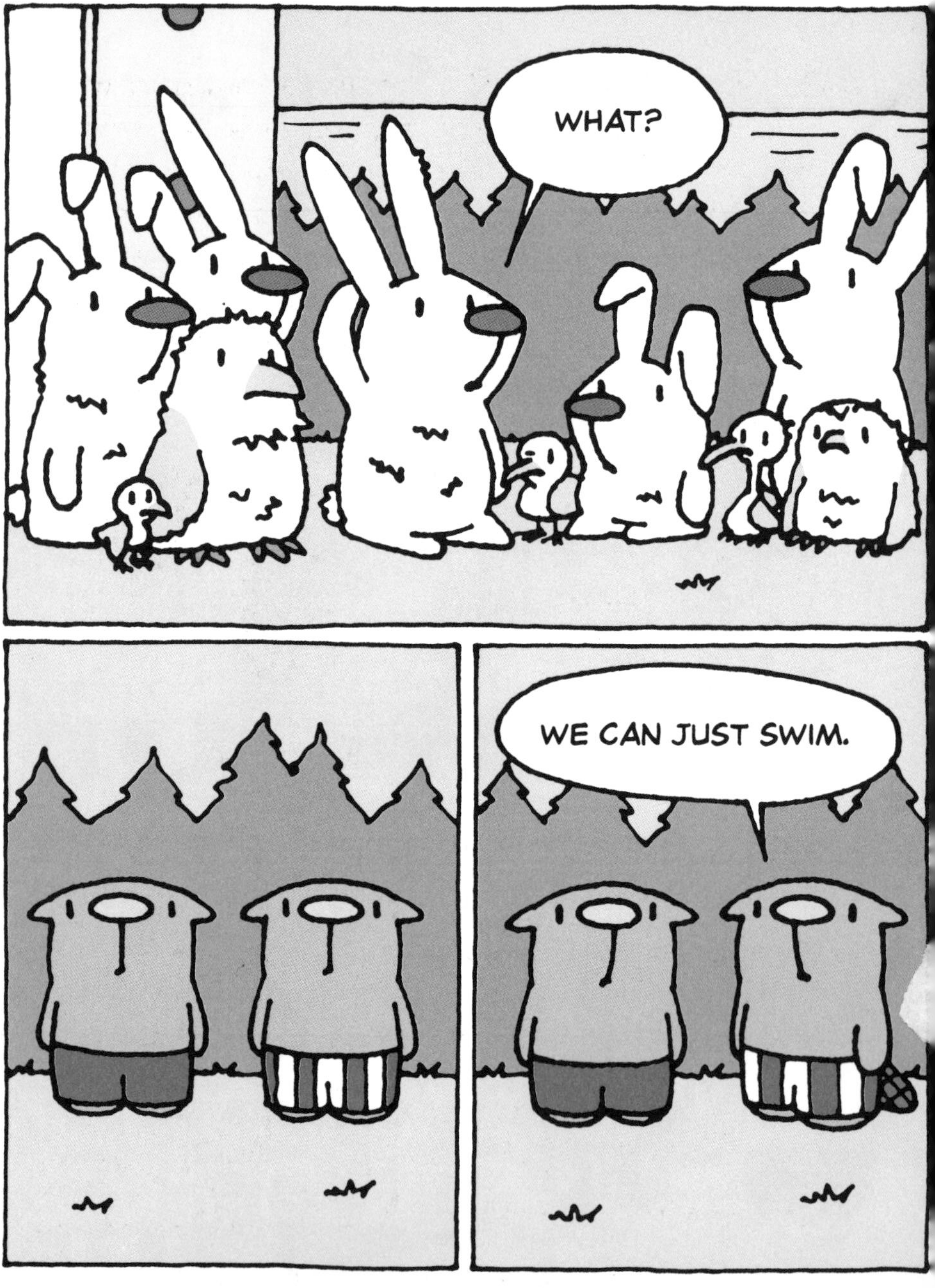
WHAT?
WE CAN JUST SWIM.